1/12

The Rune Sto

"Readers Choice Award, Be

"A nicely woven campus mystery…characters so appealing you will think of them as friends." –Romantic Times Magazine

"Like Elizabeth Peters, Mary Welk knows how to create a good
e   so using
fi   **DATE DUE**   is, author
o. .... & TWICS'mysteries

"If I was an accident victim, I would be relieved if Caroline were my ER nurse. If I were a murder victim, I would definitely want her to investigate my death. I'm already enrolling my children at Bruck University, and can't wait for my next dose of life in Rhineburg." –Donna Moore, award-winning author of GO TO HELENA HANDBASKET

"An alluring who-done-it with plenty of suspects and red herrings." –Harriet Klausner, reviewer

A Merry Little Murder

Love is Murder Best First Mystery Winner

"The novel shines for its scenes evoking the warm and fuzzy comforts of the holiday season." –Chicago Sun Times

"Highly recommended…absolutely charming…this one holds much promise." –Under the Covers Book Reviews

"Nice college town mystery with an intriguing plot and good characters." –The Baldwin Ledger

Mary Welk

The Rune Stone Murders

A Rhodes to Murder Mystery

Echelon Press

Publishing

THE RUNE STONE MURDERS
A Rhodes to Murder Mystery
Book Two
An Echelon Press Book

First Echelon Press paperback printing / June 2009

Cover Art © Nathalie Moore
Award winning Graphic Artist

Echelon Press
9735 Country Meadows Lane 1-D
Laurel, MD 20723
www.echelonpress.com

ISBN: 978-1-59080-633-3
1-59080-633-6
eBook 1-59080-634-4

PRINTED IN THE UNITED STATES OF AMERICA

10 9 8 7 6 5 4 3 2 1

For my husband, Fred –
still crazy after all these years.
With all my love and gratitude, Derf!
You're still the one.

Caroline Rhodes is patterned after the many fine nurses I've been privileged to know. Their strength, intelligence, and tenacity, both on and off the job, are attributes I've tried to duplicate in Caroline. I dedicate her existence to these women and men of nursing.

In a very special way, I dedicate Caroline to Sue Stuebe, an exceptional person and the finest nurse I've ever known.

Special thanks to Martha Eicker for keeping an eye on my grammar.

Thanks also to Jim Grundy for input on police procedures.

One

"What a glorious day to be alive!" Professor Carl Atwater, the roly-poly chairman of Bruck University's history department, threw back his head, expanded his lungs, and sucked in the fragrant scents of a mid-May morning. "Just look at those clouds, Cari. A few minutes ago they were mere powder puffs on the horizon. Now they're magnificent mountains tumbling across the sky."

Caroline Rhodes glanced up at the thunderheads gathering above the cornfields west of little Rhineburg, Illinois. A woman who knew an approaching storm when she saw one, Caroline rolled her eyes in despair.

"It's a good thing you don't teach meteorology, Carl. You'd have been sacked long before reaching tenure."

The white-haired professor ceased his deep breathing exercises. "And what's that supposed to mean?" he grumbled indignantly.

"That means your 'magnificent mountains' are jam-packed with magnificent raindrops. We'll be lucky if we aren't drenched before long."

Caroline surveyed her surroundings from the advantage of a tall-backed cedar bench parked strategically in the center of Bruck Green. The grassy oval separating St. Anne's Hospital from the campus of Bruck University was riddled with puddles from previous storms, and the cobbled walks criss-crossing the lawn still glistened with dampness.

"As if we needed any more rain," she added darkly.

Carl turned his back on the approaching cloudbank and waggled his bushy eyebrows at his friend. "Come now, Caroline. Your pessimism is an affront to this beautiful spring weather. Besides that, it's affecting my mood, which is exceptionally good considering I had breakfast with Professor Littlewort only an hour ago."

"Dr. Eccentric? You've got to be kidding, Carl."

Andrew Littlewort stood out like a sore thumb at conservative Bruck U. The Captain Kirk of English Literature, he boldly went where no other professor dared go. His required reading list included both William Shakespeare and *Rolling Stone* magazine, a combination not unreasonable except for Littlewort's attempt to prove a similarity between the two. Had his opinions been restricted to the classroom, Andrew might have fared better with his colleagues. As it was, the man had the sensitivity of a turnip when interacting with his peers. He publicly sneered at other teachers in his department, calling them 'educational cowards' whose 'slavish attachment to the status quo' reneged on their commitment to their students and the university. His acerbity cost him both respect and friendship, yet few dared criticize him to his face. Rather than deal with Littlewort's explosive temper, most of the faculty simply avoided him like the plague.

"Andy's impossible at times," Carl conceded. "But at least he's sincere."

Caroline groaned. "Pul-lease! As the good folk of Rhineburg would say, that man is downright squirrelly in the head." She reached into the brown paper bag tucked next to her on the bench and pulled out a decrepit looking plastic rose. "Now I know why you're behaving so weirdly," she said as she fixed a wire to the stem with a length of bright red ribbon. "You've been infected with Littlewortitis."

She tossed the flower to Carl who ignored her comment while making a great show of sniffing the pale pink posey.

"Ah, yes. The haunting fragrance of synthetic polymers. Robust, yet not intense. Redolent of...of...*achew*!" The professor dropped the rose and grabbed a handkerchief from his pocket.

"Redolent of dust!" Caroline rescued her handiwork from the grass. "And so bleached by the sun that it's practically colorless. These flowers belong in a Dumpster, not on a Maypole. Can't the university afford some new ones for the Festival of Knights?"

"Take it up with the Emperor," Carl said between sneezes. "He owes you one."

That's true, thought Caroline. Garrison Hurst, the president of Bruck University scornfully dubbed 'Emperor' by those who loathed his dictatorial style, was deeply indebted to her. The FBI had invaded his college over the winter holidays after a bomb decimated the psychiatric ward at nearby St. Anne's Hospital. Hot on the trail of a student terrorist, they'd disrupted the equanimity of both faculty and parents before Caroline's snooping flushed out the real killer and saved the university's reputation.

Of course, Caroline hadn't been driven purely by altruistic motives. A nurse by profession and a newcomer to town, she'd attracted the attention of FBI Agent Tom Evans after witnessing both the explosion and a subsequent murder. Evans didn't believe in coincidences. When he heard of her recent emotional breakdown following the hit-and-run death of her husband, he immediately tagged Caroline as number one suspect in the 'Mad Bomber' case.

It was only with the help of Carl Atwater that Caroline extricated herself from the mess. Thirty years younger than the septuagenarian professor, she now considered him a close friend and confidant. He'd reintroduced her to life over the course of their investigation, and for that, she'd be ever thankful.

Despite her fondness for him, Caroline recognized an alarming trait in Carl. He tended to go ballistic whenever Hurst's name was mentioned. The two men were engaged in a decade-long feud rooted in jealousy on Hurst's part over Atwater's considerable literary success. All attempts at civility had vanished last winter after Carl led a faculty rebellion against the president's proposed curriculum changes. Currently, the pair conversed only when university protocol, or unavoidable circumstances, dictated it. Sensing the professor was building up to another anti-Hurst tirade, Caroline quickly changed the subject.

"Tell me more about the Festival of Knights. How long has it been going on?"

Atwater sat down on the bench and pulled out his pipe. "The first Festival was held back in 1967. I remember it well because I was thrown by my horse during the opening ceremonies." He chuckled at the memory before catching sight of Caroline's raised eyebrows. "Don't look at me that way, woman! It may be hard to believe, but I weighed a hundred and sixty pounds back then."

"That must have been before you discovered the pleasures of Rhineburg's restaurants." Caroline glanced pointedly at her friend's waist. The professor's adipose tissue had more than doubled over the past four decades. His present girth resembled that of Santa Claus, the mythical figure he portrayed each year during the town's Winter Festival.

"Now you're going to badger me about my diet," Carl growled. "I know you're a nurse, but must you always think like one?"

Although she tried not to nag the professor, Caroline's instincts often proved too strong to resist. Today she threw up her hands in surrender.

"I'll save my lecture for the day you land in the ER clutching your chest. Getting back to the festival, whose bright idea was it in the first place? And why would the university get involved in such a massive undertaking?"

"Call it a dose of preventative medicine. You remember what it was like back in the '60s. Even staid old Bruck fell victim to flower power back then. We weren't overrun by hippies, mind you, but we did have our share of unwashed bodies littering the dormitories."

"Amazing. From the way you brag about this place, I'd have thought you survived that period unscathed."

"Let's not get nasty, Cari," warned the professor. "You Chicagoans weren't the only ones living in the Age of Aquarius. It's just that we Rhineburgers coped with the times better than most people."

"I'll bet you did! Who ran Bruck's security

department back then? The Archangels' father?"

Caroline was referring to the present day guardians of Bruck University, Michael, Rafael, and Gabriel Bruck. The triplets, who'd earned their nickname for obvious reasons, had a unique way of dealing with campus troublemakers. Those who violated university rules cut grass in the spring, raked leaves in the autumn, and shoveled snow in the winter. Apparently manual labor had an enlightening effect on most students; few ever served a second sentence.

"Their grandfather, John Bruck, was top dog back then," said Carl. "The Festival of Knights was his brainchild. He figured if the students worked together on a school project, they'd get to know each other as individuals rather than as political adversaries. Nehemiah MacCardy was Bruck's president at the time. He saw the wisdom in John's suggestion, and since Nehemiah's background was in history, hosting a Renaissance Faire was a natural for him."

"And the kids went along with the idea?"

Carl nodded. "Nehemiah persuaded the Student Senate to back the plan. Then he bullied the history and art departments into assisting with sets and costumes."

"I suppose the festival has evolved over the years."

"Sure has. In '67 we held a two-day tournament with a couple of food booths on the sidelines. Now it's a weeklong event. It opens with an evening banquet here on the Green followed the next day by a Grand Parade of Knights and preliminary jousting trials. Along with the games there are exhibitions of falconry, candle making, weaving, and other Renaissance crafts. And of course, there's the archery competition. That always draws a big crowd."

"Sounds like fun. How exactly are the students involved?"

"Each booth or event is hosted by a different student group," explained Carl. "The kids start planning their parts as early as September. Some of them even attend other Renaissance fairs during the summer, then incorporate new things they've seen into our celebration."

"I didn't realize the festival was such a big deal."

"It's become a tradition here at Bruck. It takes a lot of work to put on a decent show each year, but the kids reap the rewards of their efforts. Fifty percent of the proceeds from the fair goes to fund extracurricular activities." Carl tapped the tobacco from his pipe and returned it to his pocket. "Most of all, the students get to indulge in a little merrymaking before final exams. The festival gives them the emotional boost they need before settling down to serious studying."

Caroline couldn't argue with that. In addition to her job as a float pool nurse, she served as housemother to forty-two students living in the old nursing school dormitory attached to St. Anne's. She thought of the young people in her care.

"Considering how my gang burns the midnight oil night after night, I'd say they deserve a little fun." She returned the finished roses to the paper bag and, arching her back, rolled her shoulders. "Thank goodness that's done. Next year sign me up for something more exciting than tying ribbons on plastic flowers."

"They'll look very nice hanging from the Maypole,"

Carl assured her. "Speaking of which, those boys should have finished digging the hole for it by now."

The professor swiveled sideways on the bench until he faced north. Following his gaze, Caroline glanced over her shoulder to where a group of young men were gathered at the far end of Bruck Green. Two boys were attacking the hard packed soil with gardening spades. Several others stood nearby supporting a tall wooden pole on their shoulders. Suddenly, one of the diggers threw down his spade and began scrabbling in the dirt with his hands. The pole bearers immediately abandoned their burden and crowded around him.

"What in the world are they doing?" Carl said with a frown.

As if in answer, the boy kneeling by the hole jumped up and waved both arms in the air.

"Hey, Professor! Come see what we've found!"

Atwater clambered to his feet and extended a hand to Caroline. "With our luck, they've probably dug up a skeleton. You'd better come along, Super Sleuth."

Caroline grimaced at the title, but curiosity got the best of her. Hard on Carl's heels, she circled the fortuneteller's tent and angled across the Green to the intended site of the Maypole. She hung back when Carl approached the group. He slapped one of the boys on the back.

"What's up, guys?"

"Look what was buried here!" The erstwhile digger extended his hands to Carl. Cupped in his palms was a large rock, its surface smoothed by contact with the earth.

"Let me see that."

Carl took the stone and wiped it clean of dirt. Caroline watched as he examined it closely.

"That's a pretty hefty chunk," she said. "It must weigh at least five pounds."

"This is impossible," Carl muttered. "It can't be real."

"Let's ask Professor Littlewort," a redheaded boy suggested. "He's the expert on this stuff, isn't he?"

The redhead took off across the lawn as the others crowded around Carl, craning their necks for a better view of the stone. Caroline was bewildered by the shared excitement on their faces.

"What's so special about that rock?" she asked. "It looks quite ordinary to me."

Atwater shooed the boys aside. Cradling his prize in one hand, he pointed with the other to a series of nicks and scratches on the stone's surface. They resembled a triangle bisecting a straight line.

"I'm no archeologist. But I can assure you, if these boys' suspicions prove true, there's nothing at all ordinary about this rock. You may be looking at an ancient Viking rune stone."

"A what?"

"Atwater! Tell me I'm not dreaming!"

From the direction of the university ran a dark scarecrow of a man. His thin arms flapped in the air like the scrawny wings of a starving bird as he swooped down on the group. One oversized foot tripped over the other until he stumbled to a halt, out of breath, beside Carl.

"Is it...really...a rune...stone?" Professor Andrew Littlewort pressed one hand to his chest to ease his panting. His eyes behind horn-rimmed glasses flicked from face to face before settling on Carl's in hopeful anticipation.

Atwater shook his head slowly. Logic, that bane of all dreamers, had dampened his initial enthusiasm. He handed the rock to his colleague with a sigh.

"I'll admit, my first reaction was the same as yours, Andrew. If the stone turned out to be genuine.... But, no. We both know they couldn't have traveled this far inland."

Littlewort ignored the doubt in Carl's voice. "Look at the markings! If this isn't a letter from the futhork..."

"Hold on, Professor." Carl's tone registered gentle reproof. He touched the other man's arm in a sympathetic gesture meant to lessen the blow of his next words. "I wish for your sake you could prove your theory. But don't go jumping to conclusions. Those scratches could have been made by anyone at any time."

Littlewort pulled away from Carl's grasp. He clutched the rock to his chest, covering it with both hands, and stared stonily at Atwater. "You're jealous of me, aren't you. You know what this stone means, but you can't stand sharing the limelight with anyone. You think you're king here at Bruck. But when I prove the Vikings actually reached Rhineburg, I'll be the big man on campus, not you!"

"Andrew, Andrew," Carl said softly. "This has nothing to do with jealousy. I'm only urging you to exercise a little caution."

"Caution be damned!"

Littlewort spat out the words with a fury surprising even Caroline. She could tell by the venom in his voice that he was beyond pacifying. His hawk-like nose quivered with indignation, and the veins on his thin neck bulged rigidly as he extended his face to within inches of Carl's.

"I'll send it to Chicago for verification. The Field Museum will be honored to confirm my find." Littlewort drew back with a smirk and turned to address the redheaded boy. "Thank you, young man. Informing me of the stone's existence showed great intelligence on your part. Others, I fear," –he glared accusingly over his shoulder at Carl– "would have dismissed your report as sheer nonsense."

A stocky fellow with forearms twice the size of Littlewort's thighs, the boy glanced quickly at his companions, then dipped his head and shuffled back a step. His face had turned the color of his hair. Caroline let her gaze sweep over the other students. They seemed equally uncomfortable with the situation, and she sensed their relief when Littlewort strode away with the stone.

"You'd better get the Maypole up," she said, breaking the silence that followed the professor's exit. "It's going to rain any minute now."

The boys went back to work quite willingly. Leaving them to it, Caroline and Carl walked back to where the bag of roses lay unattended on the bench.

"Now, tell me what that was all about," said Caroline.

Carl shook his head in disgust. "I think someone's played a practical joke on Littlewort. Unfortunately, he's fallen for it." He sank down on the bench, reached into the bag, and extracted a rose. "We know these flowers are fake. Up close, anyone can tell they're plastic. But from a distance, say twelve feet up on the Maypole, most people will assume they're the genuine article newly picked from the university's garden."

"I don't think anyone will mistake those old things for real roses."

Atwater waved aside the objection. "Folks believe what they want to believe. Just wait and see. Tied up with greens and ribbon, even these decrepit blossoms will appear real to some."

Caroline grimaced. "So, what's your point, Carl?"

"Andrew wants to believe he's found a treasure, an actual runic relic left behind by ancient travelers. Common sense says it's impossible, but Professor Littlewort lacks common sense. He's like Don Quixote in academic garb, out on a quest to prove history wrong." Carl shook his head sadly. "Mark my words, he'll become the laughing stock of the university if he pursues this matter."

"Back up a minute, Carl. You lost me on the 'runic relic' part. What in the world are 'runic relics'? And that other word the professor mentioned, futtock, or…"

"Futhork. The Norse alphabet."

"Norse like in Norwegian?"

"Sort of," Carl replied. "The early inhabitants of Scandinavia—our present day Denmark, Norway, and Sweden—were called Norsemen, or Northmen. They were a fierce people, skilled in warfare and seamanship, who made a living as pirates and invaders. The Norse word 'vik' means 'harbor'. Norse warriors would 'go a-viking', sailing into bays along the European coast and raiding the villages there."

"So that's how they got their name."

"Correct. The Vikings attacked as far away as Russia, and for a time they occupied parts of Britain, Ireland, and France. They plundered Sicily and even made it to Constantinople, the capital of the Eastern Roman Empire. That was way back in the Eighth and Ninth centuries, but their influence was felt all the way up to 1050 A.D."

"Pretty powerful guys, those Vikings. But let's get back to Andrew Littlewort and his futhork. What was he talking about?"

Carl shifted on the hard wooden bench. "We sometimes call our alphabet the ABCs, right? Well, the Norsemen called theirs the futhork. The letters of the futhork were known as runes. Norse children learned to cut runes on stones much as our kids learn to write on paper. Early Norsemen used runes for scratching their names on personal belongings or on memorial stones. Over time, the memorials became more elaborate, runes intertwining with pictures and designs, like stories carved in rock. Today the word 'rune' also means a Norse poem or oral story."

"And these memorial stones still exist today?"

Carl nodded. "Thousands have been found on the Scandinavian peninsula, and one was discovered in Greenland where Eric the Red, a Viking explorer, established a Norse colony in 986 A.D. Eric's offspring, Leif Ericson, sailed as far as Newfoundland, which he called Vinland the Good, off the coast of Canada. A Norwegian expedition uncovered the remains of a Norse village there in 1963."

"I'm impressed," said Caroline. "According to those findings, Leif Ericson reached the North American continent some four hundred years before Columbus."

"It appears that way." Carl tucked the plastic rose back into the bag and took out his pipe. He pointed the stem at Caroline. "And that's why the rock those boys found is so important to Professor Littlewort."

"How so?" Caroline waited while Carl added tobacco to the pipe, tamped it down with one finger, and struck a match to the bowl. Her friend seemed distracted, even worried now. His brow was knit in a frown as he stared out over Bruck Green.

"You know how Andrew is always arguing obscure points of academia with anyone who will listen to him."

Caroline nodded. "He's fanatical in his beliefs. I remember overhearing him lecture a group of people at the faculty Christmas party last year. He wouldn't give an inch. In fact, he got downright ugly with one of the younger professors who disagreed with him."

"Andrew has a temper, alright. I've seen him in action a number of times, which is why I won't let him bait me into an argument. Much of what he propounds is just plain hogwash. Occasionally, though, the man makes a valid point. About three weeks ago, he brought up the subject of Leif Ericson at a faculty luncheon. We history buffs agreed with him that the Viking deserves more recognition. But most of the other professors pooh-poohed Andrew's ideas." Carl paused to draw on his pipe. A wisp of smoke escaped his lips and curled lazily upward, leaving behind the faint scent of vanilla. "Of course, that really angered him. If there's one thing old Littlewort can't stand, it's being rebuffed by his peers. In retaliation, he began a one-man campaign to replace Columbus Day with a holiday honoring Leif Ericson. He's been writing to congressmen and state officials ever since, trying to persuade them to take up his banner. That's why he invited me to breakfast today. He wants me to join the cause."

Caroline gazed at Carl in horror. "Tell me you didn't agree to help him."

"I sympathize with Andrew's point of view," Carl replied. "But he's gone way overboard this time. I suspect he's less concerned with Ericson's rightful place in history than with spitting in the collective eye of the faculty."

"His campaign is bound to fail," Caroline reasoned. "The Italian-American community would declare war on Congress if they even considered dumping Columbus Day. And it's sheer idiocy for Littlewort to take on the entire faculty. He'll only make enemies, and he's got enough already."

"Nobody ever credited Andrew with wisdom, Cari. But I agree with your thinking. There are plenty of folks at Bruck who would like nothing more than to cut Professor Littlewort down to size. Given this latest bit of nonsense–this rune stone charade–they may have the chance to do so."

Caroline gathered the loose bits of wire and ribbon and tossed them in a nearby waste container. "Let's hope no one gets hurt along the way," she said as she tidied up her materials. "Andrew Littlewort may deserve his comeuppance, but settling a score can sometimes get out of hand."

Little did she know how right she was.

Two

The first raindrop fell amid a low rumble of thunder. Caroline grabbed the bag of roses and, together with Carl, hurried towards Bruck Hall, the university's administrative center. Since Professor Atwater's version of hurrying differed greatly from Caroline's–his shorter legs and rotund body negating any actual attempt at speed–the two of them were moderately soaked by the time they reached shelter.

"Snow all winter and rain all spring," grumbled Caroline as she shook the dampness from her ash-brown hair. "Don't you Rhineburgers ever enjoy good weather?"

"Wait until summer," laughed Carl. He peeled off his windbreaker and hung it to dry on a rack near the Hall's front door. "I guarantee blue skies and sunshine from June through September."

"I'll hold you to that." Caroline passed her own jacket to Carl before turning to gaze out the lobby window. "Looks like the students aren't fazed by the rain. They're still out there cordoning off the jousting field." She pointed to a group of youths nailing wooden rails to fence posts at the south end of Bruck Green. "They actually seem to be having fun."

"Take a look at old Branch. He's watching those kids like a hawk." Carl gestured toward the side of the field where the university's head gardener stood scowling at the boys. "It must try his patience to see his tulip beds threatened each spring."

Caroline studied the gray-haired man supervising the activity on the Green. Stoop-shouldered from years of battling Mother Nature's darker side, Branch was thin and wiry like the weeds he so despised. His face was as bronze as the autumn asters he tended, but the sun had stained his arms an even darker color, almost obliterating the liver spots peppering his wrists. The skin around his eyes and mouth crinkled like crushed tissue paper as he scowled at the students. Standing there in a scarlet Bruck T-shirt hanging almost to his knees, he reminded Caroline of a wrinkled stick of beef jerky wrapped in bright red cellophane. Like the jerky, Branch was tougher than he looked.

"There's a good-sized patch of grass between the field and the flower beds. I doubt the spectators will trample his tulips."

"It's not the spectators that worry Branch. It's the horses." Seeing Caroline's bemused expression, Carl explained. "Jousting takes place on horseback. Unfortunately, we don't have a place to stable the nags between events. The riders are supposed to hitch their horses to lines strung between the trees, but sometimes they set them free to graze on the lawn. Many a noble steed has nibbled a bloom to the bare root."

Caroline burst into laughter. "I'd hate to own the horse that did that. Branch is as fanatical about his gardens as Littlewort is about Leif Ericson. Just last week I saw him tear into a student who picked a daffodil. Talk about tempers!"

"Actually, I'd like to," said Carl. "Talk about tempers, that is. But first, how about a bite to eat? It's almost noon."

It was closer to eleven-thirty by Caroline's watch, but she knew better than to argue with the professor. She'd learned early on in their relationship that food was never far from Carl's mind. Over the winter she'd gained not only a friend, but also six pounds and an extra inch around her waistline. Daily jogs on Circle Road had banished the unwanted weight, but Caroline now exercised a good deal of self-discipline whenever she was with Carl.

"Nothing for me," she said as Carl headed down the hallway to the kitchen. "I'll meet you in the faculty lounge."

The lounge looked nothing like it had last December when she'd first met Carl at a faculty holiday party. She'd been invited there ostensibly because her son Martin, a Ph.D. candidate at Bruck, was Carl's teaching assistant. She suspected, though, that she'd been included on the guest list for an entirely different reason. As a witness to the bombing at St. Anne's, she'd achieved an odd sort of celebrity status, a position she'd shunned from the start. As it turned out, her unwillingness to discuss the matter had branded her a troublemaker in the eyes of the killer.

Caroline shook off the memories of last winter and let her gaze wander around the room. Instead of Christmas poinsettias, outdated magazines now littered the wide windowsills bracketing the far corner of the room. To the left of the windows, the enormous stone fireplace stood empty of logs, a tarnished brass screen drawn across its gaping mouth. Tartan plaid easy chairs were grouped in pairs in front and to the right of the fireplace. To the left, on the spot previously occupied by three beautifully decorated Christmas trees, there now stood a brown leather couch and a small oak side table.

"Are you sure you aren't hungry?"

Carl entered the lounge carrying a tray of sandwiches and two bottles of beer. He placed the tray on the massive oak table in the center of the room, scooped two sandwiches onto a paper plate, flipped the cap off a beer, and settled himself at one end of the leather sofa. Caroline sank into an easy chair opposite Carl and shook her head. She refused to be enticed by the sight of dark rye piled high with thin slices of roast beef and cheddar cheese.

Diverting her eyes from Carl's plate, she said, "Tell me more about the rune stone. Why are you so sure it's a fake?"

"To tell the truth," the professor answered between bites, "when I first saw those scratches, my heart beat a little faster. The thought of finding a genuine Viking relic was overwhelming. But then my common sense took hold. Rhineburg's over a thousand miles from the Atlantic Ocean. How could a seafaring people, even those as adventurous as the Vikings, make their way this far inland? And why would they want to?"

"How about the St. Lawrence River? They might have sailed into the Great Lakes, then come ashore to explore."

Carl wrinkled his nose. "The North American colony lasted only three years. I doubt the settlers had enough time, energy, or resources to mount an expedition as ambitious as the one you suggest. Besides that, no physical evidence of Viking exploration has ever been found west of the Newfoundland site."

"So you think the stone is a hoax."

"Someone's putting one over on Littlewort," Carl said with a nod. "It may be a faculty member who's sick and tired of Andrew's temper tantrums. Or maybe a student heard about the ruckus and decided to play a practical joke. It really doesn't matter who's behind this prank. The important thing is, the professor is going to heap scorn both on himself and this university if the press gets wind of his plans."

"As it surely will if he sends the stone to the Field Museum," mused Caroline. "Maybe he'll come to his sense before he does anything rash."

"I've never known Littlewort to back down, even when it's obvious he's wrong. He just gets angry, and his anger is something to behold. You mentioned seeing Branch ream out a student for picking a daffodil. Let me tell you something, Cari. Branch is a lamb compared to old Andrew."

Carl set down his plate and stared moodily out the window. Caroline could tell he was troubled; he'd left half a sandwich uneaten.

"Don't ruin your day with worry," she said soothingly. "You did your best to stop the professor. If he continues to act like an obstinate fool, it'll be President Hurst's problem, not yours."

Carl's face brightened. "Serves the Emperor right! He's been glowing like a light bulb ever since he pushed that stadium deal through the Town Council. Littlewort's scheme ought to jar him back into reality."

Caroline chuckled. Carl was still furious over Hurst's plan to field a football team at Bruck. The school had no reputation for athletics, but the president firmly believed football would attract more students to the university while also luring sports-minded alumni into donating more cash to their alma mater. It was a plan with potential except for the fact that Hurst had no seed money to hire a coach or even buy uniforms. He'd resolved the problem by firing several untenured teachers, cutting courses, and increasing the student-teacher ratio in the remaining classes. His move had angered a good portion of the faculty, and they were fighting the changes tooth and nail. Dictating the order of battle was no other than Hurst's greatest critic, Carl Atwater.

"Your esteemed leader will suffer many a headache if Professor Littlewort publicizes his find. Before you know it, there'll be treasure hunters digging for rune stones all over Bruck Green."

Caroline's comment had an unexpected effect on her friend. Carl's eyes narrowed to thin slits as his face took on the dreamy quality of one lost deep in thought. He began to stroke his beard in slow deliberate motions.

"Oh, no, you don't!" Caroline sputtered. She'd known the professor long enough to recognize beard stroking as a classic sign of trouble to come. The grin spreading across his face only underlined her suspicions. "If you encourage Andrew Littlewort in this nonsense, you'll be as much to blame as he when all hell breaks loose."

"Now, Cari, don't be like that." Carl practically purred the words. "I'm only going to have a bit of fun at the Emperor's expense. I promise I won't let it get out of hand. And I won't involve you in it, either." He levered himself upright, his eyes twinkling with unsuppressed glee. "I was thinking more along the lines of Martin as my accomplice."

Caroline jumped to her feet at the mention of her son.

"Listen to me, Carl Atwater! Martin is your teaching assistant, not your partner in crime. He's a year away from earning his Ph.D., and you'll not get him expelled from Bruck." She paused to draw a calming breath. "Just think what Nikki would say if she got wind of your shenanigans."

"Martin's wife won't mind him helping. She detests the Emperor." Carl's voice faltered. His confidence eroded by Caroline's steely gaze, he made a last ditch attempt to smooth her ruffled feathers. "Come on, Cari. You know I'd never jeopardize your son's career. Marty will graduate with honors and probably earn a teaching post here at Bruck. Eventually, he'll take over my job as chairman of the history department. Then won't you be proud!"

"I should live so long," Caroline muttered. "You know what I think, Carl? You're as mad as your buddy Andrew. You're both obsessed with stupid vendettas, and you're both heading for trouble."

"I promise to be careful." Professor Atwater placed his right hand over his heart and raised his left in the air. "On my honor, Cari. I intend to do nothing more than tweak the nose of Emperor Hurst."

With that said, Carl suddenly remembered he had a faculty meeting to attend. He mumbled an apology and escorted Caroline to the door, then beat a hasty retreat in the direction of the Liberal Arts building. Stranded on the steps of Bruck Hall, Caroline could only stare at Carl's vanishing backside and wonder what the man was up to now.

Three

The storm had been short lived. Only a few puddles dampened the road encircling Bruck Green, and Caroline easily avoided them when she approached the parkway. The dozen or more tents scattered about the grassy oval seemed none the worse for the weather, nor did the food booths with their colorful flags, hand painted menu boards, and red and gold striped awnings.

Towering above these other attractions, the Maypole now stood firmly planted in the center of the Green. Pink and ruby ribbons extended outward from the top of the pole in a circular fashion. Anchored to the ground with lynch pins, they awaited the addition of Caroline's roses.

Unfortunately, the boys who'd raised the Maypole and were assigned to decorate it were nowhere to be seen. Caroline wondered if they'd left because they'd unearthed something else from the wet campus soil.

"Like Leif Ericson's bones," she muttered aloud.

"Enough!" she told herself disgustedly. Stuck with the bag of flowers, she tucked it under her arm and began the short walk back to her apartment in the nursing school dorm. Carl's mischievousness was a worry, but she forced it out of her mind and savored, instead, the warm spring sun beating down on her shoulders. The air was fragrant with the scent of newly mown grass, and raindrops glistened on the golden daffodils lining the Green's cobblestone paths. She stopped in the shade of a gnarled oak tree to drink in the day and admire the flowers' varying shades.

"You like my daffodils, Mrs. Rhodes?"

The gardener had appeared out of nowhere. He stood in the shadows a few feet from Caroline, his head cocked to one side as he observed her through narrowed eyes.

"I do indeed, Mr. Branch." Caroline's voice betrayed her surprise. Branch had caught her off guard, and he was quick to take note of it.

"Didn't mean to creep up on you," the older man said in apology. "I guess you're wary of that sort of thing since the business with the bomb last year."

Caroline blushed. "I admit, the murders left their mark. But I'm trying to put the experience behind me."

"Some things you never get over." Branch glanced down at the daffodils. He shrugged his muscular shoulders and added in a somber drawl, "Bein' careful ain't such a bad idea these days. Gotta protect your backside, my daddy always said."

"Hmm." Having no such pearls of wisdom to offer in return, Caroline simply joined the gardener in admiring the flowerbeds. After a few moments of uninterrupted silence, the man spoke again.

"You garden?"

"What? Oh, no. Not any more." Caroline bent over and flicked a raindrop off a drooping petal. "My gardening days ended when I moved here from Chicago. It's a pleasure I miss, living in an apartment like I do." She smiled at her companion. "You have so many varieties here, Mr. Branch. Did you plant them all yourself?"

"My daddy was head gardener before me, but he was a rose man. Roses are fine over there." He gestured towards the university buildings on the other side of the Green. "They don't work so well under these trees. I figured the walks could use some color in spring, so every fall I'd plant a few more daffies. Now all my paths are lined with gold." Branch threw back his head and uttered a loud guffaw. "That's what I tell the boys who work for me, but none of 'em understand. Not even Mr. Smarty Pants over there." He pointed a callused finger at a young man lounging against a tree trunk some twenty feet away and hollered, "Get back to your raking, Burke, or I'll report you to the Archangels."

Caroline hadn't noticed the youth before. He was a tall good-looking boy with curly black hair and an insolent manner who motioned rudely in Branch's direction before strolling off across the Green. Only Caroline witnessed the gesture; the gardener had already turned away.

"I saw you here earlier today," said Branch. "You and Professor Atwater were helpin' the students put up that Maypole."

"We weren't really helping them. We only walked over to see what all the excitement was about." Caroline described the rune stone and its effect on Professor Atwater. "He intends to send it to Chicago for verification. It's probably a fake, but I'd advise you to keep a look out for strangers bearing shovels. I'd hate to see your flowerbeds dug up by fortune hunters when word of this gets out."

Branch's jaw dropped in horror. "You think people will come looking for more of these stones?"

"It's possible. I don't mean to worry you, but it's only fair you're warned."

The gardener shook his fist in the air. "They come diggin' here and they'll get a load of buckshot in their pants. I won't tolerate no strangers messin' around on these grounds, ya hear?"

"I hear you loud and clear." Caroline raised both her hands to ward off the man's wrath. She was taken aback by the sudden fury of Branch's response. Then it came to her that his passion could be put to good use. "You should speak to President Hurst, tell him how you feel about this situation. After all," she added slyly, "he's the only one who can put a stop to this business."

Branch rocked back on his heels, his dark eyes glittering. "That's a darned good idea," he growled. "Problem is, you can never find the man when you need him."

"There's a faculty meeting going on over in the Liberal Arts building," Caroline murmured. "I'm sure the president will be presiding. I'm also sure he'll want to hear what you, as a valued employee, have to say."

"He'd better!" Branch replied heatedly. "I thank you for tellin' me all this, Mrs. Rhodes. You've been real helpful."

"I try to be, Mr. Branch. I really do."

Caroline smiled smugly as the gardener loped off across the lawn. Knowing Garrison Hurst, she was certain he'd cringe at the thought of rock hounds digging holes on Bruck Green. Archeologists were one thing, but an uncontrolled treasure hunt on his beautiful campus? No way! A few words from Branch and Hurst would surely crush Littlewort's plans. If there was a sledgehammer handy, he might even crush the stone itself.

Of course, Carl would be disappointed. But at least Martin wouldn't be dragged into his little farce, and that's what really mattered. Martin was altogether too fond of Professor Atwater. He'd follow Carl to hell and back if asked, and probably be expelled from school for doing so.

"Not while I'm around," Caroline said grimly. To paraphrase Branch's daddy, a mother had to protect her son's backside.

Four

Caroline pulled into the driveway of the Blue Cat Lounge precisely at 7 P.M. The last rays of the setting sun filtered through the gray-green boughs of the ponderosa pines guarding the graveled parking lot, illuminating it just enough for her to see Martin's old Chevy, parked halfway down the left hand aisle. A familiar red 4x4 sat near the entrance of the roadhouse. She braked beside it.

"Better late than never." Carl pushed himself off his Jeep's back bumper and opened Caroline's door. "What kept you?"

"Kerry called," Caroline said with a smile. "She was bubbling over with news about school and her new boyfriend."

"Another one?" Carl had yet to meet the entire Rhodes clan, but Caroline had regaled him with stories of her daughters. Krista was a teacher in Chicago; Kerry, a theater major in college. "What happened to the last guy? She only met him a month ago."

Caroline shrugged her shoulders. "Maybe she was just too much of a challenge for the poor boy. Anyway, Kerry says this fellow is the real McCoy." She locked her car and together they headed for the tavern. "Am I so late you had to come looking for me?"

"Shiloh sent me out to check the gutters. He says one of them is leaking."

Carl was part owner of the Blue Cat Lounge, a roadhouse outside of Rhineburg specializing in locally brewed beer and jazz. The building itself looked decrepit with brown paint peeling off the warped windows and ancient wooden siding. A jumble of mismatched shingles covered the roof, and a neon cat flashed on and off erratically above the sagging entranceway. There was no sign on the door; the cat said it all.

"It's hard to believe this place is structurally sound," said Caroline, shaking her head.

"I sank a lot of money into the Blue Cat after Shiloh and I became partners. We put in new support beams, new floors and ceilings, and we updated the electrical and plumbing. All the kitchen appliances are new also."

"And you preserved the exterior of the building in its original state so tourists wouldn't find it attractive."

"You're darn right we did," Carl said with a nod. "Rhineburg's becoming too quaint for its own good. Every week there's another grand opening of an antique store or some highbrow artsy-craftsy joint. I tell you, this town is losing its character. It's turning into a tourist trap where city folks come to gobble up bargains and gawk at the natives. Can you blame us for wanting a place of our own? A place where Rhineburgers can socialize without being bothered by a bunch of urban invaders?"

Caroline laughed. "Urban invaders? You make it sound like Rhineburg's under attack."

"In a way it is," the professor muttered. He yanked open the door and ushered Caroline inside. "Mark my words: the Vikings thought their way of life would last forever. Look what happened to them!"

"So you're still on *that* subject, are you?" Caroline rolled her eyes. "I thought after the faculty meeting you'd have given it up."

"Really? Then I guess you haven't heard the latest."

"What latest," asked Caroline, stopping dead in her tracks. "Out with it, Carl. What are you planning now?"

"The downfall of the mighty," Atwater replied with a smile. "Come on, Cari. I'll fill you in on the news during dinner."

Like Moses parting the Red Sea, Carl elbowed his way across the crowded room, roaring at the top of his lungs, "Out of my way, plebeians! The king cometh!"

"Honestly, Carl," Caroline hissed as amused patrons backed out of their path. "Act your age."

Mumbling apologies left and right, she followed the professor to a table where Martin and Nikki were waiting.

"I was beginning to think we'd have to start without you." Martin Rhodes sprang to his feet and pulled out a chair for his mother. A foot taller than Caroline, he smiled down on her with unsuppressed mirth. "Bet you were on the phone with Krista or Kerry. And here I sat waiting, so hungry I could eat the menu."

Caroline cast a sympathetic glance at Nikki. "You'd think food was a rare luxury for the boy. Is he always this bad?"

"Only when it comes to pizza," laughed Nikki. "Speaking of which, we ordered the specialty of the house. It has everything on it but the kitchen sink."

"Sounds appetizing." Caroline raised one eyebrow and motioned with her head towards Carl. "I don't suppose it's low calorie."

"Good grief, woman! It's a party, not a wake." Carl caught the shirttails of a passing waiter and ordered a round of honey beer. "We're celebrating tonight, aren't we, Martin."

"We sure are. This is an auspicious day in the history of Bruck University, a day to be remembered."

"Auspicious in what way?" demanded Caroline.

"Didn't the professor tell you? Why–wait a minute while I get these." Martin took the tray from the waiter and distributed the icy steins. A crooked smile split the rugged features of his face as he raised his glass of beer. "A toast! To Andrew Littlewort's rune stone. May its discovery benefit us all."

Nikki bobbed her head in agreement. "Amen to that."

Caroline refrained from joining the toast, something Carl quickly noticed. He smiled soulfully at his assistant. "Your mother's upset with us, Marty. She thinks we're hatching some terrible plot against President Hurst."

"Well, aren't you?" Caroline pointed her finger at Carl. "I saw that look on your face when you ran off to the faculty meeting. You were grinning like the Cheshire Cat, which meant you were up to no good."

"Now, Mom. It's not all that bad. It's more like a harmless prank than…"

"Pranks have a way of backfiring," snapped Caroline. "Can you afford that risk, Martin?"

"Your son won't be involved, Cari. As I told these two earlier, you've already done most of the work for me."

"What?" Caroline stared open-mouthed.

"You set the stage for some mighty fine fireworks when you told Branch treasure hunters might dig up his precious flowerbeds." Carl chuckled. "The head gardener came charging into our meeting, bellowing at the top of his lungs that the rune stone had to be destroyed. He was really off the wall, Cari. He called Littlewort a fool and accused President Hurst of dereliction of duty. No one disputed his opinion of Andrew. His views concerning the Emperor were another matter altogether."

"I'm sure Garrison didn't take kindly to the verbal abuse."

"He most certainly didn't. He'd just denied Andrew's request for a limited dig on Bruck Green. But Branch's little outburst left Hurst smack dab between a rock and a hard place. Everyone knows the president can't abide Professor Littlewort. But stand still for a public bashing from someone as low on the totem pole as Charlie Branch? No way! Garrison was forced to support his fellow faculty member over the school gardener."

"I can't believe it," Caroline mumbled weakly. "Hoisted on my own petard."

Nikki patted her mother-in-law's hand. "Don't take it so hard. The dig won't happen until after the Festival of Knights. By then the Field Museum folks will have proven the rune stone a fake."

"Of course, Professor Littlewort will have already spilled the beans to the press." Martin spread both hands wide. "I can see it now. Reporters will invade the campus, begging for interviews. At the same time, Bruck Green will be awash with rock hounds eagerly collecting every stone in sight."

"The Emperor will be hard pressed to explain his gullibility once the truth is known," added Nikki. "He'll cancel the dig, then pray the Board of Regents doesn't blame him for the entire fiasco."

"Which they probably will," concluded Carl. "And if so, they just might ask Hurst for his resignation."

The foolishness of her dinner companions both baffled and angered Caroline. Apparently only she understood how difficult it was to topple the powerful. Garrison Hurst had made a mistake today. Despite that, he was still a very powerful man.

"You three are daydreaming. The one most likely to get hurt by this hoax is Professor Littlewort. I'm not especially fond of the man, but he sure doesn't deserve to go down this way."

"Andrew will be all right," Carl assured her. "He's fully tenured. He'd have to kill someone before Hurst could fire him."

Caroline bit back a reply as the waiter arrived with their pizza. The aroma of garlic and onions had a potent effect on her salivary glands, and within minutes she was devouring her portion with gusto equaling her son's. By the time they finished dinner, the conversation had progressed to a less controversial subject.

"How's the new job going, Nikki?"

"I hadn't thought I'd like it, Professor, but Emma Reiser is a fantastic person to work for. She's not only Rhineburg's postmaster, but also the town counselor. It's amazing how many people drop by the post office just to seek her advice."

"So you're not disappointed that you're working outside your field?"

Nikki shrugged. "Outside of the Social Services Department at St. Anne's, there aren't many jobs in Rhineburg that require a bachelor's degree in psychology.

And to tell the truth, I'm learning a lot about people just watching Mrs. Reiser in action. She's sympathetic, but not meddling. She knows when to interject a comment or question into the conversation and when to keep still. Folks really seem to trust her opinions."

"Sounds like she could be the Postal Service Employee of the Year," joked Martin. "A woman who delivers mail and advice at the same time."

"Behave yourself!" Nikki gave her husband an affectionate punch on the arm. "Mrs. Reiser is one of those people you naturally confide in. She always has the kettle on in the back room. Folks pop in for tea and conversation whenever they please."

"And what do you do while your boss is loafing away the hours with the customers," teased Martin.

Nikki replied with a saucy toss of her curly black hair. "I sell stamps and weigh packages and sort the mail, Mr. Smarty Pants!"

Caroline glanced at her son in amusement. It was the second time today she'd heard a young man called that name. Fortunately, Martin didn't react at all like Branch's helper. Rather than replying with a rude gesture, he leaned over and gave Nikki a kiss.

As he did so, a commotion broke out in the lounge. At a table in the far corner of the room sat two men, one much younger than the other, the second more drunk than the first. The two were demanding drinks from a harried looking waiter who was clearly refusing to serve them. Caroline saw Shiloh hurry out from behind the bar and make his way towards them.

"Carl, isn't that Charlie Branch over there?"

Atwater nodded, a frown creasing his forehead.

"The other fellow is Sid Burke," said Martin. "A real piece of work. Obnoxious as hell, and sneaky to boot."

"Sid is in my History of Warfare class," said Carl. "He's an intelligent kid, but lazy. I'm pretty sure he cheats on his tests. I've never been able to catch him, though."

"I wonder why he's here with Branch," said Caroline. "They didn't seem particularly friendly when I saw them together earlier today." She told them about her conversation with Branch that afternoon and Burke's obscene gesture aimed at the head gardener. "I didn't know the boy's name until now, but Branch called him his helper. Sid didn't seem to be doing much work."

Martin and the professor exchanged amused looks.

"He was probably pressed into service," said Martin. "I'll bet he got into some trouble, and raking the Green was his punishment, compliments of the Archangels."

"But why would they be together here," asked Nikki. "Branch doesn't normally hang out with the students. And Sid doesn't sound like the type who'd buddy up to the school gardener."

Branch had risen from his chair. He grabbed Shiloh's arm, apparently to steady himself, then collapsed in a heap on the table.

"The man is totally sloshed," Carl growled. "I've never known him to drink like that." He pushed back from the table. "Come on, Marty. It looks like Shiloh could use some assistance."

Caroline watched as the two men helped ease Branch to the floor. Charlie was dead to the world. He never moved a muscle as Carl spoke first to Burke, then to

Shiloh, and finally to Martin. Martin nodded before walking back to the women.

"Professor Atwater is hopping mad," he told them gravely. "He blames Shiloh for over serving the two of them."

"Burkes looks sober enough," noted Nikki.

"Yeah, he's okay. But Branch is a goner. He drove himself here, and now my boss is insisting we drive him home."

"I don't think we have a choice in the matter," Caroline replied testily. "It may be our fault he was drinking in the first place." She noted the look of chagrin Martin exchanged with Nikki. Perhaps the two of them now understood the foolishness of their actions. Branch was an unintended but real victim of their little prank. Irritated with herself for playing a part in Carl's scheme, she slapped down her napkin and rose from the table. "Nikki and I will wait outside while you men get Charlie back on his feet."

Minutes later, Carl and Martin half carried, half dragged a very tipsy Branch out the door of the Blue Cat Lounge. "Good lord, he's heavy," exclaimed Atwater. "Get hold of his arm, Cari. He keeps grabbing my face."

Caroline peeled Branch's fingers from the professor's nose and gripped his hand in hers. The gardener gave her a tipsy smile.

"Kind of yous ta help a fella out. Would ya like ta shtroll my pash a gold?"

Caroline shook her head. "No thanks, Charlie. Maybe some other time."

The gardener blinked twice before his head lolled

forward on his chest and he passed out.

"Watch out!" cried Nikki. Branch had pitched to the left and was sliding to the ground, taking Carl with him.

"Damn it, Sid! Give us a hand!"

Burke had followed them out of the roadhouse. He stood leaning against the doorjamb, a smirk on his face as he watched the two men struggle with his erstwhile companion. Martin's frustration seemed to amuse him even more, but he did push away from the door and take a lazy step forward. He grabbed Branch by his belt.

"Sorry, Mr. Rhodes. I thought you and the professor were managing pretty well by yourselves."

Martin's only response was a growl.

"We'll put him in my Jeep," said Carl. "You follow in his car, Burke. When we're done, I'll drop you back at the university."

After much pushing and pulling they managed to cram Branch into the back seat of Carl's vehicle. Atwater told Martin and Nikki to go home, insisting he and Burke could handle the situation. Martin put up an argument, but in the end, the couple reluctantly agreed to go. Caroline was not as amenable to the professor's plan. She pulled her Jeep into line behind Branch's car and followed the others out of the lot.

Five minutes later, the three cars left the highway and headed up a gravel road leading into the forest. Their progress slowed as darkness covered them like a magician's cape once they hit the wood line. Overshadowed by thick-limbed trees, the road twisted and turned for a half mile before their headlights picked up the outline of a house set off in a clearing to the left.

Carl swung off the road, the others following him, and pulled up facing the front of the building. He left his headlights on and climbed out of the SUV. "Open up, will you?" He tossed a set of keys to Caroline. "Burke and I will bring him in."

Caroline nodded and walked up the tidy path leading to the two-storied house. The front door was illuminated by the Jeep's headlamps, and she had no trouble fitting the key in the lock. Inside, she found a long hallway with entrances to a living room on the right and a den on the left. Halfway down the hall was a staircase extending to the second floor. Beyond the staircase stood a closed door presumably leading to the kitchen.

She flipped on the lights in the hallway and living room, then took the stairs to the second floor.

"Up here, Carl!" She watched as Carl and Sid maneuvered Branch through the doorway and up the narrow flight of stairs. "Bedroom's on the left."

Carl was perspiring freely when he and young Burke dragged their drunken companion past Caroline. Huffing and puffing, the two men lowered Branch onto an unmade bed in the far corner of the room. Sid backed away as Caroline began to undress the sleeping gardener.

"Leave him," Carl muttered as he collapsed on a low wooden bench set beneath one window. "He can sleep with his clothes on."

Caroline continued to unlace Branch's boots. "Why ruin this beautiful quilt? His boots are caked with mud and grass."

Carl was more concerned with his jacket than with Branch's quilt. He sniffed the suede material and wrinkled his nose in distaste. "I'll have to get this cleaned," he grumbled. "It reeks of alcohol."

Caroline brushed a few pieces of straw from Branch's stockinged feet and threw a blanket over him. A corner of it brushed his cheek, and the slumbering man stirred. "Pash of gold," he murmured before falling back asleep.

"I doubt Mr. Branch will be tending his gardens tomorrow. He's going to have one humdinger of a headache."

"Serves him right. What the hell does he think he's doing guzzling whiskey like that? Charlie Branch is no drinker. I've known the man for years. He hardly ever touches the stuff."

Caroline shrugged. "There's a first time for everything. Perhaps Mr. Burke can explain Charlie's behavior."

But Sid Burke had left the room. Leaving Branch to sleep it off, Caroline and the professor went downstairs. They found Sid bent over the desk in Branch's den.

"What are you doing in there, Burke?"

Sid spun around. As he turned, his hand brushed against a pile of papers on the desk.

"Sorry, Professor. I got bored hanging around upstairs." He walked out of the room. "Can we leave now?"

Atwater grunted and motioned the boy to go ahead of him. When Burke was out of earshot, Carl turned to Caroline. "Are you sure it's all right to leave Branch alone like this? He won't wake up and go staggering around the house, will he?"

"I doubt it. I've had a lot of experience with drunks in

the ER. They usually don't awaken until they're sober. Considering his condition, I think Branch will sleep through the night."

Carl glanced up the staircase. "He's a good man, Cari. I wouldn't want to see him hurt himself."

"If it'll make you feel better, I'll stick around and look in on him in a few minutes. Go ahead and take Burke back to the dormitory. And on the way, try to find out what led up to this fiasco."

Carl nodded his gratitude. "I'll call you in the morning."

Caroline watched at the window as the professor pulled out of the driveway. Minutes passed and the house was quiet except for the noisy snoring of its owner. Caroline decided to check on the gardener one more time. Just as she thought, he was dead to the world.

"Sleep tight," she murmured. She pulled one end of the quilt over Branch and opened the window a crack before drawing the shade. Satisfied that all was well, she returned to the first floor. A lamp glowed in the den and she went in to shut it off.

"I wonder what Burke was doing in here."

Her eyes were drawn to the desk. A stack of seed and nursery catalogues piled left of center had toppled and now lay scattered across the wooden surface. Doubtful they held anything of interest to Burke, Caroline brushed them aside, exposing as she did so a scarred leather scrapbook. Curious, she sat down to examine it.

A faded clipping from a Springfield newspaper was pasted on the first page. Dated August 18, 1980, it gave a brief but concise account of a bank robbery in the state's capital. Next to it was taped a report from another Illinois town similarly victimized in early 1981.

Caroline leafed through the scrapbook. The first half of it contained old newspaper clippings from towns east of Rhineburg. Some of the articles originated in Indiana and Michigan while others were from states as far away as Pennsylvania. A common thread ran through all the stories. Apparently someone had plundered small town branch banks and gotten away scot-free.

The final entry was from a Wisconsin paper dated October 28, 1989. It told of yet another robbery, this one resulting in a loss of five thousand dollars. The reporter predicted the thief would soon be caught. Communities across the mid-west were acting to protect their banks by installing higher resolution cameras and, in some instances, hiring armed guards. The response apparently paid off because the album contained no further articles. Instead, the last few pages were filled with snapshots of young men posed individually and together, each one of them bearing an uncanny resemblance to Bruck U.'s head gardener.

Caroline leaned back in her chair and studied the multitude of framed photographs decorating the paneled walls of the den. Directly across from the desk hung a faded picture of a woman in her mid-thirties sitting on a rickety wooden porch swing. The woman was surrounded by five little boys whom Caroline recognized as miniatures of the youths in the album.

The adjoining walls were covered with family portraits taken over a span of years. One showed a smiling Branch decked out in formal wear and gazing fondly at his bride, a younger version of the woman on the swing. Another displayed the two of them sitting in the kitchen, an infant playing happily in the foreground.

Caroline's eyes wandered from photo to photo. There in the corner was Branch teaching his sons to fish. Below that, the five boys were captured on a tractor set in a sea of corn. Near the center of one wall a shot revealed Branch and another man standing beside a sleek black motorcycle. The two were shaking hands and grinning.

Caroline sighed. There was no sign of a wife about the house now. She'd seen no cosmetics in the upstairs bedrooms, no bottles of perfume or jars of face cream. The living room was equally devoid of a woman's touch. It had a musty, unlived-in quality about it that was accentuated by the unpolished surfaces of the tables and the general shabbiness of the furniture.

"I'll bet she's dead," she reasoned aloud. Divorced men usually didn't keep photos of their wives prominently displayed in their homes. This den had to be Branch's version of a shrine, a sacred place dedicated to a happier time in his life.

A grandfather clock in the living room began to chime the hour. Caroline glanced at her watch and was surprised to see it was already ten o'clock. She'd stayed with Branch longer than she'd planned. After one last look around the picture gallery, she flipped off the lights in the den and walked into the hallway. At the foot of the stairs she stopped and gazed upward. The sound of snoring still wafted down from the room above. Reassured Branch was still asleep, Caroline slipped out of the house, locking the front door behind her.

Five

"I didn't expect to see you again tonight."

Professor Atwater ushered Caroline into his tidy bungalow on Faculty Row. The house was dark except for the living room where the soft glow from a pseudo-Tiffany hanging lamp illuminated a trestle table set against a bay window of leaded glass. An assortment of swords, lances, and battle-axes covered the table's surface.

"Preparing for your next battle with Garrison Hurst?"

Carl wrinkled his nose. "Very funny, Cari. These are for the festival. The knights will be using them."

"You're going to let the kids duel with these swords?"

"Why not?" Carl reacted to the surprise in Caroline's voice with his typical nonchalance. "All the hand-to-hand combat is choreographed to avoid injuries. And these particular arms are fashioned of hardened aluminum. They're not at all like the real thing." He handed her a sword. "See how dull the edge is? You'd really have to whack somebody to draw blood with this."

Caroline ran her thumb along the blade. The edges were thick and blunt to the touch. The weapon's tip was round and dull.

"I suppose you know what you're doing," she said rather dubiously. She placed the sword back on the table and dug deep in her pocket. "Here are Branch's keys. I locked the front door when I left."

"I'll check up on him in the morning," said Carl as he took the keys. "You know, Cari, ever since his wife died,

Charlie's led a solitary existence. It seems to satisfy him, but I don't think it's a healthy lifestyle. He could drop dead tomorrow, and nobody would even notice."

"I figured he lived alone. There wasn't a hint of feminism in that house." Caroline told Carl about the wall of photographs. "His wife was a beautiful woman. What happened to her?"

Carl shrugged. "I'm not really sure. I saw Mrs. Branch at various university functions back when their boys were attending Bruck. She seemed the picture of health up until the time Rudy, the youngest son, graduated. Shortly thereafter she went into a decline. The word around town was that Julie had cancer, but when she died Alexsa Stromberg told me it was heart trouble."

"They were a close couple?"

"No doubt about it. From what I've heard, they spent every available moment together. But now that we're discussing it," Carl added, "I remember Rudy telling me his parents' relationship changed for the worst during those last few months of Julie's life. Of course, a disease like cancer can put quite a strain on people."

"That's true," Caroline agreed. "But it's been my experience that the stronger the relationship between a couple, the better they cope when one or the other faces a life threatening disease. Their mutual love seems to work in their favor."

"Everybody's different, Cari. Maybe the Branches just couldn't accept the inevitability of death." Carl led her into the kitchen where he clapped his hands twice. The overhead light flashed on. "How about a piece of pie? I've got lemon meringue in the frig."

Caroline declined, deciding on a cup of tea instead. She busied herself at the stove while Atwater cut himself an ample slice of the gooey dessert.

"Did you know Branch was a crime buff? He has a scrapbook full of stories about bank robbers."

"Charlie probably wishes he could catch himself a crook," Carl joked. "A big reward would let him retire in comfort."

Caroline smiled. "What are his sons doing now?"

"They all have jobs out of town. The last time I saw them was at their mother's funeral five years ago."

"So how long has Branch been tending the flowers at Bruck?"

"Must be eight or nine years now." Carl eased his belt a notch and settled down on an oversized kitchen chair to enjoy his pie. "Charlie's dad was head gardener for ages. When he died, Charlie took over the job. Before that he'd worked as a driver for a cross country freight hauling company."

"That job must have paid better than the one at Bruck." Caroline carried her tea to the table and sat down opposite the professor.

"Kept him away from home too much. Branch was a family man."

"You sure know a lot about him. Are you two friends?"

Carl shook his head. "I taught three of his boys, so I got to know a bit about Charlie from comments they made. And naturally, I attended Julie's funeral." He scraped his plate clean and pushed it aside. "As unofficial town historian, I try to keep tabs on current events in

51

Rhineburg. When I got home tonight I checked my records on the Branch family. Charlie's little binge had me worried, and I wondered if it had something to do with today's date."

"Like an anniversary of some kind?"

"Exactly. But I didn't find anything to link this situation with the past. Frankly, this entire episode has me stumped."

"I think I can explain it," Caroline replied. "I'll bet Branch is upset over the possibility of treasure hunters digging up the campus."

Carl's bushy white eyebrows shot up. "But why? The Emperor will back off his promise to Professor Littlewort as soon as the rune stone's been proven a fake."

"Branch doesn't know that. All he heard was that the President is sanctioning a dig on his territory. The news was bound to upset him. It was apparent to me this afternoon that those gardens are his pride and joy. He was genuinely distressed over the idea of strangers tearing them up."

Carl stood up and paced the room. The floorboards quivered beneath his three-hundred-pound frame, and Caroline had to suck in her stomach each time he pushed past her. After a few minutes of silent cogitation, he thudded to a halt and plopped down on his chair.

"I hate to see the fun spoiled," he said disgustedly. "Still, I'd better explain things to Charlie. If he's that disturbed over this nonsense…"

"Oh, he's disturbed all right. As drunk as he was tonight, Branch's mind was still on his beloved flowers. He calls Bruck's daffodil beds his 'paths of gold'. His speech was slurred, but I could swear he mumbled that phrase before passing out up in the bedroom."

"So?"

"Carl, obviously you don't understand the passion that burns in the heart of a born gardener. We're a breed unto ourselves, people so fixated on flowers that the highlight of the winter season is the arrival of the first seed catalogue in the mail. We tend to go a little berserk when somebody threatens to destroy our handiwork."

Carl held up one hand. "You've convinced me, Cari. I forgot you had something in common with Charlie."

"I was addicted to gardening when I lived in Chicago. For that very reason I should have known better than to get Branch so riled up this afternoon. I'm partially to blame for his drinking spree."

"It's more my fault," the professor admitted. "I'll make a point of speaking to Charlie in the morning."

With that settled, they moved on to a new but related subject.

"So why was Mr. Burke at the Blue Cat Lounge tonight?"

"*Phff*!" Carl snorted in disgust. "That Sid is a worthless lout. He claims he and Branch are friends, but we both know that's a lie. Burke was working off a punishment when you saw him on the Green today. Seems he was caught running a little con game on the freshmen. He printed up tickets to the Festival of Knights and was selling them to the more naïve students."

"But there's no admission fee for students."

"Correct. We only charge visitors, and even then it's a nominal fee. But Sid figured rightly that some of the freshmen wouldn't know this."

"I'm surprised his only punishment was raking the lawn."

"He's serving a three week sentence. Apparently he couldn't get around the Archangels as easily as he did President Hurst."

Caroline marveled once more at the Bruck brothers' disciplinary methods. The identical triplets ran a tight Security Department with Michael commanding the day shift, Rafael handling afternoons and evenings, and Gabriel manning the office at night. At times the three descendents of Bruck U.'s founder joined forces to supervise events such as the Festival. Since few students dared tangle with the blond giants, these occasions were marked by a decided lack of rowdiness. It was the ability of the Archangels to enforce tranquility that endeared them to the conservative inhabitants of Rhineburg.

"I'm glad the Bruck boys nailed Mr. Burke. But tell me one thing. Why didn't Garrison Hurst just expel the little rat? Larceny doesn't seem to fit in with the university image Hurst promotes."

"Ever hear of Edmund Burke? The guy who's always yapping to the papers about how soft the courts are on criminals? He's our local state representative, and Sid is his son."

It was Caroline's turn to raise her eyebrows. "I get the picture. Hurst wouldn't dare enrage a state rep by tossing his kid out of college. Fundraising efforts could take an unexpected nosedive."

"You're absolutely right." Atwater rose from the table and wandered to the refrigerator. "A nasty thought has entered my mind, and I'd like to run it by you," he said as he removed two bottles of beer from the bottom shelf. He handed one to Caroline, ignoring the teacup in her hand. "Burke is in my History of Warfare class. We discussed the Vikings and their raiding techniques earlier in the year. Sid is also studying literature under Professor Littlewort."

"You think he's behind this rune stone hoax?"

"The possibility has occurred to me." Carl flipped the cap off his beer and took a long pull of the dark amber liquid. "Sid is lazy and conniving, but he's also pretty bright. He could mastermind a stunt like this if he wanted to embarrass a teacher he disliked."

"If Sid's as smart as you say, Andrew must drive him crazy."

"Exactly. Burke's due to graduate in June. He's attended past Festivals. He knows the Maypole is always raised on that hilly section of the Green."

"And he had ample opportunity to bury the rock while assigned to grounds-keeping chores." Caroline shook her head. "Sid could be our culprit, but how are you going to prove it? If he did it alone, there's no one to rat on him. He's perfectly safe unless he starts bragging about it."

"Burke's too clever for that." Carl pounded his fist on the table. "I've got a gut feeling about this, Cari. That young ruffian probably overheard your conversation with Branch this afternoon. Because he's angry at having to waste his time working for the gardener, he purposely played on Charlie's fears. I'll bet he feigned sympathy for the man, then suggested they share a few drinks together."

"Shiloh denied over-serving them, didn't he? I wonder if Sid passed his own drinks on to Branch. He didn't strike me as being even slightly drunk, while Charlie was certainly intoxicated."

"I wouldn't put it past him to do something like that."

"Remember, Burke wasn't driving tonight. He wouldn't walk all the way to the Blue Cat, so he must have gone there with Branch." Caroline toyed with her unopened bottle of beer. "If we're right about this scenario, Sid Burke is one helluva nasty guy. Imagine baiting a man like Charlie just for the fun of it."

"Like I said before, I wouldn't put it past him. Sid's been in and out of trouble since the day he arrived at Bruck."

"In fairness, we should consider all the possibilities before reaching a conclusion," said Caroline. "Plenty of people had access to the Green this week. Almost anyone could have buried the rune stone. And as for Sid's presence at the lounge, maybe he went there with his buddies and stumbled on Branch by accident."

"Burke doesn't have buddies," Carl answered sourly. "He's a loner with a mean streak. Students steer clear of him because he's trouble from the word go."

"Perhaps you're letting your personal feelings get in the way of your good judgment, Carl. After all, the young man must have at least one redeeming quality."

"Sure he does," the professor exclaimed. "He's graduating this year!"

Caroline laughed as she pushed her chair back from the table. "It's almost midnight, my friend, and we're nowhere near to solving this little puzzle. I'm going to go home and crawl into my nice warm bed. I suggest you do the same." She rose and walked towards the living room.

"Once you explain things to Branch, he'll quit worrying about intruders ripping out his daffodils."

"I'll also have a word with him about young Mr. Burke. Although I seriously doubt Charlie will ever go out drinking with him again." Carl accompanied Caroline to the door. "Are you working tomorrow?"

"I'm on the evening shift in ER, so I intend to sleep away the morning. Not even an earthquake is going to rouse me before noon."

With a smile and a wave, Caroline headed for her car. She drove back to the dorm happily contemplating a rendezvous with her pillow.

Unbeknownst to her, fate was about to ruin her plans.

Six

Caroline bolted upright on her mattress. Sunlight streamed through the east window of her bedroom, and for a moment, she imagined it was the brightness that had jolted her awake. Then the telephone rang, the sound loud and insistent in the quiet apartment. She realized it was the same clamoring noise she'd heard in her dream.

She glanced at the clock and groaned. Seven-thirty. The only person who'd call this early in the day was her boss in the staffing office at St. Anne's. Some nurse had probably called in sick, and Corrine was searching for a replacement.

"There go my plans for a morning in bed," grumbled Caroline as she snatched the phone from its cradle. Because she liked Corrine, she hid her annoyance with a stream of bright chatter. "Hi there, boss. What's up, who's sick, and where do you want me to work today? Remember, I'm scheduled for–"

"Oh, Mom! Thank goodness you finally answered!"

Caroline gripped the receiver with both hands. Her heart pounded, but she tried to control her voice as she said, "What's wrong, Nikki? Has something happened to you and Martin?"

"No," Nikki sobbed. "We're okay. It's Emma Reiser. She fell down the stairs at the post office. She's dead!"

Caroline fell back against the pillows with a sigh of relief. She mentally thanked the Lord. It was just over a year since her husband Ed's death. Another tragedy in the family would have been hard to bear.

"Are you there, Mom?"

"Yes, Nikki." She pulled her thoughts together and continued more sympathetically. "I'm sorry about Mrs. Reiser, dear. How did it happen?"

"I don't know! I arrived at work a few minutes ago, and the door was still locked. Emma always opens the post office at seven on the dot, but I figured maybe she overslept this one time. I let myself in with my key and called out to her. There was no answer. I started towards the back room, and that's when I saw her. She's lying at the foot of the staircase, Mom, and–"

"You mean this all happened just now? Have you called the paramedics, Nikki?"

"Yes," Nikki sniffled. "Then I–"

"Emma may not be dead." Caroline's nursing instincts took over and she began to issue instructions to the stunned girl on the other end of the line. "She may only be in a coma from the fall, Nikki. Feel for a pulse, then…"

"I did that already. There was none, and Emma's face is so blue!"

Caroline sighed. It was probably hopeless, still she told Nikki to administer CPR until the paramedics arrived.

"Then stay at the post office, Nikki. I'll be there as soon as possible."

It took Caroline less than five minutes to pull on jeans and a sweatshirt, apply some basic makeup, and comb her short hair. She grabbed her car keys off the dresser and ran out of the apartment. Another five minutes and she had traversed the underground passage from the nursing dorm to the ground floor of St. Anne's Hospital. She took the corridor past the cafeteria, cut across the courtyard, and doubled back to ER. The department was empty of patients when she pushed open the double doors off the hallway.

"Hi, Caroline." Jane Gardner waved from behind the desk. "You're off to an early start today."

Caroline had first met Jane when the latter was nurse-manager of the Psychiatric Ward. Since then, Jane had been promoted to a supervisory position.

"Are you covering the day shift?"

Jane nodded. "I'm hoping it will be an uneventful eight hours."

"As any supervisor would," Caroline agreed. "I just got a call from my daughter-in-law. She works at the post office. When she arrived there this morning she found Emma Reiser lying on the floor. Nikki thinks she's dead."

"The paramedics notified us a couple of minutes ago. Miss Reiser was triple zero when they arrived." Jane referred to an ER term for a person exhibiting no signs of life who was beyond hope of resuscitation. "Paul took the radio call. He pronounced her in the field."

"I'd hoped Nikki was wrong." Caroline shook her head. "Poor thing. She was so upset over finding Emma's body."

"I don't blame her. It's hard when you're not used to it." Dr. Paul Wakely stepped out of the radio room. He tossed a sheet of paper on the desk in front of Caroline. "Looks like she took quite a tumble. I was told there's a nasty wound to the skull."

Caroline grimaced as she scanned the report of the

conversation between Paul and the paramedics.

"It'll be a coroner's case, right?"

"You bet," Paul said with a nod. "Emma was wearing a nightgown with a long rip in the hem. Probably caught her foot in it when she started down the stairs. Just another accident, but even so, the police will have to investigate."

"An unnatural death," Jane mused. "Old man Gordan won't be pleased."

Paul winked at Caroline. "Our poor coroner still hasn't recovered from all the activity around here last December. The paperwork alone was enough to throw him for a loop."

"Yet the voters keep electing him, don't they? He must be a real man of the people, Paul."

Dr. Wakely wrinkled his nose in disgust. He would have debated the subject, but Caroline was in a hurry. She waved good-bye and headed for the door leading to the parking garage.

Her Jeep was parked on the second level and Caroline descended at a prudent speed, then accelerated once on Circle Road. She cruised past the university before turning onto the highway leading to Rhineburg. Traffic was at a minimum there. She made good time and reached the Wilhelm exit just as an ambulance passed by going in the opposite direction. Its lights and siren were off, so Caroline guessed it was probably carrying the body of Emma Reiser.

Accustomed to sudden death from her years in the ER, Caroline's thoughts lingered only briefly on the post-mistress before the changing landscape captured her attention. Carl was right. Rhineburg was becoming a tourist trap. Cutesy shops featuring porcelain pigs, wooden birdhouses, and other non-essential items had sprung up all along Wilhelm Road. Several splendid old Victorians now sported signs advertising antiques while others had been converted into bed-and-breakfasts. All had been repainted in five-color schemes that entitled them to be designated 'painted ladies'.

Who could blame the enterprising souls of Rhineburg? They were coping the best they could with a flagging rural economy. God knew the old wooden houses required a massive amount of upkeep. Beautiful as they were, they were money pits, gobbling up incomes faster than they were earned. The homeowners may have sacrificed their privacy, but at least they weren't going bankrupt like so many of their counterparts across the countryside.

Caroline slid the Jeep into a parking space alongside the town square. The post office, a chunky two-story building constructed of pink rhyolite stone from the quarry outside of Rhineburg, squatted on the corner of Wilhelm and Kaiser, across from the square. Its thick walls blushed rosy red in the slanting sunlight, giving it an unsuitably cheerful appearance considering it was now a house of death.

Not surprisingly, a small crowd had gathered on the sidewalk. Caroline nodded to the few people she recognized and hurried into the building. She spotted Nikki behind the main counter surrounded by three policemen and the mayor of Rhineburg.

"Mom!" Nikki waved to her nervously. "I told them you were coming to help."

Caroline wasn't exactly sure what kind of help was expected from her, but she could see Nikki was a wreck. The girl's eyes were red rimmed and puffy from tears. She clutched a box of tissues. A small wastebasket near her chair overflowed with the residue of grief.

"How are you doing, hon?" Caroline asked, slipping an arm around her daughter-in-law's shoulders.

"I'll be OK," Nikki responded. "It was just such a shock seeing Mrs. Reiser that way. I still can't believe she's dead."

"Emma was practically an institution around here." Jake Moeller, Rhineburg's square-jawed Chief of Police, frowned down at the well-polished tips of his regulation black leather shoes. "People are really gonna miss her."

"But she will not be forgotten," Teddy Schoen pronounced solemnly. "From now on, this facility will be known as the Emma Reiser Post Office, dedicated to the memory of our longest serving postmaster." The ever-politically-correct mayor pursed his lips and stared at the ceiling with furrowed brow. "Of course, the Council will have to vote on it, but I'm sure everyone will agree Emma deserves a fitting memorial."

Moeller's frown deepened as he pretended to examine the wanted posters hanging on the wall next to the desk. Caroline noted the set of his mouth. She guessed the Chief was no more enamored by the pompous politician than she was.

"You have a more immediate problem to deal with," she reminded Hiz Honor with a ruthlessness bred of dislike. "The postal authorities need to be notified so they can send someone to take Emma's place. Until then, you'll have to close up shop here."

Schoen's salt and pepper eyebrows shot up in surprise. "Close the P.O.? Why should we do that when young Mrs. Rhodes can handle the job?" He turned to Nikki and flashed his signature smile. "You do know how to operate all this, don't you?" he asked, gesturing to the array of postal equipment lining the counter.

"I've only been here a few weeks," Nikki replied tentatively. "I suppose I could manage, but..."

"No buts about it, dear," the mayor boomed. "I have the utmost confidence in your ability to carry on in Emma's stead. In fact, I hereby appoint you temporary postmaster of Rhineburg. I'll see about making it a permanent position when I talk to the boys in Washington." He smiled benignly. "After all, why should they appoint some outsider to the job when we've already got you?"

Nikki opened her mouth to object, but Schoen silenced her with an upraised hand.

"No need to thank me, young lady. Only doing my job." He turned to Moeller and jerked his head in the direction of the door. "Let's go, Chief. Now that this little business is wrapped up, these ladies need to get on with their work. The last thing they want," he added with a chuckle, "is a couple of men underfoot."

Moeller rolled his eyes as Schoen made his way to the door. "If I were you," he said quietly, "I'd hang up the 'Closed' sign and give your daughter-in-law a cup of something strong. She looks like she could use it." Raising a finger to his cap, he winked at Caroline before motioning to the other officers. Together, they followed the Mayor out of the building.

Caroline locked the door and leaned against it, exasperation showing in every line of her face. "It amazes me how that man has remained mayor for so many years. What does he do anyway? Hand out hundred dollar bills at the polling places?"

Nikki stood up and wandered over to the counter.

"He may sound like a fool, but Teddy Schoen's a pretty astute politician," the girl replied distractedly. She gathered up a stack of papers and moved them from one side of the counter to the other. "These change of address forms should be placed in a rack. They're only in the way here, but Mrs. Reiser insists on..."

Nikki suddenly broke into tears. Caroline put an arm around her and guided her to the back room. Moeller's recommendation had been wise. They could both do with a cup of something strong, but Caroline figured at this time in the morning, it had better be tea. She busied herself preparing it while Nikki got her emotions under control. By the time she carried the steaming mugs of Earl Grey to the table, the young woman had recovered enough to smile her thanks.

"It doesn't bother you any more, does it?" Nikki said as she thickened the tea with honey. "Seeing people die, I mean."

Caroline considered her answer. How could she explain the change that occurred within a person after witnessing death on a regular basis? It wasn't that you stopped caring about people; you just learned to accept death as the inevitable result of living.

"Shortly after graduating from nursing school, I cared

for a patient who was slowly dying of cancer. Most of the time morphine didn't even control his pain, yet he always cracked a joke when I entered his room. I discovered that using humor was his way of staying in control of the situation.

"Over the weeks I grew quite fond of this patient and his family. One evening, only minutes after his wife had left for home, he suffered a cardiac arrest. He had never signed a DNR, a 'Do Not Resuscitate' order, so I called a code. Nikki, we worked on him for forty-five minutes–a long time for any resuscitation attempt–but it was a useless effort. When I finally left his room, I just stood in the hallway and cried. Losing him was like losing a friend. I couldn't believe we'd failed him."

"How did you handle it?" Nikki asked quietly.

"After work three of the older nurses sat me down and related their own first experiences with death. Nobody ever forgets the first time, Nikki, and all of them had felt as devastated as I did that night. But because they were nurses, they learned over time to control their feelings."

"You can't just bottle up emotions!" Nikki protested. "Once you harden your heart..."

Caroline shook her head. "I'm not talking about becoming hard, Nikki. I'm saying that if you want to retain your effectiveness, you can't allow yourself to be overwhelmed by sorrow. It's different when you're faced with the death of a family member or a loved one. Look at me," Caroline said with a sad smile. "I almost lost my mind when Martin's father died. But in my business, one has to think about facing the next patient. What kind of nurse would I be if I wore my emotions on my sleeve?

Should I cry over the patient I just lost in Room Two while I'm caring for the person in Room Three?"

"Of course not," Nikki muttered.

"Of course not," Caroline repeated. "It would only decrease my effectiveness as a nurse. I need to be thinking of that second patient, and that second patient alone, when I'm dealing with him."

"I didn't mean to imply you don't care about Mrs. Reiser. But you seem to take it all in stride while I'm sitting here like a kid who's lost a parent."

"You admired Emma Reiser, Nikki. And you've never witnessed sudden death before." Caroline leaned over the table and placed her hand on Nikki's. "Believe me, dear. There are worse things in life than dying. Loneliness and despair rank much higher on the list of human tragedies."

"I suppose you're right."

"I know I'm right. Don't mourn the dead, Nikki. They're at peace. Reserve your sympathy for the loved ones left behind."

"Mrs. Reiser didn't leave anyone behind. Her husband died years ago, and she had no children."

"No brothers or sisters?"

Nikki shrugged. "None that she ever spoke of. Of course, I'd only known her a few weeks. Maybe Chief Moeller would know if there's any family."

"We should call him," Caroline said, rising to her feet. "If there are relatives, they'll want to come by and pack up Emma's belongings."

"Will you do that while I clean up yesterday's paperwork and check the out-going mail? Ben will be here soon to pick up the bags."

Caroline nodded approvingly as Nikki walked briskly out of the room. She believed in the therapeutic value of work and hoped these routine duties would take her daughter-in-law's mind off Emma.

As for herself, Caroline was experiencing an overpowering desire for a cigarette. Smoking, which she'd given up several years earlier, had always comforted her in times of stress. Her non-smoking friends who labeled it a 'crutch' and a 'vice' simply had no idea how soothing a deep drag on a cigarette could be.

However, she was not about to get hooked on the habit again. Casting all thoughts of cigarettes out of her mind, she puttered about cleaning up the tea things as she considered why her conversation with Nikki left her feeling so emotionally drained. She'd told the girl the truth; death wasn't the curse most imagined it to be. In fact, when it came swiftly and silently, like it had to Emma Reiser, it was something of a blessing.

Still, having to defend herself to her daughter-in-law was a bit unnerving. Caroline had never before thought of herself as hardhearted. Now she wondered if her approach to life could be viewed as harsh and uncaring. She didn't think her colleagues would so consider it, but what about those outside her profession? What about her family?

"I know exactly who I am," she muttered as she rinsed out the mugs in the little sink at the back of the room. "And I'm certainly not an insensitive person."

"Of course you're not. Whatever gave you such an idea?"

Caroline spun around, coming face to face with a

puzzled looking Professor Atwater.

"Carl! What are you doing here?"

"I heard about Emma's accident and stopped by to see if there was anything I could do to help. Nikki let me in." The professor eased his enormous frame onto a less than sturdy chair. Its legs creaked ominously, but Atwater seemed not to notice as he concentrated on his friend. "So what's all this about you being insensitive?"

"Oh, nothing," Caroline replied shamefacedly. She dearly wished Carl hadn't overheard that testy remark. "Nikki was upset over finding Emma's body. I didn't react as she thought I should, and I don't think she entirely understood my explanation."

Carl stroked his beard. "You can't expect these young pups to think like you and I, Cari. They're a little short on life experience." When she didn't answer, the professor wisely changed the subject. "So what needs to be done around here? I can sort mail, or sell stamps if you want."

"You'd better ask Nikki about that. I was just about to call Chief Moeller to see if Mrs. Reiser's family was coming by. They'll need to take clothes to the undertaker."

"Emma didn't have family in these parts. She was a widow, and I believe her only kin is a brother in New York."

"*Hmm*. Perhaps we'll have to do it then." Caroline picked up the phone and began to dial. "I wonder if she'll be buried here in Rhineburg."

"I expect so. Her husband's lying in the town cemetery."

Someone picked up at the police station, and Caroline asked for Jake Moeller. She waited less than a minute before he answered.

"How's young Mrs. Rhodes doing?" The Chief's voice was filled with concern, and Caroline's liking for the man instantly grew.

"She's better now. Thanks for asking." Caroline told him why she was calling. "Professor Atwater is here, and he says Emma has a brother living out of town. Would you like us to pick out some clothes for the funeral?"

"I hadn't thought of clothes," the Chief conceded. "It certainly would help, if you have the time. I contacted the brother–got his name from Emma's lawyer–but he's laid up with a broken hip. Says he's too old and crippled to make a trip to Rhineburg and the lawyer should handle the funeral arrangements. Says he'll pray for her soul from his sickbed."

"Well, it shouldn't take the coroner's office long to clear the body. Perhaps Mrs. Reiser's lawyer knows her wishes concerning burial or cremation."

"According to Tom Crippen, he hasn't seen Emma since she made out her will three years ago. Why don't you go through her desk? Maybe she wrote something down, some instructions as to what she wanted done."

"Is it all right–I mean, legally–for me to go through her things?"

"This isn't Chicago, Mrs. Rhodes," the Chief chuckled. "We're a little looser with formalities here in Rhineburg." When Caroline didn't reply, he added hastily, "Looks to me like this was an accident, pure and simple. Emma caught her foot in the hem of her nightgown and tripped down those stairs, or else she had a heart attack and then fell. Whatever, there's no reason to treat the post office like a crime scene. You take a look around and see if you can come up with anything that would help us figure out her wishes. And if you wouldn't mind packing up her things, I'll see to it they get sent to her brother."

"If you say so, Chief Moeller." Caroline hung up and turned to Carl. "Emma left no burial plans with her lawyer, and her brother's too ill to coordinate a funeral."

"I take it the ball was thrown back into our court?"

"Yep. The Chief wants us to bundle up Emma's belongings. While we're at it, we're to search for some formal indication of her wishes. Maybe we'll get lucky," she added as she headed for the staircase. "Maybe Emma was one of those organized souls who makes lists to deal with any eventuality."

"Like what to do when the cat spits up a hairball."

Caroline laughed. "Hopefully the woman was a little more practical than that. Still, you've caught my drift. Let's go see what we can find in her bedroom."

The two friends climbed the creaky wooden staircase leading to the second floor. A narrow corridor ran the width of the building with doorways on either side of the stairs and what appeared to be a suite of rooms directly opposite the landing. Caroline crossed the carpeted hall and opened the door to Emma Reiser's private domain.

"Oh, my goodness!" she exclaimed as she flipped on the light switch. What lay before her was not the apartment of a small town postmaster, but the interior of a nineteenth century mansion brightly illuminated by a massive crystal chandelier.

Seven

Caroline and the professor were totally unprepared for the splendor that greeted them in Emma's drawing room. Everywhere they looked they saw objects that defied the notion Reiser had been an ordinary middle-class working woman.

Across from the door stood a rosewood sofa with carved cabriole legs and claw-and-ball feet. It was upholstered in deep burgundy brocade and topped with a lacy cresting rail of carved grapevines and acorns. Two matching chairs were arranged opposite the sofa on either side of a mahogany tilt-top table.

A Queen Anne highboy with carved fan and finials filled the far corner of the room. The nearer corner was occupied by an English parquetry breakfast table of rosewood, walnut, and coromandel. Heavy tapestries in rich strands of color overlaid ordinary shades on the only two windows in the room. They effectively blocked both outside light and the curiosity of passersby on the street below.

"Look at this," Carl exclaimed as he ran his hand over a marble topped chiffonier resting against one ivory painted wall. An engraved and enameled glass vase was the sole decoration gracing the mahogany cupboard. "I'll bet this piece cost a fortune."

Caroline's attention had been drawn to a knee-hole writing desk flanking the doorway. She fingered the carved shell ornamentation topping each set of side drawers.

"I'm no expert on antique furnishings," she said, shaking her head. "But this room must be worth a king's ransom. Just look at the size, design, and colors of this rug." She knelt down and turned back the edge of a Persian carpet covering the central part of the floor. "It's hand tied, not woven on a machine. Figuratively speaking, this is priceless."

"I didn't know postal employees were paid this well. Especially ones who work in backwater towns like Rhineburg."

Caroline stood up and walked over to an ebonized door at the far end of the room. "You can be sure Emma didn't acquire all this on a government paycheck. She either inherited money or... Wow! Come look in here, Carl!"

Behind the door was a bedroom rivaling the drawing room in elegance. An ornate rosewood bed in the rococo revival style stood against one wall, its ivory silk sheets rumpled beneath a turned back comforter of wine and rose satin. A matching armoire with a curved pediment of pierced scrollwork hugged the opposite wall next to a window draped in burgundy damask. A mirrored chest of drawers and a marble-topped wash stand flanked a second window. A pearl-backed hand mirror with matching comb and brush lay on the wash stand alongside antique scent bottles and a flowered porcelain pitcher and basin. Reflected in the mirror, a jewelry case carved of ebony and inlaid with ivory rested atop the chest of drawers.

On an angle to the armoire was another door leading to a walk-in cedar closet. The closet was bare except for a dozen or so rather plain dresses, two cotton and two flannel nightgowns, a good wool coat, and four pairs of sensible walking shoes.

"She sure didn't spend money on clothes," Caroline remarked as she fingered the modest material of a two-piece suit draped by a dry cleaner's plastic bag. "This must have been her Sunday-go-to-meeting outfit. It doesn't look as worn as the others."

"I guess she'll be buried in it then." Carl turned away from the closet and began perusing the paperbacks stacked on the lower shelf of the wash stand. "Can't say I admire Emma's taste in literature. These all appear to be romance novels."

Caroline walked over to his side and glanced at the books. "Does all this seem as weird to you as it does to me?"

"Definitely," the professor replied darkly. "I knew Emma a good many years, but nothing she said or did ever hinted at this kind of lifestyle. She was a plain talking woman who wore her hair in a bun and eschewed lipstick. She always came to civic events, attended church on a regular basis, and donated to any worthy cause that came up. This opulence just doesn't fit the Emma Reiser who sold stamps at the Rhineburg P.O."

"I wonder what Nikki will say when she sees this apartment."

"It might change her opinion of the postmaster."

"Undoubtedly! What do you say we go investigate across the hall? Maybe we'll discover another treasure or two."

"First I want to look through Emma's desk. It's

possible she left some final instructions in one of the drawers."

"Good grief," Caroline muttered in embarrassment. "I almost forgot the real purpose of our visit. I'll look around in here."

She had no luck in the bedroom. The chest of drawers contained only the usual sweaters, stockings, and underwear while the armoire was totally bare except for a collection of dust bunnies.

"I hope you're doing better than I," she said as she reentered the drawing room. "There's nothing of a personal nature in there."

"Nothing here either." There was a puzzled look in Carl's eyes as he gazed about. "This is more like a museum than a home."

"I have a feeling Emma was role playing in this suite, Carl. There's no trace of a postmaster here, no family pictures, no letters, not even a telephone on the desk. But there is a shelf-load of romance novels in the bedroom, and all of them are set in Victorian times."

Carl pulled on his beard, an indication he was concentrating. "You may have hit the nail on the head, Cari. If Emma was pursuing a fantasy in here, her real life probably existed across the hall. Let's go have a look at those two rooms."

The first door led to a large but simple bathroom. They checked out the medicine cabinet there, but it held nothing of interest. When they moved on to the second door, they found it locked.

"Now what?" Caroline asked disgustedly. "Unless Nikki has a key, which I sorely doubt, we're not getting into this room."

"Jake entrusted us with a task, Cari. I intend to finish it."

With that said, Carl lifted a foot and kicked the door open.

"Good lord, Carl! I don't think Chief Moeller intended we tear the place down. Are you okay?"

Carl grimaced as he rubbed his right leg. "Sometimes I forget I'm no longer a kid."

Caroline smiled sympathetically. "Come on, Mr. Macho. Let's see what Miz Emma kept hidden away in here."

The room turned out to be an office. Cabinets lined one wall behind a desk bearing a computer linked to a fax machine and printer. Three telephones stood next to the computer, each one attached to an answering machine. On the opposite wall four sixteen-inch black and white TV sets rested on a metal shelf. A second shelf below the first contained a stack of *Daily Racing Forms*.

Carl was the first to recover his voice, but what he said was unprintable.

€ight

Jake Moeller scratched his head in bewilderment. "It looks like Emma was quite the professional bookie. Beats me how I never once caught wind of her operation."

"Rhineburgers are pretty good at keeping secrets," Carl pointed out. "Especially when those secrets benefit them financially."

"And Emma didn't flaunt her winnings," added Caroline. "She invested her money in antiques rather than banking it."

"A smart move on her part," conceded the Chief. He'd already seen Emma's personal suite, and while he knew next to nothing about old furnishings, his wife ran a profitable antique store out of their aging Queen Anne over on Adams Street. He'd called her twenty minutes after arriving and insisted she hotfoot it right over to the post office. "I don't know if it's real or if it's junk," he'd told her. "But if illegal gambling paid for Emma's belongings, I'm going to confiscate every single piece of it."

"We have tough anti-racketeering laws in this country," Jake later explained. "I'm sure you've heard of RICO, the Racketeer Influenced and Corrupt Organization Act. It allows law enforcement agencies to impound assets representing the proceeds of racketeering."

"I've read about the FBI impounding cars and boats

belonging to drug dealers," said Caroline. "But I didn't know a small town police department could confiscate goods under RICO."

"I'll want to check out the finer points of the law before I do anything," Moeller admitted. "Anyway you look at it, though, gambling is a racket. I should have the right to prevent Emma's heirs from profiting off her illegal activities. Besides that," he continued mulishly, "if I auction off all this stuff, we might be able to afford to buy another black-and-white."

Caroline guessed the Chief could buy an entire fleet of cars with the proceeds of such a sale, but she kept her thoughts to herself. Better to let Mrs. Moeller break the good news after she'd appraised Emma's furniture.

"You're going to need proof of a crime before you impound anything," she reminded the policeman. She ran her hand over the computer in Emma's second floor office. "I'll bet there's a ton of incriminating information stored in here. The problem is, you can't get at it unless you know Emma's password."

"One of my deputies is a computer geek. If anybody can solve this problem, it's him." Moeller turned and walked out of the office. "I'm going to place a seal on this entire upper floor. You take any clothes you want for the undertaker, Mrs. Rhodes. But please don't touch Emma's jewelry or anything else that might rightfully belong to the town of Rhineburg."

Caroline nodded and went off to collect the suit she'd seen hanging in Emma closet. She wasted precious little time choosing burial clothes as she was anxious to get downstairs and see how her daughter-in-law was taking the news of her boss' unusual sideline. The girl had been quite fond of Mrs. Reiser. It was possible she'd excuse Emma's transgressions out of a misguided sense of loyalty.

As it turned out, Caroline needn't have worried. Nikki was hopping mad, and from the top of the stairs she could hear the girl carrying on an animated conversation with Carl and the Chief.

"I can't believe I was such a fool!" Nikki sputtered as she placed a set of mugs on the table in the back room. "I thought Mrs. Reiser was just being neighborly when she offered someone a cup of tea. Now I discover she was actually taking bets back here." She plunked down a pot of coffee and steamed off to the pantry for sugar. "She must have figured me for a regular idiot," she called over her shoulder. "Someone who'd be too dumb to catch on to her scheme." She dumped half a box of sugar cubes into a bowl and slammed the dish down next to the coffeepot. "How long did she think I'd fall for that line about folks needing a sympathetic ear? Why, if you'd counted the people lined up at her door you'd have thought half the town of Rhineburg required the services of a psychiatrist."

Caroline slid into a chair beside the professor and counted her blessings. Better for Nikki to be angry with Emma than to defend her. It was embarrassing to admit she'd been taken in by the woman, but with this outburst, Nikki had begun the process of disassociating herself from the postmaster.

"It would be helpful if you could recall the names of some of Emma's customers," said the Chief. "Those people were as guilty of breaking the law as Mrs. Reiser."

Nikki hesitated, and Caroline could guess why. Martin's wife needed the job at the post office, but would the mayor recommend her for the position if he heard she turned informer on her customers?

"Well..."

"Chief Moeller," Caroline interrupted. "Nikki's only worked here a few weeks. It could cause irreparable harm if she mistakenly identified someone as one of Emma's clients. Don't you think Mrs. Reiser kept records on the people who placed bets with her? Maybe they're locked away in those cabinets in her office. Or maybe they're on computer disks. Either way, your deputy is bound to find them."

Moeller started to object, but the rat-a-tat of knuckles tapping on glass distracted him. He frowned as Nikki hurried off to the front door. When she returned, it was with a slightly built woman with hair the color of pumpkin pie who marched over to the burly policeman and poked him in the chest with one crimson-tipped finger.

"This had better be good, Jake. I was that close–" she spread her thumb and forefinger a quarter inch apart, "to selling a complete set of Windsor china when you called and insisted I come over here. Ten more minutes and I could have persuaded that tourist it was exactly what she was looking for." She peeled off her jacket and tossed it on a chair, then turned and flashed a brilliant smile. "I adore making a difficult sale. It's like winning a battle over a worthy opponent. You never know if you've done your best until the cash is actually in your hands." She wiggled her manicured fingers at Carl. "How are you, Professor Atwater? Still drumming history into the heads of ungrateful youngsters at Bruck?"

Carl murmured a reply, but Mrs. Moeller ignored him, concentrating instead on the other two females in the room.

"You're Caroline Rhodes, the nurse who captured the Mad Bomber last winter. I saw your picture in the paper, and I must say you look better in real life than in those photographs. Oh, Nikki! You've made fresh coffee! If you could manage to find another mug, dear. And perhaps a donut or some cookies. I missed breakfast again," she confided to Carl. "And now I'm as hungry as a horse!"

Caroline suppressed a grin as she watched the little fireball whiz about the room, searching first for a teaspoon, then for a napkin, all the time carrying on her hectic monologue.

"Now tell me why you dragged me over here, Jake. Everyone's a-buzz over poor Mrs. Reiser, and because I'm the wife of the police chief, they expect me to know the gory details of the accident. Which I don't, of course, since you refused to answer even one little question when you called at the store. By the way," she said as she turned back to Caroline, "we haven't been properly introduced yet, have we? I'm Madeline Moeller, Jake's wife. My friends call me Maddy. Jake just calls me Mad."

Madeline's laughter was so beguiling that Caroline responded immediately with a broad smile of her own. She marveled over how the sober Chief of Police had somehow managed to attract this bubbly woman whose very being personified pure energy in motion.

"Mad Moeller's Antiques and Collectibles," Maddy continued. "That's the name of my shop, Caroline. Stop by some day and I'll give you a 20% discount on anything in the place."

Chief Moeller placed a restraining hand on his wife's arm.

"You've just got to cut down on the caffeine, honey."

"I don't drink that much coffee and you know it, Jake."

"Hush up, Mad. I need you to listen quietly for a moment."

"I always listen to you. You're the one who doesn't…"

"Maddy!" the Chief broke in. "Please go upstairs and appraise Emma's furniture. It's very important I know exactly what it's worth."

Maddy snapped her fingers. "No problem, Jake. If it's older than fifty years, I can put a price on it."

"I'm no expert," Caroline interjected. "But I'd say some of the furnishings were early nineteenth century, if not older."

Maddy stopped her fluttering and turned to stare at Caroline. "Are we talking American or European?" she asked gravely.

"Some of both, I think. The furniture and tapestries look like the real McCoy, and the Persian rug in the drawing room is absolutely magnificent. I'd give my eye teeth to own it."

Maddy walked over to the staircase and studied the second floor landing in total disbelief.

"If what you say is true…I mean, how in the world…" She shook her head and started over. "I'd better get to work. There's a calculator in my coat pocket, Jake.

Would you get it for me?"

Moeller retrieved the needed item and followed his wife upstairs. When they were safely out of hearing range, Carl turned to the others and growled, "How in the world does he put up with that woman? She's a whirling dervish, completely out of control."

Caroline smiled over her coffee cup. "I like her, Carl. She's smart, funny, and full of life."

Carl frowned but held his peace. "While there's a pause in the action, I think I'll call the funeral parlor and inquire about dropping off those clothes." He rose to his feet and started towards the front of the P.O. "Call me when the Mad-woman returns."

Caroline grimaced at the pun. She looked over at Nikki, expecting to see a similar reaction, but her daughter-in-law apparently hadn't heard the professor. She was leaning against the back door, her brows furrowed in concentration as she gazed at the floorboards.

"What's up, Nikki? You haven't said a word in ages."

"Hmm? Oh! Sorry, Mom." Nikki straightened up and ran a hand through her closely cropped jet-black hair. "I was thinking about something odd that happened earlier this morning. Nothing as important as Mrs. Reiser's death, but disconcerting all the same."

"Something here at the post office?"

Nikki nodded. "Ben arrived for the mail while you and the professor were upstairs. He hadn't heard about Mrs. Reiser's death, and of course he was pretty shocked when I told him. We talked a little about Emma, and then Ben offered to tag the letter bags while I loaded up the packages that came in yesterday.

"Now before I go on, I have to explain how Mrs. Reiser ran this place. She never trusted the computer system the postal service installed, so she kept a duplicate record of each and every transaction in a ledger book that sat out on the main desk. Whenever she bagged packages, she first checked them against the information in her ledger. That was her way of making sure mail didn't get lost before it left the station, and when I started working here, she taught me to follow the practice."

Caroline wasn't sure where all this was leading to, but she listened patiently as Nikki continued with her story.

"When I checked the ledger this morning, it listed five packages that were brought to this station yesterday. Professor Littlewort mailed one late in the afternoon. I'd already left for home so I never saw the box, but the record states it contained a rune stone."

"So he's already sent it off to the museum. You know, Nikki, that rock is going to cause so much trouble I wish it would just up and disappear."

"Funny you should say that," Nikki replied miserably, "because I can't find that package anywhere in this post office. It's like the rune stone has just evaporated into thin air."

Nine

"What will the mayor say?" moaned Nikki. "My first day as temporary postmaster and already I've misplaced a package."

Caroline was taken aback. "That's impossible, Nikki. This building isn't big enough to lose a package in."

"Oh, yeah? I've searched every nook and cranny. Let me tell you, that rune stone is not in this post office."

"How about the other mailbags? Maybe it got mixed up with the letters."

Nikki shook her head. "Ben and I went through them all. We checked the returned mail bin, the cabinet where we keep paper supplies, the shelves under the main counter, and even the garbage can out back. The only things we found were a old book of twenty-nine cent stamps and a mousetrap with some mummified cheese stuck to it. Needless to say, I threw both in the trash."

"Well, the only other thing I can think of is that Emma took the package upstairs."

"Why in the world would she do that?"

Caroline shrugged. "God only knows, Nikki. You have to admit, the woman was a strange bird. Maybe she decided the stone would be safer in her apartment than here. Or maybe she wanted to unwrap and examine it."

"Emma wouldn't tamper with the mail," said Nikki in a shocked voice. "That's against the law."

"Silly me," Caroline said, slapping her forehead. "I forgot she was elected Citizen of the Year by Gamblers

Anonymous. Mrs. Reiser would have never..."

"Alright already!" Nikki raised her hands in surrender. "You've made your point. Let's go have a look upstairs."

The two of them explained the situation to Chief Moeller. With his blessing they searched every room on the second floor, but came up empty handed.

"I'll have to report this to the regional office," Nikki muttered as they headed back downstairs. "Worse than that, I'll have to call Andrew Littlewort."

"You could ask Carl to do it."

"No," the girl replied with a shake of her head. "I'm in charge now, at least until a replacement arrives, so I have to be the one to break the bad news to the Professor."

Caroline admired her daughter-in-law's resolve. It would be no picnic explaining the loss of the rune stone to an irate Professor Littlewort. The man was not known for his generous nature. He'd probably chew her up and spit her out in forty different directions.

"What's going on?" Carl Atwater entered the back room as Nikki left to make her calls.

"It's a long story," Caroline said. "How about I give you the condensed version?"

"Fire away." Carl lowered himself onto a chair and listened with growing interest as Caroline explained the situation.

"Maybe Andrew wised up and returned for the box."

"I doubt it, Carl. By the time he arrived at the post office, Nikki had already left for home. It was late in the afternoon and he would have had very little time to change his mind."

"Damn it!" Carl exclaimed. "If I ever get my hands on the person who buried that stone..."

"It's unbelievable. Simply unbelievable!" Maddy waved a notebook triumphantly in the air as she and Jake descended the staircase. "You were right, my dear." Her eyes glittering with excitement, she made a beeline for Caroline and hugged her. "Just look at these figures."

Caroline gazed in awe at the scribbled numbers strung across three pages of the notebook. She'd guessed the furnishings were valuable, but Maddy's estimate astounded her.

"Are you sure?" she asked, unable to hide the doubt in her voice.

Maddy picked up a sugar cube and popped it into her mouth. "I told you, I know my stuff. I may be off by a few thousand this way or that, but on the whole, these are pretty accurate numbers." She gulped down a mouthful of cold coffee from one of the mugs on the table and grimaced. "Whew! That's bad. Didn't Emma keep some champagne around this place? We could use a bottle to celebrate our good fortune."

"I think your husband needs something stronger than champagne," Caroline noted.

Jake had collapsed on a chair and was staring off into space, slack jawed and blurry eyed. He looked for all the world like a punch-drunk fighter down for the count.

Maddy walked over and patted him on the back. "He's just stunned, poor man. It'll wear off in time. The thing to do now is set a guard on the property. It'll have to be watched day and night until everything's properly crated and ready to be shipped."

"Shipped where?"

"Why, to Sotheby's, Professor," Maddy replied with a hint of surprise in her voice. "If you want top dollar, that's the place to go."

"Let me see those figures." Atwater slipped the notebook out of Caroline's hand and flipped through the pages. When he looked up again, his expression resembled Jake's.

"Another one bites the dust," Maddy snickered as the professor's eyes glazed over. She placed her hands on his shoulders and gently pushed him down onto a chair next to her husband. "Why don't you warm up the coffee, Caroline? Our two warriors could use a stimulant to get their blood flowing again."

Caroline was in full agreement with the antique dealer. She put the pot back on the stove and began rinsing out the coffee mugs. "What I don't understand is how Emma accumulated enough money to buy all that stuff. Even with the gambling..."

"That's the part that really grates on me."

Caroline turned and stared at Chief Moeller. He'd snapped out of his trance and was suddenly angry as hell.

"Do you know how many years she had to be operating a book to earn that kind of money?" The Chief stood up and pounded his fist on the table. "Not ten. Not fifteen. Not even twenty." He glared at the others, daring them to contradict him. "Emma Reiser ran the Rhineburg post office for nigh onto forty years. She probably started handling bets the day she arrived in town." He took a deep breath to steady himself. "That woman had me hoodwinked from day one. She probably thought I was the dumbest cop she'd ever met."

Caroline and Maddy exchanged glances. Both women realized it wasn't the money Emma had made that bothered Jake. It was the embarrassment of being deceived by someone he'd trusted that stuck in his craw. That and the ridicule he'd face once the story hit the newspapers. There'd be many a joke made at his expense, many a detractor ready to question his ability when it became known that a gambling den had operated unopposed less than half a block away from the station.

"Oh, Jake!" Maddy moved to his side, but he angrily waved her off. He was in no mood for sympathy, especially from his wife. Confused as to how to help, Maddy drew back and held her tongue. Caroline took an opposite tack.

"Chief Moeller, if you'll stop pouting for a moment, I'd like to give you my take on the situation. Emma Reiser tricked a whole lot of people in this town. Folks took her for what she appeared to be, a slightly dowdy, but nonetheless upstanding, member of the community who attended church on Sundays and pedaled stamps the rest of the week. Only her betting customers knew the truth behind that innocent façade, and they weren't telling."

"You got that right," Jake grumbled.

"For all we know," Caroline continued, "Emma's illegal activities may have extended well beyond gambling."

Moeller swung around to face her. "What do you mean by that?"

"I mean she could have made some of her money stealing from the post office or its patrons. Professor

Littlewort brought a box here yesterday for shipment to Chicago. Strangely enough, it's nowhere to be found today. Perhaps it wasn't the first package to go missing from this place."

"I know you're trying to smooth my ruffled feathers, Mrs. Rhodes," Moeller remarked sarcastically. "But I'd hardly consider a rock worth stealing."

"Why not?" Carl countered. "Andrew Littlewort believes he found an archaeological treasure on the grounds of Bruck University. Andrew's not a cautious man, Jake. He's always talked too much for his own good. I'll bet he told quite a story when he posted that box."

Caroline studied the Chief's face. Moeller had calmed down, but the look in his eyes betrayed his skepticism. He wasn't buying their theory.

"There are unscrupulous collectors everywhere," Atwater reminded his friend. "One of them might have paid handsomely for what Andrew Littlewort considered the find of the century."

"You actually think Emma could have unloaded that rock?"

"She was well acquainted with the antiquities market," insisted Caroline. "She must have known collectors in fields other than her own."

"I guess it's possible," Jake conceded. "Tell me, Carl. Was this stone really that important?"

"Personally, I doubt it. But Andrew believes it's valuable, and he can be quite persuasive when he thinks he's right. I could see him trying to convince Emma Reiser of the stone's worth."

Moeller removed his glasses and rubbed the bridge of

his nose with a callused forefinger.

"Frankly, Professor, I think you and Mrs. Rhodes are barking up the wrong trail when it comes to that missing package. But I'll tell you what I'll do. If young Mrs. Rhodes doesn't find the box by this evening, I'll stop by the university and have a talk with Professor Littlewort. Right now I've got to get started on this gambling thing."

"Chief Moeller?" Nikki stuck her head around the doorway. "Mr. Gordon from the coroner's office is on the phone. If you pick up the extension, I'll transfer the call back here."

Moeller nodded his thanks and walked over to the wall phone. A second later it buzzed.

"Hi, Jerry. You got a report for me on Emma Reiser?"

The others watched with mounting curiosity as the Chief's normally solemn features grew even more sober.

"And you're sure the stairs couldn't have caused such a wound?"

Oh-oh, thought Caroline uneasily. The coroner was taking his time explaining the pathologist's report to Jake. It seemed like an eternity passed before the big policeman put down the phone.

"Looks like we'll have to start a search for that rock sooner than I expected," Jake said, eyeing the others grimly. "Emma Reiser didn't die of a heart attack or a fall down the stairs. She was hit on the head with a blunt object. Something round, smooth, and heavy. Something that left grains of dirt and rock embedded in her skull. Something, I suspect, very much like Professor Littlewort's rune stone."

Ten

The post office was now officially a crime scene closed to both the temporary postmaster and the public. No one was getting in without the express permission of Jake Moeller, not even the mayor of Rhineburg.

"I'm sure the Chief didn't intend to include me in that order," Teddy Schoen insisted upon his arrival at the P.O. "It's my duty to keep the Town Council abreast of the investigation."

Billy Wetzel had been on the force for only six months, and in many ways, was still wet behind the ears. Nevertheless, he understood his job and, in this case, enjoyed doing it.

"Sorry, Mr. Mayor. The Chief said nobody, and he meant nobody, goes in or out of this building without his okay."

"Well, why don't you go check with Chief Moeller while I..."

Schoen reached for the door handle, but the young officer blocked his way. Billy unfolded his arms with an apologetic shrug before shifting his right hand downward. It came to rest on the gun butt protruding from his holster. He countered the move with a lazy grin that didn't quite disguise the contempt in his eyes.

Teddy, however, refused to be bested by a kid straight out of the police academy. He'd seen that same triumphal gleam in the eye of worthier opponents, and to a man, none had survived to become his equal. Billy wouldn't survive either. Turning to the small crowd that had gathered on the sidewalk, the mayor threw back his head and laughed long and hard.

"Looks like I've been put in my place, huh, folks?" His sheepish grin invited empathy, and he immediately received it from most of the onlookers. Sensing victory in the offing, Schoen flung his arm around Billy and clapped him on the shoulder. "This young fellow says he has orders, and like any other good citizen of Rhineburg, I must respect them. As your mayor, though, it's my duty to see to it that you, the public, are not overly inconvenienced by the closure of this post office. For that reason I will now go and confer with Chief Moeller."

He stepped away from Billy, managing in the process to shove the officer up against the doorjamb. Billy winced as the hard stone cut between his shoulder blades. The crowd didn't notice his pain. Their eyes were glued on Teddy Schoen as he strode purposely towards the police station.

Caroline observed the entire incident from a bench in the Town Square where she and Nikki sat waiting for Professor Atwater. Earlier, she'd accompanied her daughter-in-law to the police station where the young woman made a formal statement concerning the discovery of Emma Reiser's body. A furious Andrew Littlewort accosted Nikki only minutes after she'd finished her deposition. Carl was now inside the station attempting to calm his colleague.

"Despite his smooth words, Mayor Schoen looks fit to be tied."

"He can't be as ticked off as Professor Littlewort," said Nikki. "I thought he was going to scratch my eyes out when he stormed into the Chief's office."

"You're not to blame for the loss of his precious rune stone. That's the fault of our murderer." Caroline suddenly laughed. "He did cause a stir, though, when he came bursting into the station."

Nikki giggled. "He looked so weird flapping his arms in the air and shouting at the top of his lungs. I thought the Chief was going to arrest him for disturbing the peace."

"Andrew certainly is a strange man. I hear his temper tantrums are something to behold."

"Oh yeah. I swear, one of these days that man is going to explode and end up with a stroke."

"Speaking of popping a blood vessel, take a look at Carl."

Professor Atwater had emerged from the police station and was making his way across the street. His face was beet red, and he was dripping with perspiration.

"I take it your peacekeeping mission failed," Caroline said as Carl sank down on the end on the bench.

"Miserably." Carl yanked his pipe out of his jacket pocket and tamped a wad of tobacco into the bowl with a ferocity matching his scowl. "Andrew is a complete idiot. He actually dismissed Emma Reiser's death as 'trivial' compared to the loss of his damned rock."

Caroline's eyebrows shot up. "I'd call that a rather warped point of view."

"Cold-blooded is more like it," murmured Nikki.

"He became downright apoplectic when informed his rune stone most likely was the murder weapon."

"Good grief! The more I learn about Andrew Littlewort, the less I like him."

"You're not the only one who feels that way, Cari. Andrew totally clammed up when Jake questioned him about his visit to the post office yesterday. He refused to answer anything without his lawyer being present."

"Now that's odd," said Caroline. "Why would Andrew be so skittish about answering a few simple questions?"

"I don't know," Carl said with a shrug. "But Jake's ready to give him the third degree. He wants to know what Andrew said to Emma and if she seemed overly interested in the contents of his package."

"Chief Moeller appears to be on the right trail. If the rune stone really was used to kill Emma, then either she or the murderer opened that box."

"It sure didn't unwrap itself," agreed the professor. "Which leads me to think we were right when we hypothesized the existence of some kind of collector."

"And the willingness of Emma to both steal from her customers and sell what she stole."

"Do you think the killer came from around here, Professor?" Nikki asked.

"Not necessarily. The highway runs right past town. Anyone in the state could drive here within a matter of hours."

"I wonder if the asking price was too high," said Caroline.

"You mean it was easier to steal the stone from Emma than pay for it."

"Greed has always been a motive for murder. Let me

remind you, if it happened according to our theory, there's little chance either the stone or the killer will ever be found." Caroline stood up and stretched. "I propose we leave this puzzle to the police and return to Bruck where we're really needed."

"Needed for what?"

"The Festival of Knights, Nikki. It begins tomorrow, and there's still a lot to do."

"Since I'm temporarily out of a job, I guess I could help."

"You'll have to," said Caroline. "What with all the excitement today, I totally forgot about the roses for the Maypole. I promised to deliver them to the decorations committee by noon, but it's past two o'clock already. I have to be at work at three."

"Don't worry about it. I'll see that the students get them."

"I have a couple of late classes to teach, so I'm going to head back too," Carl announced. "There'll be a general dress rehearsal for the knights and their ladies tomorrow morning, Caroline. Why don't you drop by the Green and watch the fun?"

"I just may do that." Caroline glanced at her watch. "Oh dear! Look at the time. We really have to get going, Nikki."

With a wave to the professor, the two women hurried off to their respective cars.

Eleven

Calm enveloped the Emergency Room that evening. Outside of Tommy McGruff's appendicitis and Arnold Schmidt's heart attack, little occurred to tax the P.M. shift's medical skills. By nine o'clock, the department was empty except for an embarrassed Bruck student who'd hammered his hand instead of a nail while erecting a stall for the festival.

Caroline had just finished splinting the boy's broken finger when a familiar voice hailed her from the triage area. Suppressing a groan, she discharged her patient before turning to greet the visitor.

"Back in town so soon, Mr. Evans?"

FBI Special Agent Tom Evans dismissed the question with a bored shrug. "What can I say, Mrs. Rhodes. The way you Rhineburgers persist in breaking federal laws, I just may have to set up a permanent office in your town."

"You'd resign from the FBI before you did that."

"You're probably right. Compared to Rhineburg, hell would be a downright cozy place to end my career."

Caroline shook her head in mock dismay. "Haven't changed a bit, have you. You're still the same charming person I grew to know and hate last December."

Evans grunted noncommittally as he strolled past Caroline into the ER's main room. He'd obviously lost interest in their war of words and was now busy sizing up the area. His eyes raked the empty cubicles left and right before settling on an open door behind the desk. Caroline stifled a grin when she saw him peer intently into the darkened Cast Room. She wanted to assure him that no hardened criminals lurked behind the shelves of hand splints and knee immobilizers, but she contained herself and said instead, "Your last adventure out here in the boonies proved rather nerve wracking, didn't it."

Evans transferred his gaze from the Cast Room to the ceiling. He seemed to be counting the tiles as he contemplated his answer.

"It wouldn't have been," he finally said, "if you'd come to me with your suspicions instead of tackling the murderer alone. And all that rigamarole afterwards." He shook his head ruefully. "You must have friends in high places, Mrs. Rhodes. I hadn't even finished my report before I was being pressured to re-evaluate the evidence. Seems like everyone wanted a certain person's name cleared."

"Am I supposed to feel sorry for you?" Caroline retorted. "If I remember correctly, I'd been pegged as the prime suspect in the case. You were more interested in proving I was crazy than in listening to anything I had to say."

"And if I remember correctly, you removed evidence from a crime scene. If we'd had that diary earlier, we'd have caught our man before he almost did you in."

Caroline rolled her eyes. "I doubt you dropped by to discuss old times," she said tartly. "Let's cut the small talk and get down to business. You want to question me about Emma Reiser, right?"

"Reiser was a federal employee killed on federal property. The Postal Service will be involved, but the FBI, in the person of yours truly, is in charge of the investigation." Evans glanced over at the desk where another nurse was busily shuffling paperwork while pretending not to eavesdrop. "Is there some place we could speak privately? This won't take long."

Caroline neither liked nor trusted Tom Evans, but the man did have a job to do. It was a hard job, and she was not about to make it harder.

"I'll be in the break room if you need me," she called over her shoulder. "This way, Mr. Evans."

Evans followed her to the back of the ER where a doorway led to a narrow corridor skirting the rear of the department. Half way down the corridor was a small room crammed with lockers and cast-off furniture. Caroline waved the agent in and closed the door.

"Make yourself at home. It's not exactly the Taj Mahal, but it'll do for cold dinners and short breaks."

Evans' tough boy image slipped a bit as he examined his crowded surroundings. The battered tweed couch leaning against the south wall of the room sagged precipitously to the left, its missing legs replaced by out-of-date medical books wedged between sand filled coffee cans. Scratched and dented metal lockers lined the adjacent wall below a shelf piled high with hospital scrubs. Across from the lockers, a miniature refrigerator huddled in a corner next to an ancient sink set in a boxed off countertop. A Formica cabinet, its doors long missing, clung to the wall above the sink. Packets of coffee, tea, and sugar spilled from its yellowed shelves to the countertop below. What little space remained in the room was occupied by four mismatched chairs and a scarred wooden table on which lay the remains of a pepperoni pizza and an empty two-liter pop bottle. The only modern accouterment in the room was a shiny glass coffee maker, and that, according to the penciled sign taped to the wall above it, wasn't working.

"Jeez! And I thought my boss was cheap! Is St. Anne's so poor it can't afford anything better than this junk?"

"The money goes where the public will see it," Caroline replied with as little sarcasm as possible. She pulled out a chair, sat down, and motioned Evans to do the same. "Haven't you noticed all the changes made to the front lobby? Looks more like a hotel now than a hospital."

"One of Paine's last ventures, wasn't it?" Evans asked, referring to the former administrator. "How's the new guy in charge? Or shouldn't I ask?"

Caroline shrugged. "All hospital administrators are poured from the same mold nowadays. They're businessmen, and they see their job as making and saving money." She made a sweeping gesture that included everything in the room. "Why pay for new furniture the paying customers will never see and use? Spend your money instead on whatever you think will impress the patients and their visitors."

"You're one cynical lady, aren't you?"

"You get that way after twenty years in this business. Tell me your job hasn't affected you."

Evans rubbed his jaw with the backside of one hand. "Oh, I admit I'm cynical. Why else would I have questioned your story last winter?"

Their eyes locked, and Caroline suddenly felt

ashamed. Tom Evans might not be the most congenial of men, but he'd made a career of solving tough cases through hard work and persistence. She, on the other hand, had unmasked a killer only by accidentally stumbling on the truth. What right had she to criticize the man? None at all that she could see.

"If our roles had been reversed, I might have come to the same conclusion you did, Mr. Evans."

"And I might have been just as angry about it as you were, Mrs. Rhodes. But that's all water under the bridge. I've got a new case here in Rhineburg I'd like to wrap up quickly. Will you answer a few questions for me?"

"Of course. Although I don't think there's much I can tell you about the murder."

The federal agent permitted himself the barest of smiles as he pulled a battered notebook from an inside pocket of his jacket.

"Then tell me what you know about Andrew Littlewort."

"Littlewort?" Caroline repeated in surprise. "What's he got to do with Emma's death besides taking that bogus stone to the P.O.?"

Evans sighed. "Here we go again with you asking the questions instead of answering them. Please, Mrs. Rhodes. Just tell me about yesterday morning and the discovery of this so-called rune stone."

"Don't talk down to me in that patronizing tone of voice," Caroline snapped. "You caught me off guard asking about Professor Littlewort. I thought you'd want to know about the antique collector."

"What antique collector?"

Caroline explained her theory about an unknown person who'd killed Emma after coming to Rhineburg to purchase the rune stone. Evans didn't seem enthralled with the theory and said as much.

"It's too far-fetched, if you ask me. Most crimes occur for much simpler reasons. I think this murder was committed on the spur of the moment. It was totally unpremeditated, and our killer probably regretted it immediately."

"It sounds like you have a pretty good idea of who did it."

Evans nodded. "That's why I want to hear your account of yesterday's happenings. Be as accurate as you can with the details."

Caroline related the previous day's events with a heavy heart. It wasn't hard to guess the name of Evans's prime suspect. She couldn't help but worry about the fallout from his arrest.

"Did Professor Littlewort exhibit any signs of anger when Professor Atwater suggested the stone was a fake?"

"He was a little upset, but…"

"The students who were present at the dig testified that Littlewort was more than a little upset, Mrs. Rhodes. They say he shouted at Carl Atwater before storming off with the stone. They also say the professor's well known for his temper tantrums."

"So I've heard," Caroline replied miserably. "But you have to understand how eccentric Andrew Littlewort is. He thrives on controversies like this one about Leif Erikson."

"Given to obsessions, would you say?"

"That term can be defined in several ways, Mr. Evans. I'm not sure I'm qualified to analyze Andrew Littlewort's personality."

Evans scribbled something in his notebook.

"You saw the professor today in the police station, right?"

"Andrew arrived shortly before Nikki and I left."

"He was pretty angry with your daughter-in-law, wasn't he?"

Caroline nodded.

"Was that anger real or faked do you think?"

"I haven't even considered the possibility it was faked. Professor Littlewort seemed genuinely upset both with Nikki and Chief Moeller."

"Why Moeller? Had the Chief accused him of something?"

Caroline shook her head. She knew Evans was drawing her into a trap, but she saw no way out of it.

"He wanted his rune stone back. He thought Jake should be doing more to find it."

"Well, I agree with him on that point. Moeller doesn't seem to be putting much effort into the search for the murder weapon. I may have to call in more agents if I want it found."

The hackles rose on the back of Caroline's neck. Where did Evans come off criticizing a man like Jake Moeller? Being an outsider, Evans had no idea how easily one could lose a rock in Rhineburg. Toss it in the forest, or better yet, in the quarry, and it would never be seen again.

"You're trying to pin this murder on Andrew Littlewort, aren't you?"

"He had a pretty strong motive," Evans answered mildly. "And plenty of opportunity. I believe that sometime yesterday Littlewort began to realize he'd been tricked. He regretted his decision to send the rune stone to Chicago, and he went back to the post office to retrieve it. It was late at night, and when he couldn't wake Mrs. Reiser who was asleep on the second floor, he broke into the building through the cellar door. He found his package in the mailroom, but in the process, he woke the postmaster. She came downstairs and discovered him holding the stone. They argued over the break-in and Littlewort's plan to abscond with a piece of U.S. mail. Things went from bad to worse after that."

"Without the stone…"

"Emma may have done other things for a living, but primarily she was a U.S. Postal Service employee. According to everyone I talked to today, she was very proud of her work. She never would have allowed Professor Littlewort to leave with that package."

"So you think the argument turned ugly, and Andrew hit Emma with the rock."

It was Evans' turn to nod. "Professor Littlewort has been answering questions all afternoon. He's going to crack before long and tell us the truth. Until then, I plan to gather as much testimony as to his actions and state of mind as I possibly can. This may not have been premeditated murder, but it was still pretty cold-blooded. Andrew Littlewort knew the Field Museum would label his find a hoax, and he couldn't stand to have folks laugh at him. He killed Emma Reiser to save his reputation."

Caroline couldn't fault Evans' theory. Carl had said

Littlewort possessed a short fuse. He'd fought with practically every faculty member, so it wasn't difficult to envision him taking on Emma.

"You'll probably be called to testify in court," Evans said. "I hope that's the only way you involve yourself in this case."

"Involve myself?" Caroline asked with a frown. "Would you care to elaborate on that statement, Agent Evans?"

"Don't bother trying to pin this crime on some imaginary antique collector. You were lucky once, but in this business you need more than luck to catch a killer." Chair legs scraped the floor as Evans pushed back from the table. Halfway to the door, he turned and laughed. "You know, that police chief of yours is a real riot. He actually thought he could confiscate everything in Mrs. Reiser's apartment under the RICO act." His grin grew wider. "He didn't know the law can only be employed by federal agencies like the FBI or the IRS, and you can only attach the assets of a living person. Once they're dead, you can't touch them. Moeller's not a bright cop, is he?"

Caroline felt compelled to come to Jake's defense.

"We don't see a lot of high profile crime around here, Mr. Evans. I think the Chief can be excused for misunderstanding a statute he's never before been called on to use."

Evans grunted. "Think what you want, Mrs. Rhodes, but professional lawmen ought to know the law." He started to leave, then turned back again. "I'll want a written statement from you, so stop by the police station tomorrow."

Caroline nodded her assent. She followed the agent to the door and watched him trudge back towards the ER. When she was sure he was out of hearing range, she reached for the wall phone.

"Hello?"

"Carl, it's Caroline. Can you drop what you're doing and come over to St. Anne's? I think the university has a problem. A *big* problem!"

Twelve

Caroline drove to the police station early the next morning. It took less than fifteen minutes to repeat her story to Annie Holtzbrinck, the silver-haired dispatcher who also served as Jake Moeller's secretary. Annie typed a draft of the account, and after one minor change in wording, Caroline signed it in Jake's presence.

She exited the station as inconspicuously as possible. Rhineburg was known for its active grapevine, and tongues would be wagging soon enough. She had no desire to draw attention to herself as a witness, so she was relieved to find the sidewalk empty of curious townsfolk when she made her way to the post office. Nikki waited for her at the door. She slipped inside and followed her daughter-in-law to the back room.

"I'm glad I called you before I left the station," Caroline said as she hung her jacket over the back of a chair. "I dreaded running into someone on the street and having to explain why I'd been in the Chief's office."

"I hate to burst your bubble, but I doubt your visit will remain a secret for long. Everyone's talking about Emma. I expect I'll have lots of customers this morning."

"I can't believe Tom Evans allowed you to reopen so soon. It was only yesterday that Emma was murdered."

"Apparently the FBI doesn't waste any time working up a crime scene. Still, I was surprised when Evans told me he'd taken the seal off the building. I think the postal authorities wanted the ground floor reopened for business as soon as possible."

"I wish you'd had a little more time, Nikki."

Knowing exactly what her mother-in-law meant, Nikki gave Caroline an appreciative hug.

"Don't worry about me, Mom. I'm over the shaky stage now. Mrs. Reiser's death certainly came as a shock, but now all I want to do is help find her killer. It's true Emma deceived me right along with everyone else in this town. Still, I learned a lot from her. She was kind to me, and she didn't deserve to die that way."

Their conversation was interrupted by a loud "yoo-hoo!" echoing through the post office. Nikki rolled her eyes in mock exasperation.

"The doors haven't been unlocked five minutes and already the masses are descending! Come on up front with me. You can listen in on the gossip while I sell stamps."

Caroline trailed reluctantly after Martin's wife. She'd hoped for a cozy chat with Nikki, a mother-daughter bonding session meant to ease both their minds. But the girl seemed to be handling the murder fairly well today. Perhaps she'd misjudged Nikki's resilience.

"Good morning, dear. I hope those new commemoratives have arrived."

Mrs. Bertha Meyer, the baker's wife, resembled one of the sugary delicacies displayed in her husband's shop. A diminutive woman in height, she was amply proportioned in every other way, with a face as round and plump as a Bismarck, punctuated by twin dots of licorice for eyes. Her head was capped by a crown of short fluffy hair the color of vanilla butter-cream frosting. Below a set of double chins, her figure rolled downward in ever broadening stages, her imposing bosom topping a torso aptly described as butterball in shape. All this magnificence was firmly encased in a starched white apron peppered with splotches of strawberry jam beneath a fine dusting of powdered sugar.

Standing in the doorway with the morning sun bouncing off her shoulders, Mrs. Meyer resembled nothing less than a shimmering three-tiered wedding cake festooned with red roses and baby's breath. Caroline was so captivated by the little woman she couldn't help but break into a grin.

"They haven't come in yet," she heard Nikki say. "I told you that last night when you called me at home."

The baker's wife had the decency to blush. "I thought perhaps today…"

Nikki shook her head. "Ben hasn't arrived yet today. If he brings them along with the other things I ordered, I'll put the first page aside and call you at the bakery."

Bertha heaved a mighty sigh, then broke into a fit of coughing as powdered sugar erupted from the bib of her apron.

"Oh, dear!" she cried. She swatted at the fine particles until they dispersed in the air. "I almost forgot my other reason for coming by." She waddled over to the counter and handed Nikki a brown paper sack. "I made these especially for you."

Nikki opened the bag and lifted out a fat chocolate donut. She smiled down at her benefactress. "My favorite breakfast food! Thank you, Mrs. Meyer."

"I knew you'd have lots of people coming in today," Bertha whispered conspiratorially. "It's always nice to be able to offer them a donut to go with their tea."

Caroline caught on long before Nikki and said, "I'll bet you could go for a cup of tea right about now, Mrs. Meyer. I know how early in the morning you and your husband start baking."

"That would be lovely, Mrs. Rhodes. I must say, I am a bit tired today. What with all the excitement yesterday, I hardly slept a wink all night. A little refreshment would perk me up nicely." Bertha unlatched the gate in the counter. "But don't you bother yourself over me. I know where the tea things are, so I'll start the water boiling and put the donuts out while you help Nikki with the customers. We'll be ready for company in no time flat."

With a smile and a nod of her head, Bertha vanished into the back room.

"Customers? What customers?" Nikki asked with a frown.

"Those, I expect." Caroline pointed out the front window. From both ends of the square a half dozen women were rapidly converging on the post office. "Looks like a regular Rhineburg delegation."

The words were barely out of her mouth when the door flew open and Eleanor Naumann stepped over the threshold. Tall and angular, the woman clutched an oblong package to her flat breast with long bony fingers while hard on her heels came the rest of the group.

"Good morning!" the horse-faced Eleanor trilled. She thrust the package at Nikki with a nervous smile. "Been meaning to send this book to my sister in Baltimore for weeks now and just never got around to it. Today I said to myself, 'Eleanor, get your act together before it's too late.'

I guess I was thinking of poor Emma. One tends to put things off and then, poof! The unexpected happens."

Caroline could tell none of the women believed that business about the book. Nevertheless, Eleanor's speech was well received by her companions. Heads nodding, they acknowledged the tragic eloquence of her words with a respectful silence broken only when a silver haired woman in sunglasses patted Naumann on the shoulder.

"I know exactly what you mean, Ellie. I was going to wait until Saturday to buy stamps. Then I thought, there's no time like the present for getting chores done. God only knows what tomorrow will bring."

Not to be outdone, the other ladies broke into a chorus of explanations outlining their own reasons for visiting the post office. The common thread uniting them all seemed to be a sudden distrust of the immediate future.

The temporary postmaster tuned out the chitchat as she tallied the postage on Eleanor's book and sorted out stamps for the rest of her customers. Watching from the sidelines, Caroline was not so inclined to ignore the conversation. She listened first with amusement and then with growing interest as the women expounded on Emma's personality and habits. The group seemed indisposed to leave the post office, an oddity Caroline understood only after Mrs. Meyer emerged from the back room, thumped her fist on the service bell, and announced loudly,

"There's tea and donuts in the back room, ladies. Why don't you all come in and sit a spell?"

"Don't mind if we do," Eleanor replied for her friends. Chattering happily, the six of them filed past an astonished Nikki and headed for the rear of the building.

"Won't you join us?" Sarah Sonnenschein, Rhineburg's elderly head librarian, issued her invitation to Caroline in a whisper. "We've really come to see you, you know."

Nikki continued to stand there slack-mouthed, but Caroline rose to the occasion with a smile and a murmured thank you. She followed Ms. Sonnenschein into the back room where Mrs. Meyer was playing hostess.

"Pull up a chair, Mrs. Rhodes," the baker's wife commanded as she handed Caroline a cup of tea. She pointed to a tiny woman, dressed in black, who sat at the head of the table. "Agatha here saw some peculiar goings on the night of the murder. We figured you better hear her story first hand since it might help you track down Emma's killer."

Caroline nearly choked on her tea. She lowered her cup and looked Bertha straight in the eye.

"Mrs. Meyer, I am not, and I repeat *not*, involved in this investigation. I came here yesterday only because my daughter-in-law discovered Emma's body. The poor girl was naturally upset, and I did what I could to help her."

"Oh, poo!" Agatha Hagendorf, proprietor of the Rhineburg Boarding House and Home for Gentle Women situated across the street from the post office's side entrance, registered total disdain for Caroline's statement with a toss of her blue rinsed curls. "Of course you have no *official* role in the case, but we all know that FBI agent will get nowhere without your help. Look how he botched that business with the bomber. If it hadn't been for you..."

"We really do admire your work," interrupted Ms.

Sonnenschein in a subdued voice.

"That man is not one of us," Eleanor said darkly. "He doesn't know the people of our town the way you do."

With vigorous nods and murmurs of approval, the others signaled their endorsement of Miss Naumann's viewpoint. Caroline felt her resolve crumbling under the weight of the group's flattery.

"I do feel like I'm a part of this town now," she conceded.

"I should hope so, Mrs. Rhodes," purred Bertha Meyer. "After all, you're a highly valued member of our community. Why, look at the work you do at the hospital. My John might have bled to death if you hadn't been on duty the day I brought him to ER."

"It was a very small cut, Mrs. Meyer. It only required a couple of stitches."

Bertha waved off the objection. "If you hadn't insisted he get a tetanus shot, John's hand might have become infected. I ask you now, what's a baker to do if he can't use his hands? No, Mrs. Rhodes, you mustn't underestimate your contributions to Rhineburg. Beside being an excellent nurse, you have a way of sniffing out the truth in puzzling situations."

"None of us have your talent for detecting," added Eleanor. "Or your experience."

The only thing Caroline detected at the moment was a full load of Rhineburg blarney being shoveled in her direction. Under other circumstances, it would have annoyed her to know the ladies had staged this conversation. She had to admit, though, she was intrigued by Emma's murder. She also wondered why her guests were employing such devious tactics.

"That nice Professor Atwater could help out again like he did last winter."

That 'nice Professor Atwater' was currently in Caroline's doghouse. When she'd called him from the ER the night before, he'd dismissed her concerns in a rather cavalier manner. She'd been downright annoyed with her friend by the time they'd hung up. Remembering their brief conversation, she reacted without further hesitation.

"One does have a duty to the truth, ladies. If I can help point the FBI in the right direction, then I have no choice but to become involved. Now, Mrs. Hagendorf, why don't you tell me about your experience the night of the murder."

The woman in black, as Caroline had come to think of her, waited until she had everyone's undivided attention before launching into her story.

"It was quite late, well after midnight I'd say, and I was just about to close the drapes in my bedroom when this racket erupted across the street."

"You're sure of the time?" Caroline interrupted.

Agatha nodded. "I'd been viewing the stars through a telescope just as my husband Harold–God rest his soul– did every night for fifty-two years before his premature departure from this earth. After fixing each constellation in the sky, I rolled up Harold's star charts and made my preparations for bed. I turned down the blankets before stepping to the window to close the drapes. There was no light on at the time, and my eyes were adjusted to the dark when I peered down at the street."

"Just tell Mrs. Rhodes what you saw, Agatha,"

Eleanor Naumann commanded impatiently.

Mrs. Hagendorf was not to be hurried. She took a bite of her donut, then a sip of tea before sighing, "I certainly will miss poor Emma. We shared many a fine conversation at this table."

"So did we all," Bertha Meyer muttered through clenched teeth. "Do get on with it, Agatha. I have to get back to the bakery."

Mrs. Hagendorf sniffed noisily as if to remind the other women just who was running this show. She did, however, condescend to continue.

"As I was saying, a racket erupted across the street. At first I thought it was a raccoon rummaging around in the garbage cans. But then I saw someone stumble out from behind the post office. There's a lamppost a few feet down the block, and the figure walked off in that direction. I didn't get a good look at the man, but the way he moved, I thought he must have been drinking. He was not at all steady on his feet."

"Could you describe the man?" Caroline asked.

"The first one was rather tall and broad in the shoulders," Agatha replied. "A robust, out-doorsy looking fellow. The other man appeared much shorter."

"Wait a minute! There were two men in the street?"

"I wouldn't have mentioned the second one if he hadn't been there, now would I? Of course I didn't see them at the same time, so I can't be exactly sure how tall either of them was. One man ran up towards Wilhelm Road. The second man went the opposite way down the sidewalk."

Caroline was now totally confused. She glanced at

the other women in the room, but none of them seemed to share her problem.

"I'm afraid I'm not quite following you, Mrs. Hagendorf. You say one man ran up the street…"

Agatha's head bobbed up and down. "Yes, dear. The two took off in opposite directions at different times. Looking down from the angle of my bedroom, it was difficult to compare their heights."

"I see," murmured Caroline, although she really didn't see at all. "Please go on."

"Well, as I thought he was nothing more than a common drunk, I didn't pay much attention to the first fellow. I closed the drapes, got into bed, and was just about to fall asleep when the noise started up all over again. Déjà vu, I thought, and I jumped up ready to haul open the window and give that drunk a piece of my mind. I was angry all right, but when I looked out I saw a different fellow, a skinny runt of a man whose arms flapped like chicken wings as he pranced down the street. I looked over at the post office, but there were no lights on in the building. I figured Emma had been lucky enough to sleep through the uproar." Agatha shook her head, her eyes suddenly bright with tears. "Now I wonder if she didn't hear all the ruckus because she'd already gone to her eternal rest."

There was dead silence in the room as the group contemplated Agatha's words. The little woman shook her head again, then looked up at Caroline.

"One of those men probably killed Emma," she said sadly. "Maybe you can figure out who it was."

"That's a matter for the police, don't you think?"

Eight heads swung round to face the doorway. Eight mouths fell open and then quickly shut again as Professor Carl Atwater entered the room, his eyes blazing with anger.

"What do you women think you're doing?" he roared. He pointed at Caroline. "She nearly got herself killed the last time she tried to solve a murder. Don't you think you should leave the detecting to those who are trained to do it?"

Caroline rose from her chair. "Now, Carl..."

"Don't 'Carl' me!" growled the Professor.

"I think we'd better be going," muttered Mrs. Meyer as she gathered up the last two donuts and whisked them back into the bag.

"I agree," chirped Mrs. Hagendorf. "I have quite a few chores to do."

"Not so fast," snarled Carl. He placed a hand on the elderly woman's arm as she tried to edge past him. "Your chores will have to wait, Agatha. You're coming with me to the police station where you'll repeat your story to Chief Moeller and FBI Agent Evans."

"Oh, no!" cried Agatha. "I really don't want to get involved!"

"You have no choice in the matter," Carl told her grimly. He shot a look at Caroline before dragging Agatha out the door. "Stay put 'til I get back. I want to talk to you."

Caroline bit back an angry reply. Just who did Carl think he was ordering her about? She had half a mind to follow him, but the other ladies were now closing ranks around her.

"He has quite a temper, doesn't he?" whispered Sarah Sonnenschein.

"Typical man, if you ask me," replied Mrs. Naumann.

"I think we should go over to the boarding house and wait for Agatha to return," suggested a third woman whom Caroline had not been introduced to.

"Good thinking, Myrtle," said Mrs. Meyer. "I really must get back to the bakery, but Agatha will need some cheering up when she's done at the station. I'm sure she'll appreciate you being there."

No more was said on the subject of Caroline's involvement in the case until the entire crew had filed out the front door of the post office. Then Bertha Meyer turned back and with a thumbs-up gesture called out to Caroline, "Don't worry about Professor Atwater, dear. We have every faith in your ability to handle this investigation on your own."

A crooked smile tugged at Caroline's lips. The baker's wife had opened a can of worms at this morning's tea party. She expected Caroline to clean up the mess, but it was an impossible chore. Agatha Hagendorf was very nearly an eyewitness to Emma Reiser's murder. Her explosive testimony would undoubtedly prove to be the cornerstone of the prosecution's case against Professor Andrew Littlewort.

They'll probably arrest him today, Caroline thought.

And why not? He was the only man she knew of who not only fit Agatha's description of the high stepping, arm flapping stranger, but also had a motive for killing Emma.

"What a pity," she mused aloud. "Especially since there's no way Andrew could have committed the crime."

Thirteen

Professor Atwater's mood was subdued when he returned to the post office an hour later. With little more than a cursory nod to Nikki, he passed through the gate in the front desk and trudged towards the back room where Caroline was sorting a stack of out-going mail.

"Evans means to arrest Andrew Littlewort," he said as he settled himself at the table. "He's bringing him in for questioning right now."

"I figured he would," Caroline replied without looking up from her job. "Given Agatha's testimony, he probably thinks he has a good case against the professor."

"They haven't found the murder weapon yet."

"Well, that's one thing in Littlewort's favor."

Caroline separated three letters from the pile and placed them to one side of the table. She continued to group the mail by zip code, her lips tightly compressed as she worked. Carl sat there quietly watching her. Her displeasure was obvious, and he ducked his head, concentrating his own anger on an open bag of rubber bands lying on the table. He fiddled with the bands until the silence in the room became too uncomfortable to bear. Sweeping the rubber bands aside angrily, he slapped the table with both hands.

"See here, Caroline…"

Caroline raised one hand and fixed the professor with a steely-eyed look that stopped him in his tracks.

"Don't use that tone of voice with me, Carl Atwater.

You and I are friends, but you are not my father, my guardian, or my boss. You have no right to tell me what I can or can't do, and you especially have no right to embarrass me in public."

Carl's jaw went slack. "Embarrass you in public? Cari! I was only trying to prevent you from getting mixed up in another murder! Don't you remember what almost happened the last time you tangled with a killer?"

"I could hardly forget an experience like that," Caroline answered impatiently. "How can you forget it was you who involved me in that case in the first place?"

Carl opened his mouth to reply, then promptly shut it again.

"Exactly!" Caroline slapped the remaining letters on the table. "Listen to me, Carl. I don't know who killed Emma Reiser, but I'm pretty sure it wasn't Andrew Littlewort. Andrew is under suspicion because of you. And partly because of me," she added in a less intense tone of voice. "You could have stopped this rune stone nonsense at the start if you hadn't been so intent on embarrassing Garrison Hurst. And I should never have used Charlie Branch the way I did. I thought Hurst would be swayed by Charlie's objections and forbid the dig, but it didn't work out that way."

Carl stroked his beard to cover his discomfort. "I'll admit my dislike of the Emperor may have clouded my judgment. However, knowing Andrew as I do, I think he would have mailed that stone to the Field Museum despite opposition from Hurst. If he later changed his mind and returned to claim it…"

"We know he returned here, Carl. Agatha saw him."

"What she saw was a figure running away from the post office. There's no proof it was Andrew."

"Trust me on this one. Agatha didn't tell us everything she knows, but she isn't lying about seeing Littlewort."

Atwater shook his head. "I don't want to think of Andrew as a killer, but maybe he did it, Cari."

"Good grief! Not you, too." Caroline vented her frustration on the remaining mail, tossing letters haphazardly on once neat piles. "It seems like every man I know has lost his senses in the past two days."

"What's that supposed to mean?"

"It means none of you are seeing the obvious. Look, Carl. I feel partially responsible for what's happened here. Mrs. Meyer and the other ladies have asked me to look into this matter, and I intend to do just that. I'd appreciate your help, but if you're not willing..."

"Hello, Professor. Hi, Mrs. Rhodes."

Caroline and Carl turned simultaneously towards the doorway. Michael Bruck was standing there, a ledger in one hand and a six pack of cola in the other.

"I didn't mean to break into your conversation," he said with a smile, "but I'm here on official business. Jake Moeller asked me to take a look at Emma's computer programs." The head of security for Bruck University walked over to the table and glanced down at the mail. "I see Nikki's training you as her new assistant."

"Hardly," Caroline replied with a grin. She was genuinely fond of this blond giant who'd proved so helpful during last winter's troubles. The young man had a good head on his shoulders and a sympathetic manner to match.

"I thought the Chief was assigning a deputy to check Emma's computer."

"Billy's too busy searching for the murder weapon, so I'm going to help out on the gambling end of the case."

"There's quite a setup upstairs."

"So I heard, Professor. By the way, shouldn't you be over at the college? Everything's just about set for the dress rehearsal."

Carl frowned and glanced down at his watch. "I didn't think it was this late already," he said as he got to his feet. "Will I see you at the practice, Cari?"

Caroline hesitated. "I'm not sure I'll make it. I need to stop at the hospital and a couple of other places first."

Carl frowned again, but he didn't push the matter. "Then I'll see you later tonight. Remember, the banquet starts at six o'clock."

"Don't worry. I'll meet you by the Maypole around five-thirty."

Carl headed for the front door as Michael started upstairs. When she was sure both men were out of hearing range, Caroline picked up the phone and dialed the number for Mad Moeller's Antiques and Collectibles. The Chief's wife answered on the third ring.

"Madeline Moeller speaking. May I help you?"

"Maddy? It's Caroline Rhodes. I was wondering..."

"Oh, Caroline! Thank goodness you called. I've been so upset this morning. I wanted to talk to you, but I didn't know your phone number. Are you at home?"

"I'm at the post office, Maddy. I was wondering..."

"Stay right there. I'm on my way over."

Caroline pulled the receiver away from her ear as

Madeline slammed down the phone.

"Who was that?" Nikki had entered the room and was staring quizzically at her mother-in-law.

"Maddy Moeller," Caroline answered with a laugh. "It's certainly difficult to get a word in edgewise with that woman."

"You're telling me! She's a bit on the excitable side, but I hear she's an excellent saleswoman."

"She seemed to know her business when she was here yesterday. I was hoping to pump her for a little information."

"About what?" Nikki walked over to the tiny refrigerator next to the sink and took out a pitcher of iced tea. "I made this fresh today. Would you like a glass?"

Caroline nodded. "Carl says FBI Agent Evans is building a case against Andrew Littlewort. It looks like he'll be charged with the murder of Emma Reiser."

Nikki let out a low whistle. "Littlewort's a nut case, but I never thought he was crazy enough to kill someone."

"I don't think he did, which is why I called Maddy. I'm hoping she has the inside scoop on whatever evidence Jake's gathered." Caroline accepted the glass Nikki offered and walked over to the staircase. She stared at the steps while sipping her tea. "How tall was Emma?"

"How tall? I'd say about five foot nine or ten."

"I thought so from the clothes I saw upstairs. And how tall is Professor Littlewort?"

Nikki frowned. "About the same as me, five foot five inches."

"I'd say that's about right," said Caroline. She turned to her daughter-in-law and pointed to the stairs. "You found five foot nine Emma lying dead of a head injury at the bottom of this staircase. Assuming five foot five Andrew hit her with that rock, he'd have had to stand up on the second step to generate enough downward momentum to fracture her skull." She shook her head slowly "That scenario doesn't make sense to me. The only other way he could have killed her was to swing the rock upward from the side and catch her at the base of the skull. I'm going to stop by the hospital later and see what I can find out about the autopsy."

"Caroline! Where are you!"

"That sounds like Chief Moeller's wife." Nikki put down her drink and walked to the doorway. "Back here, Mrs. Moeller. Come join us."

Fourteen

It was obvious to both women that Maddy was in a foul mood when she entered the post office. Slamming the door behind her, she crossed the lobby in long strides, swept past Nikki, and marched into the back room.

"Jake is fit to be tied," she announced querulously.

Caroline motioned for Nikki to leave them. The young woman took the hint graciously, closing the door behind her while Caroline ushered Maddy to a chair.

"What's happened now?"

"This Evans character acts as if he's God's gift to law enforcement. He talks down to Jake, like he's some hillbilly sheriff with a mushroom for a brain." Maddy's whole body quivered with indignation. "It's maddening to see my husband treated that way."

Caroline could easily commiserate with the redhead. "I know how you feel. I had my own problems with Agent Evans last winter."

"So I heard. I immediately thought of you when Jake came home last night all upset over this RICO business."

"You thought of me? But why?"

"Well, you outwitted Evans once before. I wondered if you'd like a chance to do it again."

Caroline stared at the Chief's wife in disbelief. Tangling with Evans was the last thing she wanted to do.

"I'm not sure where you're heading with all this, but I have to tell you, Maddy, I know about the mix-up with the RICO regulations. Evans came to see me at work last night. He mentioned it in passing."

"I'm sure he did," Maddy retorted. "He's probably laughing himself sick over Jake's plan to profit from Emma's estate. My husband made an honest mistake, Cari. No policeman can possibly keep track of every little nuance in the law."

Caroline considered the distinction between dead and alive to be more than a nuance, but she refrained from saying so. Instead, she sought to calm her fiery visitor with soothing words.

"You don't need to defend Jake to me or anyone else in this town. I've heard a lot of good things about him from people whose opinions I respect. It's true he's under a bit of pressure right now, but he'll survive."

"You don't understand, Caroline. My Jake is a proud man. Being made a fool of first by Emma and then by this FBI jerk is really tearing him up. I tell you, it's shaken his self-confidence."

Caroline couldn't bear to see the pain in the other woman's eyes. With a sigh of resignation, she opened the refrigerator and reached for the iced tea.

"Let's cut to the chase, " she said, handing Maddy a glass. " You said you want to outwit Tom Evans. How do you intend to do it? And how do I fit into the scheme?"

"I don't have a plan at the moment. That's why I came here." Mrs. Moeller looked Caroline straight in the eye. "Jake means the world to me, Cari. He's all I have, and I won't let him be destroyed by the gossip that's bound to spring up over this murder. People will say he should have known what Emma was up to. They'll make fun of him and laugh behind his back over this stupid RICO business." She paused and took a deep breath. "I want Jake to catch Emma's killer before Tom Evans does. I want people to respect him again, and I want him to respect himself. It's as simple as that."

Caroline nodded. Having once loved a man herself, she understood what Maddy was experiencing. "Tell me something. Do you know Evans is planning to charge Andrew Littlewort with Emma's murder?"

"Really? When did that happen?"

Caroline filled Madeline in on the morning's events. Jake's wife listened intently, interrupting only once or twice with questions. She perked up considerably when Caroline explained why she thought Evans was arresting the wrong man.

"That makes perfect sense to me. I propose we join forces, Caroline. I'll pass on every bit of information I can worm out of my husband, and you use it as best you can. If you need any other kind of help … "

"Let's settle one point before we go any farther," Caroline insisted. "I have my own reasons for getting involved in this case. None of them have to do with pursuing a vendetta against Tom Evans. True, I don't like the man, but I won't obstruct justice by withholding information if he asks for it."

"I have no problem with that," Maddy said with a shrug. "We'll just make sure Jake hears everything first."

"That's fine with me," Caroline agreed. "So what do you say we get down to work? I have lots of questions that need answering."

Maddy pulled out a notebook and a pen. "Shoot, boss."

"First of all, how did the killer get into the post office?"

"I can answer that one." Nikki walked into the room with a mail sack over her shoulder. She tossed the bag on a shelf and pulled a chair up to the table. "I take it you two are unofficially working on this case."

"We're just sharing some ideas," Madeline murmured.

"Don't worry about me blowing the whistle on you," said Nikki. "I want to help catch this killer, too."

Madeline raised her eyebrows.

"Nikki has her own special interest in this matter," said Caroline. She turned to her daughter-in-law. "If we discover anything of value, we take it to Chief Moeller. He's the action man this time. We only work on ideas. Now tell me how you think the killer got in."

Nikki pointed to a small door set back under the staircase. "That leads down to the basement. There's an outside entrance below ground level on the alley side of the building. You reach it by a flight of stairs. The way the police were swarming around back there, I figure that's how the murderer must have gotten in."

"I take it the outside door is usually locked."

"Yes, but the lock is pretty old and rusty. Not much of a deterrent for criminals."

"This upstairs door is left open?"

"It's not locked, if that's what you mean."

"Anyone could have known about that entrance." Deep in thought, Caroline turned to Maddy. "What about footprints. Did Jake find any?"

"Oh, sure. The ground back there was soft from all

the rain, so there were plenty of impressions. The problem is, there were too many impressions. Jake said it looked like an army marched past that back door."

"Nothing they could use?"

"Jake didn't think so, but then Evans arrived with his team. They took over both inside and out. Jake and his men were assigned to find the rune stone."

"And have they?"

"Not yet. I talked to Jake less than an hour ago, and they were still looking."

"If Evans pulled Professor Littlewort in for questioning, he probably got a search warrant for his house. I'm sure they'll hunt for the stone there."

"And if they find it?"

"Then we have a problem, Nikki." Caroline stood up and began to pace the room. "Andrew doesn't have the personality of a cold-blooded killer, and be assured, this was a cold-blooded killing."

"My husband said the professor has a terrible temper. He didn't seem at all concerned about Emma's death until Jake started questioning him. Then he flew into a rage and demanded a lawyer."

"Which is a point in his favor, strange as it may seem. Think about it, ladies. If Andrew had killed Emma, wouldn't he try to cover it with a show of concern rather than a display of anger? The man is a typical coward. He intimidates people with his raving and ranting, but that's as far as it ever goes. When he's done reaming you out, he simply turns and walks away."

"You're right," Nikki said distastefully. "I use to watch him in class. He always picked on people who wouldn't, or couldn't, stand up to him. Maybe they lacked self-confidence, or it just wasn't in their nature to fight back."

"Blessed are the meek," Maddy murmured.

"Emma was anything but meek." Caroline stood up and walked to the back door. "I want to have a look at the alley. Agatha says she saw two men there the night of the murder. But according to Chief Moeller, there were enough footprints to account for several people. The question is, are they old footprints, or was someone else here that evening."

Madeline and Nikki followed her outside, Nikki pointing the way to the basement entrance. The alley was a typical clay and gravel affair bordered on both sides by a wide strip of dirt. Weeds grew on the opposite side of the alley, but the strip near the post office was clean of debris.

"Emma always planted annuals back here," said Nikki. "She was waiting for Memorial Day to put them in."

"So we're in luck." Caroline stooped down to examine the churned up dirt. The ground had dried to a hardened mass since the night of the murder. Overlapping ridges and gullies could be seen on both sides of the entranceway, and there was dried mud on the steps leading down to the basement. While the signs clearly indicated the presence of more than one person, no single footprint was distinguishable from the rest. She pointed to some lighter material mixed in with the mud on the steps. "What do you think that is?"

Maddy shrugged her shoulders. "Looks like dried grass clippings to me."

"Or maybe straw," said Nikki.

Caroline glanced up at Nikki. "Think, girl. Where did those clippings come from? Where have you seen straw lately?"

Nikki's hand flew to her mouth. "Oh my gosh! Bruck Green!"

Caroline nodded. "Charlie Branch mowed the Green right before the students put up the festival tents. He was there supervising when they scattered straw over the jousting field." She turned to Maddy. "You need to tell Jake about this. He's going to want to interrogate Charlie."

"But why?"

"Branch was opposed to Andrew sending his rock to Chicago. He was afraid people would invade the campus looking for more rune stones." Caroline stood up and backed away from the stairs. "Charlie was drinking at the Blue Cat Lounge the night of Emma's murder. He got pretty sloshed, and Carl and I ended up taking him home. When we put him to bed, I peeled off his boots. They were caked with grass clippings, and there was straw stuck to his socks."

"Hot dog!" said Maddy with a grin. "It looks like we have another suspect!"

Fifteen

Caroline swung off the highway and took the road leading to the university campus. She hadn't waited for Jake to arrive at the post office, preferring instead to seek out Carl and fill him in on the news. Now, as she turned onto Circle Road, she wondered if she'd done the right thing. Pointing a finger at Charlie might help Andrew Littlewort, but it certainly boded ill for the gardener. It also increased Caroline's feelings of guilt.

If Charlie Branch had killed Emma while in a drunken stupor, it was at least partially her fault. She was the one who'd told him about the rune stone and urged him to confront President Hurst at the faculty meeting. She was also the one who'd assured Carl that Charlie was so intoxicated he'd sleep straight through the night. She'd acted unwisely on the both counts.

Charlie's boozed up state still puzzled her. Carl said he'd never seen Branch take a drink, yet Caroline's experience told her only true alcoholics recovered so quickly from a binge. Maybe Branch drank only at home. She'd seen no sign of it in Charlie's living room or den. Still, she hadn't investigated the kitchen where most people kept their liquor.

I slipped up. Some ER nurse I am.

In a deep funk over the mess she'd created, Caroline took no notice of the activities on Bruck Green as she pulled into the driveway of St. Anne's Hospital. She turned left into the parking garage, nosed the Jeep up a narrow ramp, and drove to the second level where she parked and locked the car. Minutes later she was back on solid ground headed for the ER entrance.

"Hi, Cari. How's it going?"

Jane Gardner was leaving the hospital when Caroline passed through the first set of automatic doors labeled 'ER'. She stopped to chat in the enclosed passage between the inner and outer entrances.

"I'm glad I ran into you," said Caroline. "I need some information, and you're just the person who can give it to me."

"If it's about that mix-up with the paychecks…"

"No, no, nothing like that. I need to see a copy of the autopsy report on Emma Reiser, and I need it today if possible."

"Wow! You don't ask for much, do you?" Jane replied with a grin. "I'd love to help you out on this one, Caroline, but I'm just leaving for the day. I have a class over at the university in twenty minutes, and I can't miss it."

"I understand. Do you know if Paul Wakely's on duty today?"

"Yeah." Jane thumbed over her shoulder. "He's sewing up a kid in Room One. Look, Caroline, I have to run. Are you going to the festival banquet tonight?"

"Wouldn't miss it for the world."

"Great. I'll see you on the Green then."

Jane headed out the door with a backward wave of her hand while Caroline stood in the entranceway considering her next move. Paul was probably too busy to see her, but he seemed the best bet as a source of information. It wasn't likely the morgue attendant would let her in to view Emma's body if, in fact, the corpse was still there and not already at the funeral parlor.

"Why didn't I think of the undertaker?" Caroline muttered. "He'd be able to tell me exactly where the injury was."

Probably because I've been worrying about too many other things.

"Are you going to stand there all day?"

Caroline came out of her reverie with a start. She spun around to find Paul Wakely standing in the inner doorway grinning from ear to ear.

"Gathering wool out here?" he joked.

" I feel like my brain is made of the stuff." Caroline shook her head as she walked towards the doctor. "I get so preoccupied at times I forget where I am."

"Bad sign, Mrs. Rhodes. Sounds like you're suffering from detection overload. I prescribe a nice vacation away from solving murder cases."

"And who says I'm doing any detecting, Dr. Wakely?"

Paul just laughed as he stepped back and let Caroline pass by him. The two friends walked through the triage area and into the main room where a couple of nurses were attending to half a dozen patients in various cubicles.

"Busy day," Caroline noted. She sank down on a chair behind the desk and waved to one of her co-workers who was bandaging a cut on the head of a five-year-old. "Have you got a minute to talk, Paul?"

"Sure." Paul jerked his head in the direction of the six filled cubicles. "All those folks are waiting for test results and, per usual, the lab is short of help. Until I get some answers there's little more I can do for them. So, tell me about Emma's murder. I heard Agatha Hagendorf gave you an earful."

Caroline rolled her eyes in disbelief. "I'll never understand how news travels so quickly in this town. I only met Mrs. Hagendorf a few hours ago, and already you've got the scoop on the story."

"Credit the Rhineburg grapevine. It's a marvelous instrument of communication in this town."

"So how do you manage to tap in to it when you're stuck in the ER all day?"

"Very easily. Every time another patient comes in, I simply ask, 'What's new?'. It's amazing how eager people are to tell me the latest gossip."

"*Hmm.* Well, I hope you're as eager to open up to me."

"About what?"

"I need a copy of the autopsy report on Emma Reiser."

"What for?"

"So I can find out the exact location of Emma's head injury."

Paul rocked back in his chair and ran the fingers of one hand through his short sandy hair. "Why are you getting mixed up in this, Caroline? You were almost killed last winter when you investigated the bombing here at St. Anne's."

"You're beginning to sound like Carl Atwater. The professor's not too happy with what I'm doing, but I have good reasons for getting involved. Trust me on this one,

Paul."

Paul shook his head. "Just be careful, okay? We can't afford to lose a good nurse in this place."

"Can you get me the report?"

"I don't have the authority for that. But since I pronounced her when she came in, I can tell you what killed her. Emma died of massive trauma to the brain from at least one blow to the roof of the cranium. She had a depressed skull fracture involving both parietal bones. I saw no other injuries to the rest of her body."

"Was the fracture closer to the frontal bone or the occipital?"

"The frontal," Paul answered instantly. "I'd say it was just posterior to the coronal suture and bisected the sagittal suture."

"In other words, top and center."

Paul nodded. "It was a nasty injury with some extrusion of brain matter. I don't blame the paramedics for their initial assessment of the trauma as fall related. The torn gown and the fact she was found at the foot of the staircase indicated to them that Emma took a tumble. They know skull fractures are common complications in elderly fall victims, and they automatically assumed that was the case with Mrs. Reiser. As soon as I saw her, though, I knew her death was caused by something other than a wooden stair. The shape of the wound and the amount and angle of bone depression weren't right for the scenario described by the EMTs."

"How much force would it take to create that kind of fracture?"

"I'm no expert, but I'd guess whoever did it was no

weakling. Emma's skull was pretty well bashed in."

Caroline wrinkled her nose. "Her death couldn't have been unintentional. You don't hit someone that hard without meaning to."

Paul nodded again. "I'd say that pretty well sums it up. If I were trying to analyze our murderer, I'd credit the guy with a vicious personality."

"Labs results on Mr. Miller." One of the nurses walked over to where they were sitting and handed Paul a computer printout. "His potassium level is pretty low. Do you want me to hang a 'K' rider?"

Caroline slipped away from the desk as Paul and the nurse conferred on their patient. She'd gotten the information she needed to confirm her belief in Andrew Littlewort's innocence. Now all she had to do was convince Tom Evans he was pursuing the wrong man.

Knowing the FBI agent, that wouldn't be an easy thing to do.

Sixteen

After a quick lunch in the hospital cafeteria, Caroline left St. Anne's and went in search of Carl Atwater. She found him on Bruck Green supervising a mock sword fight between two earnest young men.

"Use your shield, Tim. This has got to look real."

"It looks real enough to me," Caroline said as approached the professor. "Unless you're waiting for a little blood to flow."

"It better not," growled Carl without taking his eyes off the boys. "I don't need any more casualties among this group. We've already lost one boy to a strained knee ligament. Another one's horse stomped on his foot. Damned nag broke the kid's toes."

"Sounds like you have problems."

"I had to get replacements for both of them or we would have been short a couple of knights. It wasn't easy finding two more riders who could simultaneously control both a horse and a jousting pole. Luckily for me, Charlie was willing to help out."

"Charlie Branch?" Caroline was surprised Carl would even consider the gardener as a substitute knight.

"He's filled in for riders in the past, so he more or less knows the routine. Sid Burke volunteered for the other spot. One thing I'll say for Sid, he certainly knows how to handle a horse."

"I hate to break this to you, Carl, but you'd better look for another replacement. I have a feeling Charlie's not

138

going to be available tomorrow."

"Why not?" Carl said sharply.

"He may be spending the day in the police station answering questions about Emma Reiser's murder."

The professor's jaw went slack. Eyes glazed in disbelief, he turned and called out to the two boys on the field. "That's enough for now. Go check out your costumes, and tell the others to do the same." He took Caroline by the arm. "Let's take a walk. I'd rather the students didn't hear any of this."

They left the jousting field and strolled aimlessly about the Green, Caroline updating Carl as they walked. When they reached a row of benches stationed along the center path, he called for a halt and sank down wearily on one of the hard wooden seats.

"What a mess." The professor passed a chubby hand over his face. "It certainly would help if Agatha could identify the two men she saw in the alley."

"She could if she wanted to," Caroline replied. "Of that I'm convinced."

Carl's bushy white eyebrows shot up. "You think Agatha's holding out on us? But why?"

"I haven't quite figured that out. But I'm sure Mrs. Meyer prearranged that tea party in the post office this morning. Bertha phoned Nikki at home last night, supposedly about some commemorative stamps she'd ordered. I think she wanted to find out if I would be visiting the P.O. today. Bertha and her silver-haired buddies were the first to show up when Nikki opened for business. Mrs. Meyer brought donuts, and before you could say 'pop goes the weasel', she and the other ladies were parked around the table in the back room."

"Then she's the ring leader of the group."

"It looks that way. Bertha instructed Agatha as to what she should or shouldn't say. Along with Eleanor Naumann, she kept Mrs. Hagendorf pretty well in line during the entire conversation."

"They were setting you up."

"You've got it, Carl. First they buttered me up like I was an ear of corn at a Sunday picnic. They paid me every compliment under the sun until I agreed to help them. Then Mrs. Hagendorf described Professor Littlewort to a 'T' while claiming she couldn't really tell who he was. The other man she saw, the inebriated one, was obviously Charlie Branch. Agatha said he was tall, broad shouldered, and had an 'out-doorsy' appearance. Maybe there were a few other drunks in Rhineburg that night, but the only one I know of who had any reason at all to be near the post office was Charlie."

"They wanted you to take this story to the police," Carl said.

"I think so," agreed Caroline. "They must have thought they could keep Agatha in the clear if I was the one to rat on Andrew and Charlie. Like I said before, I'm not sure why they decided to use me, but I aim to find out. Later tonight I intend to pay a visit to the Rhineburg Boarding House and Home for Gentle Women."

"Mind if I come along?" asked the professor.

"Not at all. But I thought you didn't approve of me meddling in this murder."

Carl shifted his position on the bench. He looked out over the Green, his jaw set and his eyes suddenly less troubled.

"Knowing all this, I don't think I have any choice but to help." He pushed himself up off the bench and reached in his back pocket for his pipe. "I owe it to Andrew and Charlie. And to you."

Caroline smiled at her friend. "I knew I could count on you," she said as she hooked her arm in his and started off down the path. "We make a good team, Carl Atwater. If we put our heads together, we're bound to come up with a few answers."

"Let's just hope they're the right ones," grunted Carl. He suddenly stopped dead in his tracks. "Well, look over there now. If it isn't Congressman Edmund Burke with our dearly beloved President."

Caroline looked in the direction Carl was pointing. As usual, the sight of Garrison Hurst caused her stomach muscles to tighten in apprehension. A tall balding man in his early sixties, Hurst was as lean as Andrew Littlewort, but there the similarity ended. Where Littlewort was clumsy and awkward, Hurst carried himself like a newly crowned king. Head held high, he strutted about in suits expertly tailored to hide his spindly arms and scrawny chest. If it hadn't been for the coldness in his hooded eyes, one might have been impressed with the man. As it was, those dark pools of granite behind horn-rimmed glasses were so off-putting that Caroline felt uneasy in his presence.

Apparently Edmund Burke was not so affected by the president. Younger than Hurst by a half dozen years, Burke was taller by two or three inches with a full head of salt and pepper hair. His clothes were equivalent to

Garrison's in price and style, but unlike the president, Burke had no need to hide his physique. Here was a man who worked out on a daily basis. His shoulders were naturally broad, and his upper body was well sculptured by exercise.

Burke's brow was furrowed and his full lips were compressed in a narrow line as he listened intently to whatever Hurst was saying. Caroline imagined he'd be quite handsome with a smile replacing that frown.

"I see where Sid gets his good looks," she murmured. "Has the Congressman come for the festival, or do you imagine he's here because of Emma's murder?"

"He usually attends any major activity here," said Carl. "It's good for his image. He's also bound and determined his son will graduate from Bruck. He's smooth-talked Sid out of more than one jam since the boy arrived here."

"Oh dear, Carl. It looks like they've seen us. They're coming our way."

Atwater groaned, but he held his ground as the two men approached.

"Good afternoon, Professor Atwater." Hurst nodded to Carl before turning to Caroline. "Mrs. Rhodes, I would like you to meet Congressman Edmund Burke."

Burke extended a hand to Caroline. "I'm pleased to meet you, Mrs. Rhodes. President Hurst tells me you saved the university from quite a bit of embarrassment last winter."

Caroline returned the Congressman's smile with one of her own. "It was unfortunate the FBI felt it necessary to include the students in their investigation," she replied.

"Still, it's understandable in a case like that. The police are forced to suspect everyone."

"The Congressman and I were just discussing the problem of Emma Reiser's murder," Hurst purred. "I was hoping I could persuade you to lend your talents to the school one more time."

"In what way could I be of help, President Hurst?"

The President glanced at Edmund Burke, but the Congressman kept silent. His face was set in a look of polite interest only.

"Congressman Burke thinks it would be better if we left this matter to the police," began Hurst. "I, on the other hand, feel the school has a responsibility to protect its faculty if at all possible. As you probably know, Andrew Littlewort has been detained by the police. They apparently feel that unfortunate business with the rune stone gave Andrew some kind of motive for killing Emma Reiser. Of course that's a lot of nonsense, but we all know how stubborn the police can be once they've decided on a course of action."

"From what I've heard, they have a pretty good case against your professor," said Burke. "I really think it's unnecessary to waste this lady's time, Garrison."

"Do you realize the kind of publicity we'll get if Littlewort is put on trial?" Hurst's voice soared from petulant to shrill. "Last winter was bad enough, Edmund. We fielded calls from dozens of worried parents after the newspapers linked Bruck to the bombing at St. Anne's. Think of the possibilities if word gets out now that one of our teachers is a murderer! Parents will start pulling their children out of school. If it turns into a mass exodus, the damage to Bruck will be irreparable."

"You're getting worked up over nothing," Burke said soothingly. He clapped Hurst on the shoulder in a reassuring manner. "The FBI know what they're doing. They'll make a quick arrest and this'll all blow over during the summer break. Come September, you'll find your classrooms full again." Burke smiled at Caroline. "Don't you agree, Mrs. Rhodes?"

"Actually, Congressman…"

"President Hurst is right when he says we'll lose students," interrupted Carl. He glanced at Hurst who stared back in shock and suspicion. "We agree on very little, Garrison, but this time I'm backing you. Neither Caroline nor I believe Andrew Littlewort is a murderer. Given a little time, and the cooperation of the university, we intend to prove Andrew's innocence."

Burke threw back his head and laughed. "Get lucky once and you suddenly think you're smarter than the police. Well, who am I to stop you? Just keep me informed, all of you. I hate to be caught unawares by the press."

Edmund nodded to Caroline and Carl, then strode off in the direction of Bruck Hall. Hurst watched him go with obvious annoyance.

"Burke's a typical politician." The President spat out the last word as if it had a filthy taste. "He profits from his association with Bruck, but he couldn't care less what happens to us." He squared his shoulders. "Well, we'll have to proceed without his blessing. Let me know if I can be of any help to your investigation, Mrs. Rhodes." His eyes swiveled in Carl's direction and he nodded slightly.

"Good day, Professor Atwater."

Carl chuckled as Hurst hurried off after Burke. "If Garrison's worried now, just wait until he hears about Branch."

"I almost feel sorry for the man," said Caroline. "It's bad enough having one Bruck employee suspected of murder. Having two of them detained by the police is a downright nightmare."

"It couldn't get worse than that, could it."

If Carl had been a betting man, he would have lost his shirt on that last statement.

Seventeen

"Make a way for the Duke and Duchess of Rhineburg!"

"No, no, no! Not 'make a way'. It's just plain 'make way'!" A frazzled looking woman in an olive drab sweater and beige slacks pounded her fist on one of the long wooden tables set up for the evening's feast. "How many times must we go over this before you people get it right?"

Caroline suppressed a grin as she meandered about the Green watching the students practice. Most of them had their parts down pat. Others, obviously new to the game, looked about in confusion when asked to perform. On the whole, the rehearsal was going well. The week ahead promised to be interesting.

Caroline was almost abreast of the fortuneteller's tent when she spied Edmund Burke standing near the jousting field. The Congressman was deep in conversation with Charlie Branch. While she couldn't make out their words, she could tell the two men were arguing. The discussion ended abruptly with the arrival of Sid Burke.

Edmund said something to his son. Sid seemed to object, but he fell silent when the elder Burke suddenly turned on his heel and strode off towards Bruck Hall. Sid hesitated before jogging off after his father. Charlie started to follow also, but was brought up short by Jake Moeller who called to him from across the lawn. The Chief was down on one knee gathering bits of straw from the jousting field. He motioned Branch to join him.

"Milady seems troubled by what she sees."

Caroline spun around to find a young girl standing at her elbow. The child was perhaps ten years old. She was dressed in the same medieval garb as the other performers, though on her the clothing seemed to be normal attire rather than a costume. The cross-laced maroon bodice covering her long-sleeved collarless blouse was patched and faded from wear. It barely overlapped the waistband of a long coffee colored skirt that grazed the tips of scuffed black slippers. Greasy stains streaked the cotton a dark walnut where grubby fingers had rubbed the material, and the hemline was frayed and torn.

None of this seemed to bother the girl who gazed up at the older woman with a bearing that belied her age. Through eyes the color of violets in spring, the child briefly studied Caroline before continuing the one-sided conversation.

"Perhaps my grandmother could be of assistance."

Before Caroline could reply, the child took her by the hand and led her to the entrance of the fortuneteller's tent.

"Wait in there." She pulled back the flap and pointed to the dimly lit interior where a table and two folding chairs filled most of the visible space. "I'll go get her."

The child ran off leaving Caroline with no choice but to enter the tent.

Why am I doing this? She sat down on one of the rickety chairs. Any moment now some college student would appear and go through the pretense of predicting her future with a phony crystal ball. Well, it was all part of the fun of a Renaissance Faire, and the kids did need someone to practice on before the big show started

147

tonight. *It might as well be me.* Caroline sighed in resignation.

"The child says you are in need. The little one is rarely wrong."

Caroline had expected her 'gypsy' to make a grand entrance at the front of the tent. Instead, the grizzled old woman now walking towards her had emerged from behind one of the many curtains lining the inside walls. Wrapped in a black shawl and supported by a cane the likes of which Caroline had never seen, the woman stopped just short of the table and stared at her guest through narrowed eyes.

"Yes, I see you are indeed worried. Something is very wrong, isn't it?"

Her speech was so guttural and heavily accented that at first Caroline had difficulty understanding her. Then she realized that part of the problem was due to the woman's coarse breathing. Caroline rose from the table and crossed to the fortuneteller's side.

"Let me help you," she said as she pulled out the other folding chair. "How long have you had this lung problem?"

The old lady waved Caroline off. "Too many years to count. Some days are worse than others. Today is one of them." She sank onto her chair, then motioned Caroline to do the same. "There are several methods for divining the future. You may choose tarot cards, runes, or..."

"Did you say runes? Like in rune stones?"

"The runes are pictographic symbols of forces in nature that affect our lives. Some early alphabets were comprised of runes, and at one time runes were carved into stone to tell stories or serve as memorials."

Caroline leaned forward, suddenly anxious to hear more from this woman. "Wait a minute, please. I was under the impression that this fortune telling business was...well, just a fun kind of event run by the students. But you're not...I mean..."

The old woman smiled. "No, I am not a student at this school. My name is Maria Gregori, and I am Rom. To you, Rom means gypsy. To me, it means family. The Rom are my people, my family."

"And this is how you earn your living?"

"In the summer my grand-daughter and I go from fair to fair doing what we know how to do. The little one, Bricole, takes after me. We have what some call 'second sight'. I call it a gift."

She's for real. Or at least she thinks she's for real.

"I'd like you to tell me about one particular rune." Caroline dismissed her qualms regarding Maria's 'gift' and pulled a scrap of paper and a pen from her pocket. She drew a vertical line intersected on the left side by two horizontally slanted lines that came together to form a point. "I saw this carved on a stone the other day."

Maria looked at the drawing and shrugged her shoulders.

"That is Thurisaz, the rune associated with protection and luck, except in your drawing it is reversed. If the arrow pointed to the right, the rune would indicate unexpected good fortune. When it is reversed, it may mean your luck is running out. You must make no hasty decisions at this time. They are based on a weakness within yourself, and you will live to regret them. If you deceive yourself concerning your motives, you will create problems you may not be able to rectify."

"You've got to be kidding. That one rune says all that?"

"I do not kid when it comes to reading the runes," Maria said, a trace of annoyance in her voice. "Now I will see why you are so bothered, and what will come of it."

Taking a deck of cards from the pocket of her long black skirt, she shuffled them before placing one card at a time face up on the table. Each move in the deal brought a deeper scowl to her face until it appeared she could stand it no longer. She gathered up the deck and thrust it back into her pocket.

"What's wrong," asked Caroline.

Maria rose unsteadily from the table. "I do not know what is happening here, but there is something wicked in the air, something that threatens us all. We are surrounded by death, and there is no way to stop it. No way at all."

The old gypsy swayed on her feet. Fearing she was about to fall, Caroline jumped up and rushed to Mrs. Gregori's side. Maria shook her off. Leaning heavily on her cane, she trudged towards the back of the tent. She pushed aside the curtain, then turned and pointed a bony finger at Caroline. The look on her face was one of fear.

"Go now, lady, and do not come back. I beg you, stay away from Bricole!"

Eighteen

Caroline returned to the nursing dorm to change into something more appropriate for the banquet. A breeze had sprung up, flushing the scent of lilacs through the open screens on the apartment's third floor windows. The day had been warm for May, but it was bound to get cooler as the evening wore on. With that in mind, Caroline slipped into a gray ribbed turtleneck sweater and navy corduroy slacks.

Maria Gregori occupied her thoughts as she dressed. The nurse in her worried about Maria's breathing problems. If the woman traveled as much as she said, she probably didn't see a doctor on a regular basis. That alone portended trouble for the old gypsy.

On a more personal note, Caroline wondered what she'd said or done to disturb Maria so badly. The woman had pushed her away when she'd tried to help, and her warning to stay clear of Bricole seemed more a command than a request.

It had to have been the tarot cards that did it. Caroline knew next to nothing about tarot reading. She'd once worked, though, with an ER registrar who firmly believed in the power of the cards to predict the future. The little she'd gleaned from conversations with the woman led her to believe that certain cards, when placed next to each other, foretold death and destruction.

The deck must have fallen that way this afternoon. Perhaps in Maria's mind, the coming disaster was linked to Caroline, maybe even caused by her. That would certainly account for the sudden change in the fortuneteller's behavior.

Satisfied she'd solved that puzzle, Caroline grabbed a fleece lined jacket from the closet, slipped a pair of brown suede gloves into one pocket and a pale blue scarf into the other, and left the apartment. Outside, the wind had died to a whisper. The excited laughter of students drifted towards her from the Green as she stepped onto Circle Road. She was about to cross the street when a jaunty little sports car pulled up to the curb. Madeline Moeller rolled down her window.

"Just the person I was looking for. Hop in, Caroline. I've got lots to tell you."

Maddy swung back into traffic as Caroline buckled on her seatbelt. "I've been all around town today, and did people ever clam up when they saw me coming! I felt like the Black Plague descending on Europe."

Caroline chuckled. "You mean no one rolled out the red carpet for the police chief's wife?"

"Hardly. The only placed I scored was at the Dip-N-Do. There was a bevy of women in the beauty shop when I arrived, but by the time Dolores finished my cut, rinse, and set, I was the only one left. Since Dolores can't resist passing on the latest gossip, I let her yak away to her heart's content."

"I assume you inserted a few appropriate questions into the conversation."

Maddy looked properly shocked. "But of course! And, boy! Did I get results." She pulled into the university parking lot, nosing the car into a slot between two pick-up trucks. "First of all, though, let me tell you about the rune stone. It still hasn't been found. The FBI searched Andrew Littlewort's place today. Practically tore the house apart according to Jake. They also went up and down the alley behind the post office. They raked through every patch of weeds and emptied every garbage can without success."

"Evans may never find that rock. It could be in the bottom of the river by now. Or the killer might have thrown it away in the forest."

Maddy nodded in agreement. "Jake says it'll take a miracle for that stone to show up."

"What about Charlie Branch? I saw your husband earlier this afternoon gathering samples of straw from the jousting field. He called out to Charlie, but I was distracted by a little girl and didn't see what happened next."

"Jake pulled him in for questioning. Charlie won't admit to anything other than being drunk that night. Tom Evans was no help either. He claimed the straw and grass we found could have come from anywhere around here. With so many farms surrounding Rhineburg, he does have a point."

"Yes, but give me the name of one farmer who had a motive to kill Emma."

"Someone who couldn't pay off his betting debts?"

Caroline sighed. "There's always that possibility. Until Michael Bruck comes up with some answers from Emma's computer, I'm afraid we're stuck on that one."

"Maybe not," said Maddy. "Dolores had quite a bit to say about some people and their possible gambling habits. Come on. Let's go find Nikki and the men. I'll tell you about Dolores while we're walking."

Bruck Green was a beehive of activity. Students rushed about putting the final touches on the tables under the watchful eye of Bruck's catering crew. Fires glowed at the north end of the lawn where several large grills had been set up, and the smell of barbecued chicken and ribs filled the air. Caroline's mouth watered in anticipation.

"Something tells me I should have brought a bib," said Maddy. "Ribs are my absolute favorite food, but I always end up wearing the sauce."

"You should have borrowed one of those plastic capes Dolores uses when she cuts hair. It would have saved you a trip to the cleaners."

"A raincoat would have served just as well. Speaking of Dolores…"

"Hold that thought," said Caroline as she caught sight of Martin and Nikki in the distance. "I'd like the others to hear your story, too. Will you and Jake join us at our table?"

"We'd love to, and thanks for asking." Maddy's eyes suddenly welled up with tears. "Jake is so embarrassed over this business with Emma that he didn't even want to come tonight. He thinks people will be laughing at him." Her voice caught in her throat. Ducking her head, she swiped at a pumpkin colored curl that had broken loose from its lacquered companions. She tucked it behind one ear in a quick, angry gesture. "I told him it's better to stand up and face the crowd than hide away at home like he had something to be ashamed of. Who cares what the town thinks anyway? Jake's been a darned good chief of police for a long time now. One little incident shouldn't turn folks against him."

"Of course not, Maddy. And truthfully, I haven't heard anyone criticize your husband. I'm glad you talked him into coming tonight. Both of you should try to relax and simply enjoy the evening."

"Hi, Mom. Hello there, Mrs. Moeller." Martin Rhodes bounded up to the pair and gave his mother a hug. With his dark hair and rugged good looks, Caroline's tall lanky son was a handsome young man, especially when he smiled, like now. "Nikki picked out a table close to the dais so you'll get a good view of the Duke and Duchess. The knights will be seated on both sides of the platform along with their ladies. They'll be attended by squires and pages."

"Weren't pages quite young back in medieval times? And squires...."

"I know what you're thinking." Martin's smile widened to a grin. "And you're right. College students would look kind of silly playing those roles. That's why we use local high school boys as squires and grade school kids as pages. They enjoy being part of the show. A lot of parents come to the festival just to see their kids in action."

"I should have known better," Caroline laughed. "Carl told me the Festival of Knights was first held in 1967. By now the coordinators must have everything down pat."

"No slip-ups allowed," said Martin.

The three of them crossed the lawn, still talking about the history of the evening's event. The Green was rapidly becoming more crowded as townsfolk and visitors alike arrived for the banquet. Some of the guests wandered about the grounds checking out the craft and exhibit booths. Others were content to merely sit and visit with their neighbors at the long wooden tables set in rows near the dais.

Caroline noticed only a smattering of children among the banquet's attendees. She commented on this to Nikki when they met at their table.

"I don't know how it started," her daughter-in-law replied, "but it seems to be a tradition that the Friday evening dinner is an adults only affair. You'll see plenty of children here Saturday and Sunday, and the school kids come with their teachers during the week. The only ones here tonight are the children of parents who couldn't find babysitters."

"And the fortuneteller's granddaughter."

Caroline spied the little girl crouched behind the trunk of an imposing oak. The youngster was watching them, but she ducked out of view when Caroline waved.

"A cute little ragamuffin," Maddy remarked when the child skittered out from her hiding place and ran towards her grandmother's striped tent. "Is she the girl you met earlier today?"

Caroline nodded. "She approached me while I was watching Jake collect straw. She's a persistent little thing, quite grave for her age."

"She's had a tough childhood."

Professor Atwater's booming voice sounded behind them as they watched Bricole scamper away. Maddy turned and smiled at him.

"Well, hello there, Professor. Sneaking up on us, are

you?"

Carl's eyes twinkled merrily. "Given my size, it's hard for me to sneak up on anyone, Mrs. Moeller. I cast a large shadow."

Maddy's smile faded and a glazed expression settled over her face. Lips pursed in concentration, she stared off into the distance.

"Behave yourself, will you?" Caroline hissed in Carl's ear. "The woman is a wreck worrying about her husband."

Carl rolled his eyes. "What did I do wrong?"

"Absolutely nothing." Maddy snapped back to attention. She patted Carl's arm reassuringly. "What you said makes perfect sense, Professor. I just hadn't looked at it that way before." Aware she'd confused the others, she motioned to the table. "Let's sit down. I want to run something by you."

"This better be good," Carl muttered as he cautiously lowered himself onto one of Bruck's ancient folding chairs.

"Hush up, Carl." Caroline glared at Atwater, then nodded at Maddy. "Go on, Mad. Tell us what you're thinking."

Maddy pointed a finger at Caroline and the professor. "Yesterday at the post office, you two suggested that Emma might have been killed by an antiquities collector."

"That's right," said Carl. "We thought maybe she contacted a buyer for the rune stone."

"It's a plausible argument," said Martin. "After all, there has to be an explanation as to why the stone was unwrapped. Showing it to a potential buyer is as good a reason as any."

"There's only one problem with that theory," Maddy said smugly. "Do you really believe Emma Reiser would have discussed business with someone while dressed in nothing but a nightgown?"

Silence descended as the others stared at each other in consternation. Caroline was the first to react to Maddy's bombshell.

"You're right, of course. I don't know how we missed that."

"Another thing, Professor," Maddy continued. "When you said that about a big man sneaking up on someone, it suddenly flashed through my mind that it's not easy for anyone to sneak up on anyone else. I mean, people are naturally noisy, and they're especially noisy if they're stumbling around in the dark. Agatha Hagendorf insisted there were no lights in the post office. But Emma was found at the foot of the stairs."

"Could the murderer have been waiting at the top of the landing?"

"It doesn't make sense, Nikki," said Caroline. "Paul Wakely examined Emma's body when she was brought in by the paramedics. He said there were no visible injuries except for the skull fracture. If Emma was struck at the top of the landing and then tumbled down the stairs, there would have been bruises somewhere on her body, not to mention blood from the head wound on the steps or on the wall." Caroline shook her head. "If you look at all the possible scenarios involving a buyer, you can easily punch holes in each one of them. Say Emma did contact some out-of-town collector. If the person arrived at the agreed upon hour, Emma would have been dressed, and Agatha would have seen a light on in the post office."

Martin raised his hand. "What if the buyer became greedy and didn't want to pay Emma's price? Maybe he broke in after Emma went to bed, then killed her when she discovered him snooping around downstairs."

"That scenario won't work either. There's a light switch on the second floor landing. If she'd heard someone moving about on the first floor, Emma would have turned on the lights before checking out the noise. She'd never have walked down those steps in the dark."

"You're still missing my point," argued Madeline. "If Emma was found lying with her head on the first step, and she didn't take a tumble from the landing, then how did the killer sneak up behind her on the staircase?"

"That's easy, Maddy. The answer is, Emma wasn't killed where she was found."

All eyes were glued on Caroline as she explained. "Tom Evans wants to pin this murder on Andrew Littlewort, but it won't work. Andrew is short, and Emma Reiser was quite tall for a woman. According to Dr. Wakely, the blow was delivered to the crown of the head. That means Andrew would have had to be standing above Emma on the staircase in order to gather enough force to fracture her skull with the rune stone.

"He couldn't have hit her when she was standing on the landing because he wasn't tall enough to reach up and deliver that kind of blow. And we know she didn't fall down the stairs because there were no other injuries to her body and no blood except on that first step. So we have to assume she descended the staircase on her own." Caroline glanced at Carl before continuing. "Those stairs are old and creaky. Carl and I walked up to the second floor, and we made enough noise to wake the dead. Nevertheless, Agent Evans apparently thinks Andrew either went up to the landing and then followed Emma back down, or he crept around her and climbed just high enough on the staircase to give her a good whack on the head. Evans must also be assuming Emma was totally deaf."

"There's no way she wouldn't have heard her killer."

Caroline nodded. "Exactly, Carl. And that's why I believe Emma was killed somewhere else in the post office. Paul told me it would take a powerful person to crush Emma's skull that way. I think whoever did it was bigger and stronger than Mrs. Reiser. I think that after he hit her with the rune stone, he picked up her body and placed it at the foot of the stairs. He laid her head on the bottom step to make it look like she'd fallen so we'd all believe it was an accident."

"And he did this all in the dark?"

"I don't see how, Martin. I think Agatha lied when she said she saw no light on in the post office."

"But why would she do that, Mom?"

Caroline lifted one shoulder. "There's only one obvious answer: Agatha Hagendorf is protecting someone."

Nineteen

"My lords and my ladies! Make a way for the Duke and Duchess of Rhineburg!"

Caroline fought to contain her laughter as she watched the poor woman who'd worked so long and hard to teach the boy that line. If she'd appeared frazzled earlier, she now looked ready to cry. She sat bent over on a bench, her face buried in both hands.

"I can't believe he said it wrong again," Caroline told the others. "She made him go over that line at least a dozen times during dress rehearsal."

"Which goes to prove, practice doesn't always make perfect."

All heads turned at the sound of a new voice in their midst.

"Jake! I'm so glad you're here." Maddy jumped up and rushed over to her husband. The way she gathered him in her arms reminded Caroline of a sad little puppy trying any trick to make its master smile. It was almost too pathetic to watch.

"Whoa there, woman. You're going to squeeze the life out of me." Jake disentangled himself from his wife with a sheepish grin. "She's not usually so demonstrative."

"Demonstrative is sometimes nice," Caroline replied with a smile. "Come sit down and watch the show with us. You're just in time for the knights' grand entrance."

The words were hardly out of her mouth when a lone trumpet sounded in the distance. A hush fell over the crowd as out from behind Bruck Hall came a string of horsemen preceded by a band of young men beating drums. The knights were dressed in closely woven mail shirts and bright surcoats emblazoned with their heraldic arms. Their heads were bare and they bore no weapons as they guided their hooded and bedecked horses across the campus. Beside each knight walked a young squire bearing a banner in his master's colors. Behind the knights rode their ladies.

The women wore pastel gowns with embroidered bodices and dropped waists under hooded cloaks of pale brown or gray and rode sidesaddle on their horses. They were followed by a group of peasant girls carrying baskets of spring flowers. The girls scattered blossoms before a horse-drawn cart trailing the main body of the procession by two or three yards. Aboard the cart on a cushioned seat sat the Duke and Duchess of Rhineburg.

"Look at that," Caroline exclaimed delightedly. More than two dozen pages walked solemnly in line behind the Duke and Duchess. Playing wooden flutes and rattling tambourines, the children preceded twenty trumpeters and a company of armed foot soldiers.

"I can't believe Carl is missing all this," she muttered to her daughter-in-law. "He said he had some business to attend to, but I didn't think he'd be gone this long."

Nikki's eyes never left the parade. "I wouldn't worry about the professor. Look, Mom. They're lining up right in front of us."

Each squire led his knight to a designated spot next to the dais while the ladies positioned themselves in front of the raised platform. The banner bearers and the drummers stood off to one side, with the pages gathered in front of them. When the jangle of spurs and the creaking of leather saddles subsided, the Duke's cart, which had halted some yards back, trundled forward to the sound of a trumpet fanfare.

"Lords and ladies of the realm! All rise for His Lordship, Duke Richard of Rhineburg!"

The speaker bowed with a flourish and extended his hand in the direction of the cart. Down stepped a heavyset man, his rotund body enveloped in a forest green, ermine-edged cloak. The hood of the cloak was also edge in fur and hid the man's features. When he turned to accept the applause of the crowd, it slipped back to reveal a familiar face.

"Carl!"

The Duke's blue eyes twinkled as he winked at Caroline.

"Her Ladyship, Duchess Alexandra of Rhineburg."

Carl extended his hand to his silver haired 'wife' amid cheers from the knights and their ladies. Duchess Alexandra acknowledged the ovation with a smile before lifting the hem of her cobalt blue gown and stepping daintily to the ground. The applause continued as the royal couple ascended the stairs to the top of the platform. Two attendants dressed in the livery of the Duke's court met them. One young man accompanied the Duchess to the center of the dais where stood a pair of tall-backed thrones upholstered in dark red velvet. The other attendant handed Carl a scroll that he unrolled and began to read from.

"Let it be known to all here that, having acquitted himself well as both page and squire, Guy Freeborn of

Rhineburg will, on the morrow, be awarded the rank of Knight of the Realm.

"On the occasion of his knighting, I hereby declare a week long tournament commencing with a banquet in honor of Guy Freeborn. While our candidate remains in solitude tonight preparing in body and spirit to assume his knightly duties, let us make merry at this opening celebration of the Festival of Knights.

"Lords and ladies of the realm, I welcome you to Bruck Green and invite you to partake of the hospitality of our court. May good fortune embrace you in all your endeavors. And now, kind visitors, let the feasting begin!"

Twenty

"I managed to surprise you, didn't I?"

Having finished his third helping of chicken and ribs, Duke Richard had abandoned the dais to mingle with his guests. He was now enjoying a cup of mulled cider with Caroline.

"You certainly did. I had no inkling what you were up to."

The professor stroked his luxuriant beard with one hand while reaching for his pipe with the other. "I'm too old to ride a horse or fight in a mock battle, so the students graciously assigned me this role."

"They were lucky to get you, Carl. You make a grand Duke of Rhineburg."

"I'll second that." Jake Moeller guided his wife to the table where Carl and Caroline were sitting. "You fit the part perfectly."

"The same can be said for the lovely Alexandra," added Maddy. "She looks beautiful in that dress."

"Who's playing the Duchess," asked Caroline. "I don't believe I've seen her before."

"That's Judith Applegate, Garrison Hurst's secretary." Carl sighed. "She's an absolute jewel, Cari. Not only pleasant, but also efficient, organized, and discreet. I wish she worked for me and not the Emperor."

"Did you say she's discreet?" Jake seemed to perk up at the thought. "If that's so, maybe I'll try to lure her away from here. We could use someone in the office who knows how to keep police matters confidential."

Carl grinned up at the big policeman. "Has Annie been talking too much again?"

"Annie Holtzbrinck is the number one purveyor of gossip in this town," Jake responded as he sat down across from the professor. "Say she takes a call about a domestic disturbance in the trailer park. First she tells me, and then she phones every single one of her cronies. Annie has friends up and down the grapevine. They're privy to every bit of news that hits the station."

"Why don't you just fire her?"

"He can't, Cari," replied Madeline smugly. "Annie's husband was Chief of Police before Jake, and she used to run the office for him. Harry died quite suddenly. When my soft hearted husband took over, he promised Annie she could stay on as long as she liked."

"She is a good secretary," Jake admitted grudgingly. "This business with Emma Reiser has her hopping mad. Harry was Chief for a long time, and apparently Emma bamboozled him, too. Now Annie's determined to find out the names of Emma's customers. She wants to personally nail their hides to the barn door."

"Maybe her tendency to gossip will prove helpful this time," said Caroline. "She might hear something that you, as Chief of Police, would never be told."

Maddy bobbed her head up and down. "That's right, Jake. Maybe she can confirm what I heard at the Dip-N-Do this afternoon." She turned to Caroline. "We got sidetracked earlier when I started to tell you about this, and I didn't want to ruin Jake's dinner with talk of the murder."

"So what did Dolores tell you?"

"Well, Cari, it seems Mayor Schoen may have been one of Emma's best clients."

"Teddy a gambler? I don't believe it."

Madeline looked down her nose at Professor Atwater. "And why not, pray tell? The office of Mayor doesn't pay all that well, and you know, most of their personal wealth was in Martha's name. Teddy didn't inherit a penny from his wife."

Martha Schoen had died in the December explosion at St. Anne's Hospital. Due to the terms of a tontine established by her predecessors, Martha's money had passed to her nearest living blood relative, the already wealthy Alexsa Stromberg Morgan.

"What exactly did Dolores say," asked Jake.

"Dolores told me that Martha came into the shop every Friday for a wash and set. More often than not, she arrived angry over something Teddy had done. Most of her complaints had to do with money. Once she said the Mayor had lost a packet on the Super Bowl. Martha was furious because he'd gambled with funds she'd earmarked for a new roof on their house. Another time she found a bundle of cash stashed in the Mayor's sock drawer. When she asked him about it, he said he'd gotten lucky on a basketball game."

"That's all very interesting, Maddy, but you know if I go to Mayor Schoen with this story, he'll deny everything. I sure as heck can't question Martha, and Dolores' testimony is only hearsay."

"Then you should talk to Bertha Meyer, the baker's wife. Bertha has her hair done at the Dip-N-Do also.

Dolores said that on several occasions, Bertha left very large tips. When Dolores tried to thank her, Mrs. Meyer blew it off saying she'd made a little extra that week and could afford to be generous. A couple of times Dolores overheard Bertha gabbing with the other customers about sporting events. She thought it was kind of funny because all these women seemed pretty knowledgeable about teams and statistics. That's not a trait you'd usually associate with the likes of our local librarian, Miss Sarah Sonnenschein, or the church secretary, Eleanor Naumann."

Caroline's eyebrows shot up. "Those are the very ladies who asked me to investigate Agatha's story about the night of the murder. I'll bet you anything Mrs. Hagendorf is withholding information. I think she saw someone else outside the post office that night. Someone besides Andrew Littlewort and–"

"Good evening, ladies. Chief Moeller." Edmund Burke emerged from the crowd and favored the foursome with a broad smile. "Congratulations on a nice performance, Professor Atwater. You look like a real English noble in that outfit."

"Thank you, Congressman. The students worked very hard on the costumes this year."

"So I see. Hey there, wench!" Burke signaled to a young woman in a long flowing skirt and shirred bodice moving through the crowd with a tray of cider. He took the tray from her hands and passed it to Caroline.

"This should cover it." He drew a fifty-dollar bill out of his wallet, handed it to the astonished student, and dismissed her with a wave of his hand. "Now come on, everyone. Drink up!" Burke turned to Jake. "So tell me, Chief Moeller. How's the investigation going? Did you got the goods on that professor?"

Jake took a sip of the spicy cider. "I'm sorry, Congressman. There's not much I can add to what you already know. My office is cooperating with the FBI."

"Oh, come on, Chief," interrupted Burke. "The press is already hounding my people with questions about Mrs. Reiser's murder. As Congressman of this district, I have to supply them with some answers or end up in hot water myself."

"I understand your position, but certain aspects–"

"I'm not asking for confidential information. Just tell me if you have a good suspect, somebody who may be charged soon."

Jake relented. "We haven't found the murder weapon yet, Congressman. Without the weapon or an eyewitness, it'll be hard to charge anyone with the crime. Still, we have interviewed two men in connection with the case."

"Two men?" Burke looked uncomfortably surprised. "You're investigating someone other than Andrew Littlewort?"

"We brought in a man named Charlie Branch for questioning today. Charlie is head gardener here at Bruck."

"Really."

"Personally, I don't think Charlie had anything to do with Emma's murder, but he may have been at the post office that night."

"*Hmm*. Do you have any other leads?"

Jake shook his head. "Nothing so far."

Burke set down his cup. "Well, I wish you luck, Chief. If you ask me, that Littlewort fellow is your man. I've heard he has quite a temper." He bowed to the women. "It's been a pleasure, ladies. I hope to see you all tomorrow. Nice meeting you again, Professor." He nodded to Carl, then walked quickly away.

Professor Atwater drained his cup and set it down on the tray. "Maybe I'm just prejudiced against politicians, Cari, but I don't trust Edmund Burke. The man's a little too slick for me."

"It's strange how Burke reacted when Jake mentioned Branch's name. He pretended not to know Charlie."

"That doesn't surprise me," said Madeline. "Bigwigs like Burke don't hang around with university gardeners."

"Oh, really?" retorted Caroline. "Then how come I saw him carrying on a long conversation with Charlie just this afternoon?"

Twenty-one

"I may have an explanation for what you saw," Carl said after hearing Caroline's tale of the meeting between Branch and Burke that afternoon on Bruck Green. "If you recall, young Mr. Burke is working off a punishment meted out by the Archangels. He pulled three weeks duty as Charlie's helper."

"He was probably trying to smooth things over for his boy," said Jake.

"I think so," said Carl. "It wouldn't be the first time Edmund ran interference for his son. Sid is always getting himself in trouble."

"Speak of the devil. Here comes Sid now." Caroline pointed him out to Maddy. "Good looking kid, isn't he."

Dressed in tan knee breeches and a loose fitting red shirt with bloused sleeves and an open v-neck, Sid cut a dashing figure as he sauntered by.

"Makes your heart beat a little faster," said Maddy with a sigh. As if she could feel Jake's eyes boring into her back, she quickly added, "I mean, it would if you were a teenager."

"Why don't we go take a look at some of the booths," her husband suggested. "I saw a nice necklace in one that ought to take your mind off all the young lions prowling the Green."

"Oh, Jake!" Maddy winked at Caroline as she linked

her arm in the chief's and strolled off.

"They make a nice couple," said Carl.

"They certainly do," agreed Caroline. "It's good to see them enjoying themselves. Maddy was very tense earlier tonight. She said Jake didn't even want to come to the banquet."

"Why not?"

"He's got it in his head that people are going to poke fun at him over this gambling business."

"He still thinks he should have caught on to Emma long before she died."

Caroline nodded. She pulled her coat closer around her. "It's getting chilly. Why don't we walk around a bit?"

The professor struggled to get up off the bench. "Something tells me I shouldn't have kicked in the door to Emma's room. I think I pulled a muscle in my leg."

"That'll teach you to act your age."

The two of them wandered up the Green, stopping along the way to view a candle maker at work in one of the booths and a potter at her wheel in another. Caroline bought a ring and a beaded necklace from a man hawking hand made jewelry. Carl indulged in his favorite hobby—eating—at a stall featuring a dozen varieties of fudge.

"Don't you dare mention the word cholesterol," he said as he wiped his mouth with a napkin. He handed her a piece of the gooey confection. "Here. Have your dessert."

Caroline couldn't resist. She downed her fudge without complaint.

"Caught you!"

Caroline swung around. Her son and daughter-in-law stood there grinning, Martin holding up a small white box.

"I bought you a present, a pound of chocolate bark that I forbid you to share with anyone. Enjoy it in front of TV tomorrow."

"Why, thank you, Marty. What makes you think I'll be home watching television?"

"Did you forget the Cubs are playing the Cardinals tomorrow? I was sure you'd tune in to it."

"I'd rather listen on the radio. Pat and Ron make the game fun even when the Cubs lose."

"Martin feels the same way," said Nikki as she eyed her husband mischievously. "But he misses yelling at the umpires while throwing pillows at the TV set."

Martin made a face at his wife. "You exaggerate, woman. I pride myself on my self-control. Dad was the one who went nuts over the Cubs."

Caroline smiled. "And the White Sox. Ed was a fan of both teams. He never missed a game when he was home."

It was strange how easily she could speak of her dead husband. Six months ago that would have been impossible. A lot had changed in six months. Mostly, she had changed.

"Look," exclaimed Nikki. "There's a portrait artist working over by the Maypole. Why don't we ask him to draw your picture, Professor? You can be immortalized as the Duke of Rhineburg."

Carl protested, but in the end he gave in. The four of them trooped over to where the artist had set up his easel in a canvas-covered stall. Money exchanged hands, and the man set about preparing to sketch the royally robed professor.

A small crowd gathered to watch. Some of the people knew Carl well, and they cheered when he tossed aside his cloak and struck a lordly pose in his red velvet doublet and knee breeches. With his chin held high and one bushy white eyebrow arched in regal disdain for those standing on the sidelines, Carl fit the part of the aristocratic Duke Richard to perfection.

Caroline glanced at the people standing opposite her. While most seemed to be enjoying Atwater's performance, she noticed two who appeared completely detached from the merriment.

The first was Maria Gregori's granddaughter. The little girl's face was screwed up in a look of intense concentration as she stared not at Carl, but at the man who was sketching him. As Caroline watched, Bricole stepped away from the ring of people surrounding the professor. She edged closer to the artist, rising up on tiptoe and craning her neck to get a better look at the emerging portrait. Her gaze flickered repeatedly between the picture and its creator, her eyes taking in every stroke of charcoal on paper.

Positioned a few feet to Bricole's left and directly across from Caroline was Alexsa Stromberg Morgan. The ninety-year-old matriarch of the wealthy Morgan clan looked profoundly sad as she stood there leaning on her cane, her attention riveted on the gypsy child. Head cocked to one side, she seemed intent on every move the girl made. Caroline wondered what it was about Bricole that merited the old woman's interest.

Caroline hadn't seen Alexsa since the funeral of Mrs. Morgan's granddaughter-in-law in January. Alexsa seemed older and weaker than she had last winter. That was probably due to the emotional aftermath of Elizabeth's tragic death. Caroline guessed the consequences of that event were far from resolved for either Alexsa or Elizabeth's husband Jim.

She wasn't sure Alexsa would speak to her. Their last meeting had ended on a cool note, due to Caroline's discovery of a Morgan family secret. Still, she couldn't quite ignore the old woman's presence. Determined to make at least an attempt at cordial conversation, she circled the artist's stall and came up behind Alexsa.

"Good evening, Mrs. Morgan. Oh! Hello, Bill."

Caroline hadn't noticed Bill Morgan standing there in the crowd, but Alexsa's son had obviously seen her. The graying owner of Stromberg and Morgan Auto Sales greeted her like a long lost friend.

"Long time no see, Mrs. Rhodes. How's that Jeep we sold you?"

"It's a wonderful car, Bill. I really enjoy driving it."

"That's great, really great. Now if it ever gives you any trouble, you just bring it in to the service center, and we'll whip it back into shape."

Caroline thought the man was being overly hearty. When she looked at Alexsa, she figured she knew why. Up close, the elderly woman's face appeared gray and pinched. She'd lost considerable weight, and where she'd feigned a fragile condition last winter, she was now truly frail.

Without putting it into words, Bill communicated his fears for his mother. His eyes darted back and forth from Caroline to Alexsa as he cheerfully rambled on about nothing in particular. This forced bravado didn't fool Caroline one bit. She recognized a coping mechanism when she saw one, and Bill's way of coping was certainly not unusual. By acting as if everything was normal in his life, he was denying the fact it wasn't.

When he finally began to wind down, Caroline broke in with a question for Alexsa.

"I noticed you watching little Bricole. Have you met her grandmother, Maria Gregori?"

Alexsa's eyes took on a far away look as if she was seeing something in the distant past.

"We met many years ago in Europe."

The brevity of the statement coupled with the expression on Alexsa's face discouraged further discussion of the Gregori family. Caroline took the rebuke in stride. She was about to offer an innocuous comment on the evening's festivities when Alexsa suddenly said, "I understand Agatha Hagendorf came to see you today."

Caroline marveled at Mrs. Morgan's continued ability to keep up with events in Rhineburg. While the old woman's physical health had deteriorated, her mental agility was not curbed in the least.

"She was part of a delegation that tracked me down this morning. The purpose of their visit, so they said, was to enlist my aid in discovering the identities of two men Agatha claims she saw on the night of Emma Reiser's murder."

"I suppose she'd been spying on the post office through her telescope."

Caroline nodded. "It sounds like you've already heard Agatha's story."

"Only the bare bones of it. The friend who called me was unable to supply any details."

Carl had once said Alexsa was privy to inside information on every family in town. Knowing what she did now, Caroline guessed Mrs. Morgan's primary source of information was Chief Moeller's loquacious secretary, Annie Holtzbrinck.

"Perhaps we could sit down," Alexsa said, pointing to a bench a few feet away. "It's been a long evening, and I seem to tire easily these days."

She motioned Bill to stay put. With Caroline at her side, she walked the short distance to a flag-stoned pathway cutting diagonally across Bruck Green.

"That's better," she said as she sank down on one of the rough-hewn wooden benches placed strategically on either side of the trail. "You're probably wondering why I'm interested in what Agatha had to say."

"The question did cross my mind," replied Caroline.

Alexsa rested both hands on the carved knob topping her walking stick and gazed out over the Green. "I was told Charlie Branch was brought in for questioning by the police."

"That's right. Jake Moeller spoke with him this afternoon."

"I was a friend of his wife. Julie worked for me up at the house."

"Carl told me she died several years ago."

"Yes, that's true. Before she passed away, she asked me to keep an eye on Charlie and the boys. Of course I said yes, even though I didn't see how I could do anything for them. Her sons were grown men by the time their mother died, and Charlie isn't the sort to ask for help from anyone."

"It does sound like a strange request."

"It was typical of Julie. She worried too much about her family, especially during those last months."

"What did Julie die of?"

Alexsa hesitated before answering. "Heart trouble. Anyway, I feel I have an obligation to do what I can for Charlie. I'm sure he's not a murderer."

"Agatha described two men she saw outside the post office. The police think one of the men was Andrew Littlewort. The other was apparently a drunk who fit the description of Charlie Branch." Caroline told Alexsa about the incident at the Blue Cat Lounge. "Carl said Charlie never touched liquor, but it's been my experience that only confirmed alcoholics recover that quickly."

"Charlie's a secret drinker," said Alexsa. "He started after Julie died, mostly out of regret, I think. He doesn't go to bars, though. He only indulges at home."

"How do you know all this?" Caroline asked the question out of curiosity, although she already had a pretty good idea of what the answer would be.

"There aren't that many places in town that sell booze. Word gets around."

"The Rhineburg grapevine at its busiest and best."

Alexsa waved off the comment. "Charlie's not the only person in town with that particular vice, Caroline. Agatha might have seen someone else the night of the murder, and simply mistaken him for Charlie."

"It's possible," Caroline conceded. "But Charlie had a motive. He didn't want to see a dig here on the Green. He

was furious over the idea of his flower beds being ruined."
She pointed to the row of bright daffodils lining the walk.
"Charlie called those his paths of gold. He seemed very
concerned they might be uprooted by rock hounds. In his
drunken state...well, who knows what he may have
done?"

Alexsa stared at the flowers. "Paths of gold," she
murmured. "That might be enough to kill for." She
struggled to her feet. "This evening has taken more out of
me than I bargained for. I think I should be getting home."

Caroline rose from the bench and accompanied
Alexsa back to the artist's booth. The old lady seemed
unsteady on her feet, and she leaned heavily on her cane
as they walked.

"This stick belonged to my late husband. It's probably
one of the most useful things he left me when he died."

Caroline glanced down at the cane. "It has an unusual
handle. That's a cobra, isn't it?"

"A rather worn cobra," said Alexsa. "It was carved in
England and given to my husband as a gift. He took it
everywhere he went, but he never had to use it for its true
purpose."

Caroline looked puzzled, and Alexsa explained. "It's
a sword cane actually. The snake's head is attached to a
blade."

"Are you ready to leave, mother?" Bill Morgan came
striding towards them, but stopped when Alexsa held up
her hand.

"Just one minute, Bill." She turned to Caroline. "You
said Sid Burke was in the roadhouse with Charlie."

"Yes. They were drinking together."

"Be careful, Mrs. Rhodes. Sid's father wields a lot of power in these parts. He can be nasty when opposed."

"You mean he'll protect Sid regardless of what the boy does."

"That, and other things. Edmund Burke is a conniver who clawed his way to the top. Today he wears the clothes of a Congressman, but he's looking to go farther. He'll do what's necessary to get what he wants."

Having said her piece, Alexsa walked off with her son. Caroline was left alone in the gathering darkness to ponder the old woman's warning.

Twenty-two

By nine o'clock the crowd on Bruck Green had thinned considerably. The balmy temperatures of daytime had vanished along with the sun. It was at least twenty degrees cooler now, and a stiff evening breeze ruffled the flags on the festival booths. The combination of cold and wind had sent many folks scurrying for their cars.

Caroline was glad she'd chosen her fleece-lined jacket over a windbreaker. She might not look as fashionable as the students in their thin costumes, but she surely was a heck of a lot warmer. She was remarking on that fact to the professor when Madeline Moeller came hurrying towards them from across the Green.

"Yoo-hoo!" Maddy yodeled. She waved both arms in the air. "Cari! Wait up!"

"Good grief," Carl growled. "It's the Mad woman again. I thought we'd managed to lose her for the evening."

"You're terrible," Caroline said, shaking her head. She sent him a wicked smile. "Be a gentleman and behave yourself."

"I'm always a gentleman," murmured Carl. "Even when faced with adversity such as this." He raised his voice along with one hand. "Well, hello, Mrs. Moeller. How nice to see you again."

Maddy slid to a halt, ignoring the professor. "You won't believe what I just heard," she panted. Grasping Caroline's arm, she squeezed it with both hands. "I'm so excited, I can hardly breathe!"

Carl grumbled something under his breath about the effects of oxygen deprivation on the brain. Caroline shot him a withering look before turning her attention to Madeline.

"You certainly look excited," she said as she peeled Maddy's fingers off her arm. "What's going on?"

"It's Emma's code. Michael Bruck has broken it!"

"The computer code?" Professor Atwater was suddenly interested in what Madeline had to say. "I knew Michael was good at that stuff, but even for him, that's fast."

"He said it wasn't all that difficult to do. Either Emma was sloppy, or she thought no one would ever see her records."

"There's a third choice," said Caroline. "Maybe Emma wanted someone to break the code."

"But why, Cari? That doesn't make any sense."

"Sure it does, Carl. Just think about it. Emma was no fool, so she had to realize there was some danger in running a book. What if one of her customers decided to wipe out a big debt by wiping out Mrs. Reiser? Emma had to make sure no one even considered doing such a thing. She probably told each new bettor his name was encoded in her records, but it was encoded in such a way that any computer geek could figure it out. She may have hinted at the existence of multiple disks stashed away in safety deposit boxes. Or maybe she said her lawyer kept copies of all her accounts."

"You're saying Emma insured her life by making it easy for the law to catch up with her clients."

"Exactly, Maddy. I don't think Emma was the sloppy type, nor have I heard anyone accuse her of stupidity. Emma ran a very business-like operation out of her second floor office. She didn't miss a trick, and I'll bet that included insuring her own survival."

"So you're discounting any of her clients as the murderer."

"I think it's highly unlikely that one of them killed Emma and then left without destroying her records. But they can all be checked out if Michael deciphered their names."

Madeline looked over both shoulders, then quickly checked the landscape behind Caroline and Carl. It appeared they were the only people left in the immediate area.

"I don't want anyone to overhear us," she said quietly. "When Michael tracked us down by the cider booth, all he said was, 'I've done it'. I didn't know what he meant, but Jake got all excited and slapped Michael on the back. Then he told me to wait for him by the booth while he and Michael discussed police business. They walked away, and for a minute or two I thought nothing of it." Maddy paused and performed a second visual check of their surroundings. Satisfied they were still alone, she continued her tale.

"Then I remembered what Michael was up to. Of course I was curious to know what he'd found out, so I worked my way from tree to tree until I was close enough to hear them talking. Michael was being very careful not to mention any names. But I heard him tell Jake that the 'top man in town' had been placing bets with Emma for years." Madeline drew closer to the others and said in a meaningful way, "None of us need to be told who the 'top man in town' is, now do we?"

"Mayor Teddy Schoen," murmured Caroline.

"Exactly," agreed Madeline. "Now we know why the Mayor hotfooted it over to the post office so quickly the day Emma's body was discovered. He was scared stiff over what Jake might find there."

"It would also account for the scene he made the next day," said Carl. "He came storming into the police station, demanding to see the official records of the investigation, when an officer refused him entrance to the P.O."

Maddy wrinkled her nose in disgust. "Jake says Teddy's been an absolute pain in the neck. He visits the station at least three times a day wanting information on the case."

"This corroborates what Dolores told you," said Caroline. "But I still don't see Teddy as a murderer."

"Well, I also heard Michael say something like 'the gardener was in on it'. He must have been talking about Charlie Branch."

"I could see Charlie as a gambler," said Carl. "I always wondered how he could afford tuition at Bruck for five sons. It's not a cheap school, you know."

"Betting with a bookie is a risky way to subsidize your kids' education," said Caroline. "What if he lost more than he won?"

Carl pooh-poohed her objection. "Gardeners don't make much money, Cari. He probably did better when he was driving a truck, but I'll wager a good portion of his income came from betting. When Julie was alive, the family never seemed to lack for anything. Julie drove a nice car, and Charlie tooled around on a swanky motorcycle."

Caroline recalled the photographs she'd seen in Charlie's den. One of them had featured Charlie and another man standing beside an expensive looking cycle. The picture had seemed quite ordinary at the time, but something about it bothered her now. She couldn't imagine what it was, but it would come to her eventually.

"What else did Michael say?" she asked Maddy.

"Not much after that. He handed Jake a piece of paper, and I could tell my husband was surprised by whatever was on it. I assumed it was a list of names because Jake looked up at Michael and started laughing. Then he shook his head and said, 'What a bunch of petty criminals'. He told Michael to keep quiet until he'd had a chance to check out things."

"He's not going to turn the list over to the FBI?"

"I don't think so, Cari. Jake really wants to crack this case on his own. I heard him tell Michael he was going to talk to Charlie in the morning. I backed off then because the two of them began walking back to where I was supposed to be waiting."

"So Jake doesn't know you overheard this conversation."

Maddy shook her head. "He said he and Michael had some business to attend to, and he'd meet me back at the house later tonight. We have to help Jake, Cari, but he mustn't know we're doing it. You understand, don't you?"

Caroline did understand. The Chief's pride had suffered one blow already. If he found out his wife was snooping around on his behalf, it would upset him even more.

"We'll just have to be careful not to appear too curious when we're around your husband. Don't ask too many questions when you're alone with him at home. Don't give Jake any reason to suspect the three of us are investigating this murder."

"I can do that," Maddy replied emphatically. "I know how to keep my mouth shut."

Carl rolled his eyes, but fortunately Maddy's attention was riveted on Caroline.

"So what do we do now? Should I try to get my hands on that list?"

Caroline shook her head. "Definitely not. Leave the list to Jake, and instead, get friendly with Annie Holtzbrinck. If Jake's secretary is the gossip he claims her to be, she'll be eager to tell you everything that's going on over at the police station. We need to know what Tom Evans is up to. Is he ready to charge Andrew Littlewort, or is he considering anyone else as a suspect."

"Try to find out what evidence he has," added the professor.

"I'll work on it tomorrow," Maddy promised.

"Good. As long as you're free for a while, how about driving into Rhineburg with me?" Caroline glanced up at the sky. It was a clear night and the stars were shining. "I want to pay a call on Agatha Hagendorf."

"What are you up to now," Carl asked suspiciously.

"I'd like to check out Agatha's telescope. It would be interesting to see how powerful it really is."

A broad grin split Carl's face. "That's hard to tell

unless you have something to look at. Maybe I should go stand across the street from Agatha's house."

"Why not? I'm sure Mrs. Hagendorf will be stargazing on a night as beautiful as this. Don't you agree, Madeline?"

But Maddy wasn't listening. She was staring over Carl's shoulder at a stand of trees a few yards away. By the look on her face, Caroline could tell she wasn't happy.

"What's wrong, Maddy?"

"Someone was eavesdropping behind those trees. Look! There he goes!"

Caroline turned in time to see a shadowy figure jog away across the Green. Despite the electric torches set at intervals in the lawn, it was too dark to make out who it was.

Twenty-three

"Good evening, Mrs. Hagendorf. I hope it's not too late for a little chat."

Agatha visibly paled when she saw Caroline and Maddy standing on her doorstep. "I was just about to go to bed."

"Then it's a good thing we arrived when we did." Caroline slipped past Agatha and entered the foyer of the old Victorian. "What a lovely place you have. You take in boarders, don't you?"

"Yes," whimpered Agatha. She closed the door behind Maddy. "Five other ladies live here."

"Are they all home tonight?"

Agatha glanced nervously at the staircase. "I...I imagine so. In fact, I know so. I know they're here, I mean. Here in the house." Her voice trailed off to a whisper when she caught sight of Maddy lusting over a mirrored hallstand. Tearing her eyes away from the pert little antique dealer, she said, "Why don't we go into the living room."

"I'd much rather go upstairs," replied Caroline. "That way you could show us your telescope."

"My telescope?" Agatha squeaked. "Why do you want to see that?"

"It's a beautiful night outside. We thought you could show us the stars."

"The stars?" Agatha blinked in surprise. One blue-veined hand flew to her throat as she looked anxiously towards the second floor landing. Apparently her boarders were all tucked away for the night; no one appeared to rescue her.

"I've always been interested in the stars," Caroline said glibly. "And Madeline dabbles in astrology. She knows everything about the constellations."

Madeline shot her a look indicating she knew nothing at all about the subject. Caroline winked at her friend and walked to the staircase.

"Your telescope is up there, I presume."

"Yes, Mrs. Rhodes, but–"

"Then up we must go." Maddy took their hostess by the arm and gently propelled her towards the steps. "You know, Agatha, your hallstand is an excellent example of Renaissance Revival craftsmanship. If you ever decide to sell it…"

Mrs. Hagendorf disengaged her arm from Maddy's grip and gazed at her in horror. "I wouldn't think of parting with a single piece of furniture in this house. Why, Emma Reiser told me that hallstand alone is worth…"

Agatha's eyes widened in distress when she realized what she'd said.

"You were smart to ask for Emma's opinion," Maddy countered smoothly. "Mrs. Reiser was quite knowledgeable about antiques."

Agatha erupted into a paroxysm of nervous giggles. Turning on her heel, she fled up the staircase.

Caroline waited on the second floor landing. "Which way do we go?" she asked sweetly.

Agatha motioned towards a door midway down the hallway. Caroline gestured for her to lead the way. Rattled by the turn of events, Mrs. Hagendorf meekly complied.

The room she took them to was situated at the front of the house. It featured two large windows facing Kaiser Street and lent a clear view of the entire block. Directly across, and in a line with the windows, stood the Rhineburg Post Office.

A large cloth-covered object was tucked away in one corner of the room. Caroline walked over to it and removed the covering. "My goodness," she remarked in surprise. "This is quite a telescope."

"Harold only bought the best." Agatha ran her hand over the smooth black tube that comprised the body of the instrument. "It's a eight inch compound reflector telescope on a German equatorial mount." She pointed to a shorter compact tube attached to the top of the telescope. "This is a finderscope."

Agatha visibly relaxed as she lectured them on the finer points of the telescope.

"The mirror inside is eight inches in diameter, so you can view even faint stars with this telescope. Harold always wanted a twenty-inch telescope, but they cost way too much money. He had to be content with this."

"It sounds like your husband loved astronomy."

"Oh, yes. Harold read everything he could on the subject. He taught me how to use a starfinder chart to recognize the constellations and the locations of the planets."

Caroline leaned forward and looked up at the sky through the window. "What stars can we see tonight?"

"The constellation Virgo should be visible," answered Agatha. She dragged the telescope across the floor. "Open the window, Mrs. Moeller. It swings to the side instead of up and down. So much easier for maneuvering the telescope." She switched off the lights, pointed the scope towards the west, and squinted through the finderscope. "Spica is the brightest star in Virgo, so I'll look for it first. Mars should also be visible this month. Ah! There we are."

Agatha twisted a knob to focus the telescope. Then she stepped back and let Caroline take her place.

"What a beautiful sight," Caroline murmured. She slowly swung the scope around so it faced the post office. Then she lowered it until Carl came into view leaning against the lamppost.

The professor had been watching the window. When he saw the telescope point in his direction, he waved his hand in the air, then straightened up and walked off down the street. He stopped and made an about face at the far corner before heading back towards the post office. Reaching the alley, he stepped behind the building and was momentarily lost from view. A few seconds later he emerged and began walking briskly towards Wilhelm Road.

Caroline backed away from the telescope, satisfied with what she'd seen. She motioned to Maddy who nodded in return.

"Let's go downstairs," Madeline said to Agatha. Once again a look of confusion entered the old woman's eyes. Maddy gripped her arm and guided her gently towards the door.

"I'll be along in a minute," said Caroline. "After I close the window."

Agatha nodded mutely. Caroline watched as Maddy ushered their hostess down the staircase. Stepping back into the room, she took one last look outside, then closed and latched the window. Apparently the professor had returned to his car because the street below her was now deserted.

"It sure wasn't this quiet on the night of the murder," she reminded herself. That evening there'd been plenty of people roaming the street. All but one had been gamblers.

Caroline left the room and walked down the hall, knocking on doors as she went. A few minutes later she headed downstairs, preceded by five very frightened ladies.

"It's time to get a few things straight," she said as she motioned each woman to a chair in the living room. Agatha was already seated on the sofa with Maddy hovering nearby. The little redhead crossed the room to stand silently beside Caroline.

"First of all, there are a few of you here whose names I don't know, even though we shared a cup of tea at the post office this morning." Caroline smiled at the silver haired lady she'd last seen wearing sunglasses. "Why don't we start with you?"

"I'm Marie Moser," the woman said nervously. "I'm a widow, and I've lived here since I sold my house seven years ago."

"Very good. You see, ladies? It's not all that hard to tell the truth." Caroline turned to the woman seated next to Mrs. Moser on the sofa. "And you?"

"Myrtle Jennings," came the reply. "I'm Marie's sister. I moved in a year ago when Angela Cummings died and her room came up for rent. I used to live in Ohio. I'm single by choice."

"Welcome to Illinois, Miss Jennings." Caroline pointed to a third woman huddled on the couch. "I've seen you at the hospital, but we were never formally introduced."

"I'm Emily O'Hara, and I'm the medical librarian at St. Anne's. I also work part time in Accounts and Billing."

"How long have you boarded with Mrs. Hagendorf?" Caroline asked the rosy-cheeked little woman.

"Ever since Mr. O'Hara passed on four years ago. My children wanted me to move in with them, but I'm young yet, and I prefer my freedom."

Mrs. O'Hara was sixty-five if she was a day. Despite that, she was the youngest of the lot. Caroline appreciated her desire to remain independent.

"Mrs. Naumann and Miss Sonnenschein I know, and it goes without saying that Mrs. Hagendorf indelibly impressed herself upon my memory." Caroline introduced Madeline. "I'm sure you're all acquainted with Mrs. Moeller."

The six women nodded in unison.

"So now that the introductions have been made, let's get down to business." Head down and hands clasped behind her back, Caroline began to pace the room. "This morning the six of you arrived at the Rhineburg P.O. with a most unusual story. Supposedly Mrs. Hagendorf saw two men outside the post office on the night of Emma Reiser's murder."

"But I did see two men," insisted Agatha. "I didn't make that up."

"Of course you didn't, dear." Ellie Naumann reached over and patted Agatha's hand. "Don't let her ruffle your feathers. You know we're all behind you a hundred percent."

"You'd better not be," snarled Maddy, "or you'll be charged with obstruction of justice just like Mrs. Hagendorf."

Mrs. Naumann opened her mouth to reply, then apparently thought better of it. She clamped her lips shut and contented herself with a 'who-do-you-think-you're-talking-to?' look aimed at Madeline.

Agatha's other boarders were not so smart. Refusing to take the insult lying down, they broke into a babble of protest directed at Chief Moeller's wife. Maddy merely glared at them.

"May I continue?"

Caroline's raised voice penetrated the din. One by one, six heads swung in her direction. She stared each of the women into silence. When she was sure even Maddy had calmed down, she continued to outline the events of the morning.

"With the assistance of Bertha Meyer, you tried to lure me into acting as a mouthpiece for Mrs. Hagendorf. You wanted me to repeat Agatha's story to Jake Moeller, including her amazingly accurate descriptions of Professor Andrew Littlewort and Charlie Branch."

Her audience exchanged worried looks, but no one attempted a denial.

"Your little plan didn't work. Professor Atwater interrupted our tea party and dragged Agatha off to the police station. There she was interrogated by FBI Agent

Tom Evans. I know how hard that must have been for you, Agatha," Caroline said, her voice softening as she directed her words to the unhappy Mrs. Hagendorf. "Agent Evans questioned me last winter. He's not a very gentle man."

Tears welled up in Agatha's eyes. "I was afraid of him. He made me repeat myself three times."

"Which is hard to do when you're not telling the complete truth." Caroline stopped pacing and planted herself in front of Agatha. "Why did you do it, Mrs. Hagendorf? Were you protecting your friends?"

"Oh, dear," whispered Miss Sonnenschein.

"Be quiet," commanded Mrs. Naumann.

Caroline ignored the two ladies and continued to grind away at Agatha.

"You own a powerful telescope, but you don't always use it to look at the stars. Sometimes you aim it at the alley behind the post office." She paused to let her words sink in. "One night you saw people passing in and out of that alley. When it happened again, you began to suspect they were visiting Emma Reiser. Eventually you got up the nerve to ask her about it."

Myrtle gasped when Agatha nodded. The others appeared equally shocked, but Caroline gave them no chance to speak.

"Emma was forced into telling you her secret. She paid for your silence by giving you tips on betting, and you began making money on the deal. No one can blame you for wanting some extra cash, Mrs. Hagendorf. A widow's life can be difficult, especially when you have a large house to keep up and very little income."

Agatha sighed. "Harold's pension didn't even cover

the utility bills. With him gone, I only get a minimum payment from Social Security."

"So what you won on the horses helped a great deal."

"Oh, I never played the ponies, Mrs. Rhodes." Agatha seemed shocked Caroline would even think that. "It's much too risky. I just threw a few dollars in the football and basketball pools, and I was lucky enough to win."

"You gambled on sports?"

Agatha's head bobbed up and down. "Harold was a great fan of the Bears and the Bulls. He taught me all about statistics and averages. Since he died, I've also kept up with baseball and hockey."

Flashbulbs popped in Caroline's brain. She thought of the box of fudge lying on the seat of her car.

"The Cubs are playing a four game series against St. Louis starting tomorrow. Did you put money on the games, Mrs. Hagendorf?"

Agatha realized she'd said too much. She looked about wildly, her gaze sliding over the faces of her friends in a futile search for support. When none of them spoke up, she dropped her head in defeat.

"Tell me the truth, Agatha. Did you place a bet with Emma on the night she was murdered? Or were you simply on look-out duty for these other women?"

"How dare you!" thundered Mrs. Naumann. "You have no right to accuse the rest of us just because Agatha admitted to gambling."

"But Ellie…"

If looks could kill, Eleanor's would have sent Sarah Sonnenschein to an early grave.

"Keep still," she hissed at the librarian.

"We can't keep still." Emily O'Hara stood up and walked over to Agatha. She placed an arm around the other woman's shoulders. "I'm sorry, dear. I guess I was just too afraid to speak up earlier." Emily looked up at Caroline. "Are we all going to jail?"

"I doubt the Chief will press charges if you agree to cooperate." Caroline glanced over at Madeline who nodded in agreement. "You'll have to go see him first thing in the morning, though. He won't be understanding if you put it off."

"How did you find out about us?" asked Mrs. Moser.

"Michael Bruck has been deciphering Mrs. Reiser's records for the police. Emma kept a list of the people who placed bets with her. Your names were on it." Caroline pulled up a chair and sat down facing Agatha. "Let's go over your testimony again. And this time, don't leave anything out."

"We'll help you," Myrtle said kindly.

Agatha smiled weakly. She patted her friend's hand, then cleared her throat and plunged into her story.

"You were right about the baseball games, Mrs. Rhodes. We all intended to bet on them, but we never got the chance. The night Emma died, the six of us were gathered in this room discussing which team to back and by how many points. By the time we finally decided on our picks, it was well after eleven o'clock."

"Almost eleven thirty," grumbled Mrs. Naumann who had decided to go along with the crowd rather than face the music alone. "We argued so much about the scores that we lost track of time."

"*Some* people argued about the scores." Agatha

corrected the other woman without bothering to look at her.

"The time didn't matter, though," Emily reminded them. "We couldn't have gone to the post office any earlier than we did. Emma had too many customers coming and going that night."

"That's true," Agatha conceded. "And since we didn't want the rest of the town knowing we did business with Emma, we had to wait until the coast was clear."

"Agatha offered to keep watch while the rest of us freshened up in our rooms."

This latest offering came from Sarah Sonnenschein. Per usual, the librarian whispered her comment. Caroline had to lean forward to hear it.

"So you all went upstairs, and you, Agatha, used your telescope to spy on Emma's visitors."

"I wouldn't call it spying," retorted Mrs. Hagendorf. "Everyone in Rhineburg knows about my telescope. If anyone had seen me in the window, they would have assumed I was stargazing."

"Then you admit you saw Charlie Branch and Professor Littlewort through your scope."

Agatha nodded. "I didn't want to get them in trouble, but the other ladies said they might be involved in Emma's murder. I thought if I described the two of them, you'd figure out their identities on your own."

"What time did you see them?"

"That part of my story isn't a lie, Mrs. Rhodes. Charlie arrived at the post office at a quarter past midnight, and it must have been ten minutes later when I saw Professor Atwater in the alley."

"Did you see either one of them enter the building?"

Agatha shook her head. "The back entrance is not in line with my windows. I only saw them go into the alley and come out again. Then they left, one going up the street and one going down, exactly like I told you this morning."

"Who else did you see that night?"

Agatha squirmed in her chair. Caroline had to remind her that Chief Moeller already had a list of Emma's customers.

"You can only help them by telling me who you saw. Unless you do that, every person on that list will be dragged in for questioning as a potential suspect in the murder."

"How horrible," Agatha murmured with a shudder. She continued in a more subdued tone of voice. "John Meyer arrived soon after I set up the telescope. He was followed by Arch Tillar, the quarry foreman. Next came Albert Miller and Harry Lee. After they left, Emma turned the lights out in the post office." She looked down at her feet. "The next person I saw down in the street was Charlie Branch."

Caroline was acquainted with John Meyer. The baker was short, fat, and elderly. All three characteristics left him out of the running as the killer.

"Tell me about Arch, Albert, and Harry. I don't think I've ever met those men."

"Arch Tillar is sixty-five, and he has emphysema," Emily stated flatly. "There's no way he'd have the strength to kill anyone."

Caroline nodded at the medical librarian. The woman was sharp in an unprepossessing way.

"I take it he's been a patient at St. Anne's."

"Like I said, I work part time in Accounts and Billing. I must have sent a half dozen statements to his home in the past year. He always pays after the first one."

With his winnings from gambling, Caroline guessed.

"And the other two men?"

"Albert Miller and Harry Lee share a room at the Rhineburg Retirement Home. Albert's plagued by arthritis, and Harry had a hip replacement in January."

"You've made your point, Mrs. O'Hara."

That left Charlie and Andrew Littlewort as the only two viable suspects. Unless Agatha was leaving someone out.

"Are you sure those are the only people you saw near the post office?"

Once again, Agatha hesitated before answering. When she did speak, though, it was with conviction. "I'm sure of what I told you," she said.

Caroline suddenly thought of something. "You said you were going to bet on the baseball games, but you never got a chance. What did you mean by that?"

"Good grief, Mrs. Rhodes. Haven't you figured it out by now?" Eleanor Naumann arched her eyebrows and glared disapprovingly at Caroline. "It was nearly one in the morning when Agatha finally trooped over to the post office with our money. By that time, Emma was already dead."

Twenty-four

Madeline walked into Professor Atwater's kitchen and sat down next to Caroline at the table.

"Jake's not home yet, and he's not answering his cell. I left a message on both phones telling him I was here so he wouldn't worry."

"Looks to me like you're the one doing all the worrying," said Carl. He plunked a plate down in front of Maddy. "Relax and eat your sandwich. Jake's probably busy checking out folks on that list."

"Speaking of the list, Cari, how did you know Agatha and her buddies were on it?"

Caroline put down her roast beef sandwich and wiped her lips with a napkin. "It was just a good guess, Maddy. You said Jake laughed when Michael showed him what he'd found in Emma's records. Then you quoted Jake as saying, 'What a bunch of petty criminals'. It occurred to me that Jake wouldn't laugh if Teddy Schoen or Garrison Hurst showed up on that list. But he might find it amusing if his gamblers turned out to be the six elderly ladies living at the Rhineburg Boarding House and Home for Gentle Women."

"You were already suspicious of Agatha," said Carl.

"Her story left a lot to be desired. Her descriptions of Charlie and Professor Littlewort were a tad too accurate for a woman who claimed she couldn't name the men she saw in the alley."

"That's where our little experiment came into play."

"Yes, Carl. You were leaning against the lamppost when I first looked out Mrs. Hagendorf's window. In the light I could see you fairly well. But when you walked away, you were just a figure moving through the shadows. Agatha's telescope changed all that. Through the scope I could make you out perfectly. That instrument is so powerful I could even see the wrinkles in your forehead."

"It's comforting to know my wrinkles are showing," grumbled the professor. He slapped three spoonfuls of ice cream on top of an enormous piece of apple pie and sat down to console himself with food.

"There was another thing that caused me to wonder about Agatha and her friends," Caroline said. "Emma's bookmaking operation was fairly common news by the time they came to see me, yet they never mentioned it. It's hard to believe something that sensational wouldn't merit a comment from one of them."

"And there was that little slip-up by Agatha when I was admiring the hallstand," said Maddy.

Carl looked up from his dessert. "What slip-up?"

"Agatha told me that Emma advised her on antiques."

"When I was upstairs gathering the other five ladies, I managed to peek into each of their rooms. Every one of them owned at least one really good piece of furniture," added Caroline.

"What's so important about that?"

"Emma invested her money in antiques, Carl. I think she counseled Agatha and the others to do the same. That way their illegal earnings didn't show up on any bank records, and they didn't have to pay taxes on the money. If the day ever came when one of them really needed cash, she could simply sell her investment."

"Emma Reiser was one clever woman," said Carl, shaking his head. "She figured out every angle, didn't she."

Madeline toyed with her sandwich. "In a way, I feel sorry for Agatha and the others. They're all making do on Social Security and whatever pensions they have. Who can blame them for trying to hit the jackpot with Emma Reiser?"

"I know what you mean," said Caroline. "Although I'm surprised you feel any pity for Eleanor Naumann. She's one tough bird."

"I get the feeling she calls all the shots in that house."

"Maybe she did in the past, but I wouldn't be so sure about the future. Emily O'Hara seemed to be in charge tonight."

"She did step up when no one else came to Agatha's rescue," admitted Maddy. "I think I liked Emily the best of all of them."

"I only hope she can persuade Agatha to name the other person she saw that night."

"She saw someone else?" The professor stopped eating long enough to look up in surprise.

"I'm convinced of it. She hesitated twice when I asked her about it. The second time she gave me some lame reply about being sure of everything she'd told us. That's not quite the same as saying, 'No, I didn't see anyone else'."

"I wish I'd reached Jake," lamented Maddy. "He could have gone over to Agatha's place tonight."

"I spoke to Emily before we left the house. She

promised to get her landlady over to the police station first thing in the morning. I told her I suspected Agatha was holding out on us, and she said she would talk to her. Don't worry, Maddy. Jake will hear the whole story tomorrow."

Madeline looked at her watch. "I guess you're right. It's almost eleven-thirty. Agatha's probably tucked up and asleep in her bed already. A few more hours of waiting won't hurt."

That was the first mistake the three of them made.

Twenty-five

The morning dawned bright and clear. The forecast was for a sunny day with temperatures in the mid-seventies followed by increasing clouds in the afternoon. Thunderstorms were predicted for the late evening, but the festival organizers weren't too worried. Rhineburg's weatherman had been wrong before, and besides, the local celebration had never suffered a rain out. No, they all said. Nothing was going to ruin this year's Festival of Knights.

Caroline was feeling as upbeat about the festival as the people in charge when she stepped onto Bruck Green at nine o'clock that Saturday morning. The Grand Parade wasn't scheduled to begin until ten, leaving her an hour to select the best spot from which to photograph Carl and the knights.

The procession was due to start at the north end of the Green and travel south past the site of the archery competition. From there, the parade would wend its way through the exhibitors' area, past the Maypole and the fortuneteller's tent, and on to the jousting field where a pavilion had been erected for the Duke's entourage. The knights had pitched their own brightly colored tents across the field opposite the pavilion. Movable bleachers had been placed on the other two sides for the public.

Caroline decided to take a panoramic shot of the parade as the riders passed the first stand of trees on the route. Pointing her camera towards the trees meant she could avoid capturing the university buildings in the picture.

"This looks good," she murmured to herself as she squinted through the viewfinder on her camera. "Nothing but green lawn and trees."

"And lots of blue sky."

Caroline lowered the camera and saw a solemn-faced Bricole Gregori watching her from a distance.

"You forgot about the sky," the child said seriously as she walked forward. "It'll show up in the picture, you know."

"I guess it will," Caroline replied. "Silly of me not to think of it."

"Don't feel bad. Lots of people forget about the sky because they're so used to seeing it everywhere." Bricole bent down and picked a blade of grass. "Do you ever get up real early in the morning?"

"Only when I have to work the day shift. I usually stay up late at night."

"The night's okay," Bricole conceded with a shrug, "but you don't see any colors in the dark. At night the grass is just plain black. Early in the morning it's silvery gray and shimmery."

Caroline laughed. "I think you've made up a new word, Bricole. But I know exactly what you mean. When the grass is wet with dew it sort of twinkles in the sunlight."

Bricole drew back and gave Caroline one of those 'must-I-teach-you-everything?' looks. Then she said quite patiently, "Grass doesn't twinkle, Mrs. Rhodes. Stars twinkle."

Caroline raised her hand. "I stand corrected. By the

way, Bricole, how did you learn my name?"

"I asked someone." The child's eyes suddenly widened. "Hey! Do you want to see what happened to the flowers over there? I'd be really mad if they belonged to me."

"Don't tell me the horses have been nibbling at them already." Caroline followed the little girl across the lawn to one of the paths crisscrossing the Green.

"I think it was squirrels." Bricole tossed the statement casually over her shoulder as she pointed to a bed of daffodils lining the walk. "See what I mean?"

Caroline frowned. A row of perfectly round holes had been dug in the ground. Next to each one lay a dead flower, its stalk still attached to the bulb.

"Squirrels dig up nuts and things, don't they?"

"They do when they're hungry." Caroline picked up a daffodil and examined it. The bulb was intact without so much as a scratch on its surface. She checked the other bulbs and found them equally free of marks.

"This feels funny."

Bricole had crouched down on the path next to the flowerbed and thrust her hand into one of the holes. Her arm was buried in soil almost to the shoulder. She pulled it out and grinned up at Caroline.

"These holes are really deep."

Too deep for daffodils, thought Caroline. She tossed the dead flowers back on the ground. "I'd better find Mr. Branch. He's the gardener here at Bruck, and he'll want to know about this."

Bricole stood up and brushed the dirt from her arm. "I wish I could go along, but Grandmother will have a fit if she sees me with you. She says you're unlucky."

Caroline's eyebrows shot up. "Oh, really?"

"She saw it in the cards yesterday. She says you're headed for trouble. I hope she's wrong."

"Is she wrong very often?"

Bricole shook her head. "Hardly ever at all."

They walked back to where they'd met, and Caroline said good-bye to the child. "Before you leave, would you mind if I took your picture?"

Bricole rolled her eyes. "I guess it's all right. But don't let Grandmother see it, okay?"

Caroline snapped two quick shots before the child ran off.

"Having fun?"

Martin waved to her as he and Nikki approached from the direction of the university.

"That Bricole is a remarkable little girl," Caroline said as the two came abreast of her. "I don't know what it is about the child, but I feel like I'm under some kind of a spell when she's around."

"Did you see her checking out the artist who drew the picture of Professor Atwater," asked Nikki. "We stopped to watch him work, but I was totally distracted by Bricole. She was fascinated by the man and kept edging closer and closer until she was standing right next to him."

"The guy was really nice about it," said Martin. "It didn't bother him at all that this kid was practically panting down his neck. He just kept on drawing, and when he was finished, he handed Bricole his charcoal stick. He told her to take it home and draw something."

"I'll bet she did exactly that," said Caroline. "She has

an artist's eye for colors and shapes. Maybe she'll be one some day."

Martin checked his watch. "The parade will be starting soon. The way this crowd is growing, we'd better find a place to stand along the route or we'll end up having to watch it over somebody's shoulder."

After a brief search, they found an open spot near the Maypole and claimed it for their own. Caroline told the others about her plans to take a panoramic shot of the procession. She promised to return as soon as she'd snapped a couple of pictures.

The parade was already underway when she arrived back at the north end of the Green. Today the trumpeters were leading the procession, followed by the drummers. All were dressed in black tights covered by long red tunics belted at the waist. Embossed on the front of each tunic was a golden lion in an upright pose.

The musicians were followed by a posse of armed foot soldiers wearing chain mail shirts with attached hoods over long leather leggings. The shirts extended to their knees, and over their hoods each man wore a conical steel helmet with a noseguard. The first three rows of soldiers bore long spears with leaf shaped heads. The rest of the men held a variety of weapons ranging from fine edged battleaxes to swords, maces, halberds, and spiked flails. All of them carried round shields covered in leather and rimmed with steel.

Behind them rode the knights. They were also dressed in mail shirts called hauberks, and their leggings and shoes were made of the same material. Over the hauberks they wore sleeveless cloth surcoats of blue, red, gold, or green imprinted with the individual knight's heraldic symbols. Each man wore a broad leather belt from which hung a sword and scabbard. Some of the knights wore mail mittens while others were bare handed.

The horses were blanketed in long saddlecloths complementing their riders' colors. The bridle reins were looped through bands of gold or silver material, and some of the horses wore hoods matching the color of their blankets. Beside each one walked a young squire carrying his master's banner.

Caroline recognized Charlie Branch riding in the procession. Dressed in a sea green surcoat emblazoned with two diagonal black stripes bisected by a gold leaf, he wore mail mittens and a mail hood, but no helmet. She could tell by the look on his face that he'd heard about the destruction of his garden. Charlie's expression was grim, and he sat rigidly in his saddle, his hands gripping the reins like they were rods of steel instead of strips of leather.

Charlie's horse clearly sensed his rider's emotion. It reacted predictably, prancing sideways out of line, tossing its head and rolling its eyes each time Charlie jerked on the reins. At one point the horse reared up, nearly throwing the gardener to the ground. It was only when another rider turned to him and said something that Branch seemed to realize he was disrupting the parade. He slackened the reins and leaned forward to rub his horse's neck. The frightened animal calmed down almost immediately, and the cavalcade continued across the Green.

When they reached the first stand of trees, Caroline

lifted her camera and snapped a picture. She continued photographing the parade as it wound its way across the Green. When the last man passed her, she dashed back to join the others.

"I hope the panoramic shots come out all right," she said to Nikki. "I bought one of those throw-away cameras for the wide photos and used my own for close-ups."

"One of Martin's buddies promised to develop our film at the school this evening. Would you like us to give him yours, too?"

"That would be great. It'll save me a trip into town."

The musicians were almost upon them. Martin and Caroline raised their cameras, Caroline focusing on individuals and her son aiming for longer shots of the parade. Both concentrated on the Duke and Duchess as they brought up the rear of the procession.

"Miss Applegate and the Professor look stunning this morning," Nikki commented when the cart bearing the two rumbled past. "Judith always carries herself well, but today her appearance is regal."

"That gorgeous outfit helps a lot." Caroline fell in line with the crowd making its way to the jousting field. "Cobalt blue goes perfectly with her pink complexion and silver hair."

"Carl looked pretty spiffy, too," said Martin. "I noticed he wasn't wearing a sword over his surcoat like the rest of the knights."

"They probably couldn't find a belt long enough to buckle around him," Nikki giggled.

"Careful, woman. That's my boss you're talking about." Martin wrapped an arm around his wife's waist and squeezed her to his side. "You know what they did in the old days to wenches who made fun of their masters, don't you?" He made a cutting motion across his throat with one finger. "Off with their heads."

Nikki responded to the kidding with a clever retort, but Caroline didn't catch it. A break in the crowd had given her a clear view of Edmund Burke leaving the fortuneteller's tent. She watched curiously as the congressman stopped near a tree and drew a pack of cigarettes from his pocket. His hand trembled noticeably as he attempted to light up. Caroline wondered why he appeared so shaken.

She glanced back at the tent. Mrs. Gregori leaned on her cane in the doorway. The old gypsy was also watching the congressman, but the look on her face was hard to decipher.

Caroline hung back as Martin and Nikki moved on with the crowd. Her curiosity piqued by the oddness of the scene taking place before her, she flattened herself against the side of a booth and observed the unlikely pair with growing interest. A few seconds later, a third person entered the picture.

Sid Burke strode towards his father from the direction of the jousting field. He was dressed in the garb of a knight with a sword hanging at his side. His normally handsome features were marred by the presence of an angry scowl. When he reached the congressman, he leveled a clenched fist at the man. Edmund took a step back, but apparently the boy had no intention of hitting him. Instead, he dragged a dirty plastic package out of the pocket of his leather breeches and threw it on the ground.

His head bobbed forward, then he jabbed a finger at his father and said something Caroline couldn't hear. Edmund started to reply, but his son turned on his heel and stalked off.

The congressman seemed frozen in place. Head hanging, he stared at the ground for a long moment before slowly bending down and retrieving the package the boy had thrown at his feet. Thrusting it into his coat pocket, he walked off in the direction his son had taken.

Caroline stepped away from the booth. Her gaze traveled once again to the fortuneteller's tent where Mrs. Gregori stood hidden by the shadow of the tent flap. When she saw Caroline staring at her, she moved into the sunlight. Their eyes met, and the gypsy woman slowly shook her head.

Twenty-six

In his official role as lord of the manor, Carl was welcoming his guests to Rhineburg when Caroline took her seat in the stands next to Martin and Nikki.

"We were wondering where you'd gone to," said Martin. "Is everything okay?"

"Everything's fine," Caroline said with a smile. Her eyes swept the audience. "Why are there so many knights and ladies sitting here in the bleachers? I thought they'd all be down by the pavilion with the Duke and Duchess."

"They're alumni," Nikki explained. "Bruck grads who took part in previous festivals like to come back every year for a mini reunion. They wear their old costumes so they can blend in with the current crop of nobility."

"And when the fun dies down here on the Green, they all go off to the Blue Cat Lounge to celebrate." Martin pointed to two young men sitting in the stands opposite them. "Look over there. We've even got a couple of Friar Tucks in attendance today."

"And there's another one," said Caroline, indicating a third brown-clad figure approaching the dais. The boy in the monk's habit climbed onto the platform and replaced Carl at the front of the stage. He gestured to two young men standing off to the side, beckoning them forward. One of the men dropped to his knees before the pavilion. The other, dressed as a squire, stood tall behind him.

The monk began speaking in a clear voice that reached every corner of the field thanks to the tiny microphone he wore. He delivered a sermon on the duties of knighthood, including protecting the weak, righting wrongs, and honoring fair womanhood. He finished with a flourish, and the youth kneeling before him rose.

Two more squires entered the field bearing a wooden pallet on which lay a complete suit of armor. As the crowd in the bleachers watched, the three squires began buckling pieces of the armor onto the knight candidate.

First came a breastplate covered with etched engravings that connected to a plain backplate. These were followed by the tasset, a reversed-U-shaped piece that encircled the waist with the arms of the U extending downward over the surcoat to cover the knight's thighs. Hinged plates were strapped to the young man's arms and legs, and metal pads, called pauldrons, were attached to cover his shoulders. The squires then slipped jointed gauntlets onto his hands and tied a metal collar, called a gorget, around his neck. Lastly they placed a visored helmet with four rows of neck-guard plates on the candidate's head.

Due to long hours of practice, the dressing of the knight aspirant took only a few minutes. With visor raised, the young man climbed the pavilion steps and knelt before Duke Richard of Rhineburg.

Carl rose from his seat and accepted a sword from an attendant. He lifted the sword and laid it flat across the youth's right shoulder. In a booming voice, he then solemnly proclaimed, "In the name of God and St. Michael and St. George, I dub thee knight. Be brave and loyal."

The audience broke into cheers as the new knight

rose to his feet and bowed to Duke Richard. He then turned to Duchess Alexandra and bowed again. The Duchess nodded graciously, after which she tied a blue silk handkerchief on the young man's helmet as a sign of her favor. The crowd roared again when the knight descended the stairs and the Duke's attendant came forward to announce the start of the tourney.

Two mounted knights armed with ten-foot lances and kite-shaped shields entered the field. They were dressed in light armor, and they took up positions at opposite ends and on either side of a short wooden barrier. They waited until the attendant announced their names before kicking their horses into action. Riding at a gallop, they charged towards each other, their lances lowered and their shields raised. Each knight got in a glancing blow as they passed in the center of the field. Neither having been unseated, they turned and charged again. This time the knight farthest from Caroline took a blow to the center of his shield. He tottered in the saddle, then pulled on the reins to slow his horse before sliding to the ground in a faked fall. He lay there until his squire came running up and helped him to his feet.

"At least he had a soft landing," Caroline said to Nikki. "There must be six inches of straw padding the field."

"They practice those falls, Mom. It's all choreographed."

"That's what Carl told me. It's a good thing the tips of those lances are encased in wooden blocks, though. A pointed lance could really hurt someone."

"They're made of ash," Martin told her. "They bend

easily when they hit the shields, though occasionally you'll see one splinter and break."

A second set of knights positioned themselves for battle. Once again, one of the men was unseated on the second attempt, but this time he jumped to his feet and drew his sword. The other knight dismounted and took up the challenge. Weapon clashed against weapon as the two circled the field in mock combat. Finally, one of the knights slipped and went down in the straw. His opponent placed his sword against the man's chest, and the supine knight quickly conceded the fight.

After taking the defeated knight's horse and weapon, the victor left the field amid shouts from the audience while the loser stumbled off with the assistance of his squire. They were quickly replaced by two more combatants and the jousting began again.

Caroline was cheering as loudly as the other people in the stands by the time the fifth set of knights was announced. When only one man rode onto the field, she was as surprised as the rest of the crowd.

"Sir Charles," the attendant proclaimed more loudly as he frowned in the direction of the mounted knights gathered to the left of the pavilion. "Will Sir Charles please take the field."

One of the squires emerged from the pack of horsemen and hurried over to the platform. The boy carried a sea green banner crisscrossed by two black stripes. He called out something to the attendant who in turn relayed the message to Carl. Carl took the news in stride, waving a hand at his helper as if to say, 'Get on with it'. As he did so, a knight wearing a purple surcoat beneath his armor rode onto the field. The attendant sighed in relief and announced, "Sir Sidney will replace Sir Charles. Let the joust begin."

"Those colors belong to Charlie Branch," said Caroline. "I saw him riding in the parade."

"It's not like Charlie to back out on his obligations," Martin noted. "I wonder where he is."

Caroline scanned the field for a glimpse of the gardener, but there was no sign of him anywhere. She glanced over her shoulder at the tents set up nearby as changing rooms for the students. She saw several horses grazing in the area, but once again, no Charlie. She wondered if Jake had pulled him in for more questioning, or worse yet, arrested him.

She swiveled on the hard bleacher seat, craning her neck to get a clear view of the booth area. Her breath caught in her throat when she saw Bricole Gregori running towards the stands. Tears streamed down the little girl's face.

"Something's wrong!" Caroline jumped up and hurried down the bleacher steps. She pushed her way through a knot of people and jogged across the lawn to where Bricole had collapsed on the grass. She gathered the child in her arms.

"What is it, Bricole? What's happened?"

"Grandma," Bricole sobbed. "I think she's dead."

Caroline transferred the little girl to Nikki who along with Martin had followed her from the field.

"Call the paramedics. Then stay with Nikki," she instructed her son before running off in the direction of the fortuneteller's tent.

Panting and out of breath, she pushed back the tent flap and called out to Maria. The gypsy didn't answer. A quick look around told Caroline the forward part of the tent was empty. She hurried to the back where a black velvet curtain separated the working area from the Gregoris' living quarters. Flinging the curtain aside, she entered a combination bedroom and kitchen. The heavy canvas walls blocked most of the daylight from entering this part of the tent. The room lay in shadows with only a narrow stream of sun forcing its way through a partially opened window flap.

Even in the dimness Caroline could tell that no one was in the tent. She raced back outside, shouting Maria's name. A low moan came from somewhere behind the tent.

"Mrs. Gregori!"

Caroline circled the tent and found Maria crumpled on the ground. There was still life in the old woman, but her breathing was weak, and her pulse, while present, was thready. Her head was covered in blood from an ugly gash on her forehead.

From the pale clammy look of her skin, Caroline guessed Maria had suffered a heart attack. The laceration probably occurred when she fell to the ground. Caroline placed her fingers on the either side of Mrs. Gregori's head and gingerly searched for signs of further damage. She felt no depression at the base of the skull and no protrusion of bone in the neck. Her hands came away free of blood, which was something to be thankful for. She knew her simple exam didn't guarantee the absence of a skull fracture or bleeding inside the brain. She could only hope for the best.

She heard a siren wail in the distance and checked Maria's pulse and breathing again. Assured nothing had changed, she made a rapid trauma assessment, looking for other injuries. Maria's left leg was shorter than the right, her foot rotated outward until the toes nearly touched the ground.

'Fractured hip,' Caroline thought. She carefully removed the woman's shoe and felt for a pulse in the foot. Then starting at the shoulders, she ran her hands down the woman's arms and gently probed her chest, abdomen, and pelvis. Mrs. Gregori moaned weakly, but her eyelids remained closed.

"You're going to be all right," Caroline whispered in Maria's ear. "We'll get you to the hospital very soon."

She looked up as an ambulance skidded to a halt in front of the tent. "Back here!" she shouted.

The two paramedics quickly placed an oxygen mask on Maria's face and connected her to a heart monitor. One of them started an IV drip while the other took Maria's blood pressure and circled her neck with a hard plastic collar. As they worked, Caroline gave them a rundown on Maria's injuries.

"We'll notify the police about the other body," one of the men said as he and his partner logrolled their patient onto a backboard. "You'd better wait for them."

"What other body," Caroline asked in confusion.

The paramedic pointed to a spot behind her. "That one."

Caroline turned and saw Charlie Branch slumped against a nearby tree. There was a wicked looking blade stuck in his chest, and he was very, very dead.

Twenty-seven

At four-fifteen in the afternoon, Maria Gregori died in the Intensive Care Unit of St. Anne's Hospital. Twenty minutes earlier she had opened her eye and murmured the word 'mon'. Since no one understood what she was saying, the nurses assumed she was speaking in her native tongue. None of them bothered to report it to the policeman stationed outside her room. Caroline would have been left in the dark also if she hadn't arrived just as the alarm signaled a flat line on Maria's heart monitor.

Because Mrs. Gregori had left no papers indicating her wishes in the matter, every attempt was made by the ICU staff to restart her heart. One nurse began chest compressions while another injected epinephrine and atropine into Maria's veins. A third nurse pumped air into the woman's lungs with a blue vinyl bag attached to a mask and oxygen. When the doctor arrived, he quickly inserted a breathing tube into Maria's trachea and attached the bagging device to that.

Every few minutes CPR was stopped while a staff member checked for a pulse. Each time this happened, the heart line on the monitor flattened to little more than a squiggle. Round after round of drugs were given, but when twenty minutes passed with no sign of sustainable life, the doctor called an end to the code.

One of the nurses clamped off the IV lines, then cut and tied each with a tight knot. Another nurse scooped up the long strip of paper that had recorded their efforts on the heart monitor. She folded the paper fan-like and tucked it in Maria's chart. The third member of the team cut the intubation tube, leaving just enough for the coroner's exam, and gently closed the dead woman's lips and eyelids. Together, the three nurses removed the monitor leads from Maria's chest and covered her with a clean gown and a sheet.

Caroline had watched the code from the doorway. Now she stepped into the room.

"Her heart was just to weak," said one of the nurses. "We did all we could."

"I know," Caroline replied with a sad smile. "It's always hard to lose one, isn't it?"

The nurse nodded mutely and left the room. Caroline moved over to the side of the bed and lifted one of Maria's hands. She stroked the old woman's arm tenderly.

"You tried your best," she whispered. "Don't worry about Bricole. We'll take care of her."

"I'll see to that."

Caroline glanced over her shoulder. "Hello, Alexsa. I didn't hear you come in."

"I've been sitting in the waiting room." Mrs. Morgan shuffled forward. She leaned heavily on her cane as she stared down at Maria's face. "I owe this woman my life. Now I can repay the debt by looking after her granddaughter."

"Is Bricole an orphan?"

Alexsa was about to say something when the chaplain walked into the room. A middle-aged woman with graying hair and sympathetic eyes, she crossed to the bedside and nodded to Alexsa. Caroline backed away when she noticed a nurse beckoning to her from the doorway.

"My name is Amy Wallace," the young woman said. "Because Mrs. Gregori had no doctor, and the circumstances surrounding her heart attack are unknown, this will have to be a coroner's case."

"I understand the rules." Caroline pointed to Alexsa. "Mrs. Morgan knew your patient much better than I. You'd better talk to her about final arrangements."

Caroline waited with Amy until the chaplain finished her prayers. After speaking briefly with Alexsa, Amy led her to the desk where the unit receptionist handed Mrs. Morgan a form.

"I'm sorry to bother you with this," said Amy. "But so far the police have been unable to supply us with the names of any family members."

"Maria had no one but her granddaughter Bricole," said Mrs. Morgan. "Her husband's been dead for over a decade. Bricole's parents were killed in a car accident three years ago."

"No brothers or sisters?"

Alexsa shook her head. "Maria's entire family perished in a concentration camp during World War II. They were among the thousands of gypsies rounded up by the Nazis during the war." Her voice quivered with emotion. "Most people think the Jews were the only ones who suffered in the camps. They don't know that Hitler annihilated over ninety per cent of the gypsy population of Europe. He pursued them ruthlessly. Most of them died in his gas chambers."

"But Maria escaped?"

"One of the chambers in her camp malfunctioned. Enough gas spewed in to kill the very weak and the very young, but some people survived. Maria was one of them. Her lungs were badly damaged by the gas. She would have died except three days later the camp was liberated by Allied troops. She was taken to a hospital and treated by American doctors. That's where she met her future husband."

"He worked there?" asked a fascinated Amy.

"He was an Army corpsman assigned to her ward. They married in England after the war."

"No wonder she had difficulty breathing," Caroline remarked. "I'm surprised her heart lasted this long under that kind of stress."

"She was a strong willed woman with an amazing gift for predicting the future," said Alexsa. "She was never truly healthy, but she was determined to live long enough to see her granddaughter grown and out on her own. Whatever happened on the Green today must have been more than she could handle."

"The police are saying she stabbed Charlie Branch."

"That's ridiculous," Alexsa snorted. She shook her finger at Amy. "Don't you go spreading that kind of gossip. There was no reason on earth for Maria to hurt Charlie."

"He was killed with her sword cane," Caroline told Mrs. Morgan. "I noticed the cane the first time I met Mrs. Gregori. It struck me as an unusual piece, then last night I saw you had one exactly like it."

Alexsa lifted her cane and showed the cobra head to Amy. "Maria gave this to me many years ago. I brought it to the banquet so she'd know I still treasured her friendship." She unscrewed the head of the cane, withdrew the eighteen-inch blade, and let the two women examine it. "It's meant to be used only for defensive purposes. The Maria Gregori I knew was a gentle woman. If her sword was unsheathed, it could mean only one thing. Maria was being attacked by someone."

"I tend to agree with you, Alexsa. I only wish Mrs. Gregori could have told us what happened before she died. Did she say anything at all while you were caring for her, Amy?"

"Well," hedged the nurse, "she did mumble something shortly before she died. It sounded like she said 'mon', but that doesn't make sense, does it."

It certainly didn't, thought Caroline.

"I guess we can't fill out this form if Mrs. Gregori had no relatives." Amy dropped the form on the desk. "If there's no one left to bury her, the coroner's office will have to do it."

"I'll arrange for Maria's burial," Alexsa said quietly. "Dr. Talens, the county pathologist, is an old friend of mine. I'll call him to find out when the body will be released."

"That's very kind of you, Mrs. Morgan."

Alexsa waved off Amy's praise. "I must be going. Will you walk with me, Mrs. Rhodes?"

"Of course."

Caroline accompanied Mrs. Morgan out of the ICU. As they made their way to the elevator, she noticed Alexsa had shed a good deal of the feebleness she'd exhibited earlier. Her shoulders were squared and her stride seemed more confident. It was almost as if she'd come away from her friend's deathbed with a new a sense of purpose.

"How long have you known Mrs. Gregori?"

"We met by accident in England. The war had recently ended, and my husband had business to settle in London. I accompanied him solely for pleasure, but the city depressed me with its bombed out buildings and ever-present soldiers. I decided to take a train up to Scotland for a few days. I met Maria while waiting in the station."

"She was traveling also?"

"No. She was standing on the platform looking up at the train I was about to take. She was crying and begging people not to board it. She kept saying she'd dreamed of a crash, of people dying. No one believed her. Eventually a conductor came rushing over. He threatened to have Maria arrested if she didn't leave."

"Did you intervene?"

"Maria was just a slip of a girl back then. I took her by the arm and told her to come away. She'd done her best to warn the passengers. If harm came to them, they had only themselves to blame. We spent the day together waiting to hear the bad news."

"Did the train crash?"

"Oh, yes," Alexsa replied quietly. "They said it was a problem with a switching mechanism. The track didn't quite meet where two lines separated, and the train derailed. Several people were killed. Many more were injured."

"But you were safe."

"I believe in second sight. Some people are gifted that way, and Maria convinced me she was one of them.

We became close after that, exchanging letters over the years. Then her husband died leaving her with nothing but debts. I urged her to come live with me. But she was too proud to accept what she saw as charity. She went back to her roots, living on the fringe of the American gypsy community. She used her gift to work as a fortuneteller. She came to Rhineburg each spring to participate in the festival as a favor to me."

"So Maria adopted Bricole when her parents died."

"She was only four then. Speaking of Bricole, where is she?"

"At my son and daughter-in-law's apartment. They brought her here earlier. She got to see her grandmother in the ER before Mrs. Gregori was transferred up here. The poor kid was devastated. She seemed to sense Maria was dying, but she went quite willingly when Nikki suggested they leave."

Alexsa nodded solemnly. "If you don't mind, I think I should be the one to tell her Maria's gone. Bricole knows me quite well. She'll take it better if I'm there with her."

"Of course." Caroline wrote down the address of Martin and Nikki's apartment. "Will Bill drive you there, or would you like me to take you?"

"My son is waiting downstairs. There's only one thing I want from you, Caroline. Find out who caused Maria's death. If you do that, you'll also find Charlie's killer."

The elevator doors opened and Jake Moeller stepped out. He tipped his cap to Alexsa as the matriarch of the Morgan family brushed by him and entered the lift.

"In a bit of a rush, isn't she?" the Chief said gruffly.

"She was a close friend of Maria Gregori. She's gone off to break the news of her death to the granddaughter."

Jake rubbed his nose with the tip of one finger. "I don't envy her that job. That poor kid has nobody left in the world now."

"Not for long, she doesn't. I have a feeling Alexsa intends to take Bricole home with her."

"Really?" Jake's eyebrows soared. "Tough job for a ninety-year-old woman."

"Alexsa has tremendous strength of character. She also has a great deal of money. Between the two, she'll get by." Caroline accompanied Chief Moeller down the long corridor leading to the ICU. "So tell me, Jake. What's the situation with Andrew Littlewort? Is Tom Evans going to release him now that Charlie's been killed?"

"Are you kidding? He intends to bring formal charges tomorrow. He's just wrapping up what he calls 'loose ends'."

"You mean he really thinks Maria stabbed Charlie Branch?"

"That's what he says. Several people have testified that Charlie was furious over some damage done to his flowerbeds. Evans figures the Gregori kid wrecked the flowers and Charlie went to have it out with the grandmother. Supposedly they had an argument and Maria stabbed Charlie before collapsing with a heart attack."

"Maria was a frail old woman with a bad heart and bad lungs. She didn't have the strength to kill Charlie, much less the personality according to Alexsa Morgan."

"Maria Gregori was a gypsy," Jake said quietly. "That's enough to convict her in Evans' eyes."

Caroline stared at Chief Moeller in shocked silence.

"I know what you're thinking, and I don't like it either."

"All Frenchmen drink, and all gypsies steal," Caroline muttered. "That was one of my grandmother's favorite lines. Call me stupid, but I'd hoped that kind of prejudice didn't exist in the FBI."

"The term 'gypsy' has gone out of style. Today the police call them the Eastern European Travelers Organization. I know all about the EETO because I checked out Maria Gregori the first year she pitched her tent at the Festival of Knights."

"Did you find anything on her?"

Jake shook his head. "Maria was clean as a whistle. Look, Caroline, Tom Evans wants to close the Emma Reiser murder case and get out of town as quickly as possible. As far as he's concerned, whatever happens in Rhineburg is small potatoes compared to the stuff he works on back in the city. He doesn't like small towns. After last winter, he especially doesn't like our small town."

"But you're not Tom Evans."

"You're darned right I'm not. The way I see it, these three deaths are connected to each other. Evans wants no part in the Branch murder, which is fine with me because now I'm back in control. I can investigate Emma's death any way I see fit as long as I believe it's somehow tied to the murder of Charlie Branch."

"If it helps any, I can assure you Bricole had nothing to do with the ruined flower bed. She knew the bed had been dug up. In fact, she took me to see it today. But she thought squirrels caused the damage."

"And in your opinion they hadn't?"

Caroline shook her head. "No way. Someone used a bulb planter to carefully lift each daffodil out of the ground."

"You mean one of those metal things you push in the dirt and it pulls out a handful of soil."

"Right. It's a gardener's tool that leaves a round hole just deep enough to bury a bulb. Except these holes were deeper than usual for daffodils. Bricole reached down into one this morning. The ground level was above her elbow."

"Maybe Branch buried his bulbs deeper than most people. Maybe he figured they were better off that way."

"I had a great garden back in Chicago, Jake, and I never buried a bulb that deep. Besides, Charlie's daffodils had been lifted whole. The flowers were still attached to the bulbs."

Jake stopped suddenly and stared at her. "Vandals aren't usually that careful. They like to rip things out so they're totally destroyed." He rubbed his chin thoughtfully. "I wonder if there was something else beside bulbs buried in those holes."

"That's exactly what I was thinking. Listen, Chief. I've heard a lot about Charlie from different people here in town. Some of the things I've been told don't jive with my impression of the man. I saw a photograph in his house the night Carl and I rescued him from the Blue Cat Lounge. Something about that picture bothers me, although I don't know exactly what it is. I'd like to go back and take another look at it if I can."

Jake dug in his pocket and produced a key. "You're

welcome to search the entire place if it'll help solve this case. Just keep me informed of anything you find there."

"I will. There's something else I think you should know. Sid Burke was working off a three-week punishment as Charlie's helper. Sid had access to the gardening tools, and he sure as heck didn't seem to like Mr. Branch. Yesterday morning I saw his father arguing with Charlie on the Green. Congressman Edmund may have been pleading Sid's cause. On the other hand, maybe Branch was threatening to have Sid's punishment extended. I understand the boy is rather troublesome."

"Sid might have a motive in the vandalism case—if it was vandalism—but I don't see how any of this ties in with Emma Reiser's murder. Still, you can be sure I'll have a talk with the young man."

"Have you found the rune stone yet?"

"No. Evans figures Andrew threw it away in the woods. We may never find that rock." Jake began walking again and Caroline followed. "Maddy told me about your visit with Agatha Hagendorf last night. If Agatha identifies Andrew as having been outside the post office the night of the murder, it'll clinch the case for Agent Evans."

"Didn't Agatha come into the station this morning?"

"No. And she wasn't home when I called her around eight o'clock. Apparently Emily O'Hara drove her to Newberry for her cousin's granddaughter's wedding. I'll talk to her when she gets back tonight."

"*Hmm.*"

"I have to say, before Charlie was killed, that nutty professor made a good suspect. He had motive and opportunity, and he's got a reputation for a bad temper. He lied to us about being near the post office, although after Agatha fingers him, he may start singing like a bird. As for Charlie, he lied, too. I was on my way over to the festival to question him about it when I got the call he'd been murdered."

"What a mess. You're satisfied, though, that Emma wasn't killed by one of her customers."

"The folks who were placing bets with her? I doubt it. Nevertheless, I've got a man checking out all the names in Emma's records. I personally interviewed the four other men Agatha supposedly saw. I'm positive none of them were involved. Dr. Talens set the time of death between midnight and one A.M. Agatha must have entered the post office only minutes after the murderer left. If she'd called me like she should have, we might have gotten a better jump on him. As it is…" Jake shrugged his shoulders.

Caroline knew exactly how the Chief felt, and she sympathized with him. She still couldn't figure out who Agatha was shielding. She was surprised, though, that Emily hadn't kept her promise to escort Mrs. Hagendorf to the police station. Maybe the two had thought they'd be stuck with Agent Evans all day and miss the wedding.

"I have to get moving, Caroline. Keep me informed of what you're up to, okay?"

"I will, Chief. I hope your day doesn't get any tougher."

Jake laughed. "It's been a wild one so far. As if I don't have enough on my platter already, one of the students stopped me on the way in here to complain about a missing costume. Somebody lifted his friar's habit from the changing tent, and the kid was hopping mad. I told him to take it up with the Bruck boys. They're in charge of festival security, thank goodness."

He punched a metal plate on the wall and the doors of the ICU swung open. Caroline watched him walk to the desk where Amy sat, charting on her patients. Something he'd said sparked a new idea in her mind. She turned and hurried back to the elevator, suddenly sure she was on the right track.

Twenty-eight

Caroline pulled up in front of Charlie Branch's house at six o'clock and switched off the headlights on her Jeep. What had been a beautiful day an hour ago was fast becoming an ugly evening. Gray clouds heavy with rain scudded across the western sky and slid eastward, darkening the already dusky horizon. A blustery wind accompanied the changing weather. Sweeping aside all in its path, it rattled through the branches of the ponderosa pines and stripped the blossoms from ancient forsythias lining the gardener's driveway.

The wind grew in ferocity as Caroline exited her car. It whipped the leftover leaves of autumn into whirlwinds of brown and old gold that skittered across the lawn like madly dancing elves. Thunder rolled in the distance, and the first fat raindrops splattered on the brick pathway. Caroline hurried to the house while silently berating herself for forgetting her umbrella.

Sliding the key from her pocket, she was about to insert it when she noticed the door was slightly ajar. She paused, unsure whether to proceed or retreat. Jake would never have left the building unlocked, but unlocked it was. That could mean only one of two things. Either someone had entered the house soon after the police left, or someone was in there now.

She pushed open the door, a shiver running down her back. The hallway was layered in shadows. The rooms on both sides were also dark. Outside of the wind and rain beating on the windows, silence filled the house.

She recalled turning on the hallway light the last time she'd been here. The switch was on the right hand wall only a few inches from the door. She reached in quietly and tripped it.

Nothing happened.

With her heart beating a tattoo on her ribs, Caroline backed slowly down the path. Rain pelted her head and shoulders. Sheltering her eyes with one hand, she looked quickly around her, then turned and ran to the car.

Safe inside the Jeep, she consciously slowed her breathing, forcing herself to relax. She locked the doors, switched on the engine, and turned the heater on full blast. Then she put the SUV in reverse and swung backward in a half circle until her headlights, powered up to bright, pointed straight at the open door.

The front of the building leaped into view. Peering through the arcs made by the windshield wipers, Caroline scrutinized the house for signs of life. She saw no movement within. The thought that she was alone calmed her. She reached forward, intending to power down the headlamps, when a sudden flash of lightening illuminated the yard.

To the left of the house, a figure dashed through the downpour and disappeared behind the garage. Caroline threw the Jeep into reverse and spun the wheel to the right, braking as the nose of the car swung into line with the garage. Straining to see through the dark and the rain, she eyed the wooded area ringing Branch's property.

It was a useless task. The headlights bounced off the trees revealing nothing more than wet shrubs bent to the ground by the force of the wind. Convinced the intruder had escaped, Caroline gave up and reached for her cell phone. She dialed the police station.

Ten minutes later, Jake Moeller pulled up in a black and white, mars light flashing, siren turned off. His yellow slicker was streaked with rainwater, but the storm that had caught him in town had already passed over Caroline. She stepped out of her car and greeted the Chief beneath a dark sky still rumbling with thunder.

"Sorry to pull you away from dinner, Jake. When I got here, someone was inside the house. He ran out the back door and crossed the lawn behind the garage. I lost him in the woods."

"Did you get a good look at him?"

Caroline shook her head. "It was pouring, and the wind was blowing every which way. I sensed it was a man, not a woman, and he seemed athletic, but not heavy set. He dodged between those trees and kept on running."

Jake heaved a sigh. "Let's take a look in the house."

"He must have tampered with the lights," Caroline said as they walked up the path. "The switch in the hallway isn't working."

Jake pulled out a flashlight and shined it through the open door. He motioned for her to wait outside, unclipped his holster flap, and placed his palm on the gun butt. Caroline watched him work his way quietly down the hall. He disappeared for a moment beneath the staircase. Then suddenly the light near the front door flashed on.

A second black and white turned into the driveway and ground to a halt near the Chief's car. A grizzled policeman in his late forties jumped out and rushed over to

Caroline.

"You okay?" he said in a low voice.

She nodded and pointed to the house. "Jake went in a minute ago. He got the lights working again."

With that, a lamp went on in the living room. Jake waved at them through the window.

"I guess we can go in," said the policeman. "Stay behind me."

Caroline followed the man through the door into the hallway. Chief Moeller was standing in Charlie's den staring at the dozens of pictures on the walls. He turned when she entered the room.

"Wait for us here while we check out the rest of the house." He motioned to the other officer. "You take the upstairs, and I'll look out back."

Caroline stepped to the center of the room and let her gaze wander over Charlie's photo gallery. There was something about the arrangement of pictures that displeased her. She moved closer to examine them.

The Branches' wedding picture hung where it belonged, as did the photo of the two of them sitting in their kitchen. But the shot of Charlie teaching his sons to fish had been moved from its spot.

Most people wouldn't have noticed the tiny nail protruding from the paneling near the corner of the den. Fortunately, Caroline had developed a memory for details over the course of her nursing career. She knew the photo now centered on the adjoining wall had originally hung in this spot.

Who moved it? And what had it replaced?

She scanned the gallery a second time before it came

to her. The photo of Branch and his motorcycle was missing from the room.

Perplexed, Caroline sat down at the desk to consider the matter. She brushed aside the pile of seed catalogues still littering the surface and rested her elbows on the scarred wood. Propping her chin in her hands, she gazed about the den.

Nothing else looked out of place. The metal filing cabinets appeared untouched, their drawers tightly closed. Beside them, a row of gardening books stood undisturbed on a wooden shelf. A second shelf held a pile of magazines.

"Why?" Caroline muttered. She glanced down at the seed catalogues and suddenly realized something else had been taken from the room. Branch's scrapbook was no longer on the desk.

"No sign of anyone in the house or outside," Jake said as he reentered the den. "If I may say so, you look like a drowned rat, Cari."

Caroline pushed back from the desk. "I feel like one, too. Let me find a towel for my hair. Then I want to show you something."

She left him and headed up to the second floor. In a linen cabinet squeezed between two tiny bedrooms she found a couple of well used but clean towels. One she threw over her shoulders. The other she used to dry her hair. She ran a comb through it hastily before returning to the den.

"Whoever was in here took at least two objects from the house." She led Jake to the corner where the fishing picture had once hung, then pointed out its new spot on the wall. She described the missing photo in detail.

"There was another man standing near the motorcycle. He seemed to be friends with Branch. I didn't recognize him, but there was something about him that struck me as being familiar. I swear I've seen him, or someone who looks very much like him."

She told Jake about the missing scrapbook. The Chief scratched his head when she finished her story. "This is weird," he said. "I don't see any connection between Emma Reiser and the missing objects. There should be one if Charlie's death is tied to hers."

"We should probably search the house before jumping to any conclusions. I suspect they were stolen, but Branch may have moved them himself."

Search they did, but there was no sign of the missing photograph or scrapbook anywhere in the home.

"We may as well call it a night," grumbled Jake. "We're getting nowhere here."

"How did the thief get in?"

"He broke a back window and climbed in. He was probably on his way out the front door when you arrived." Jake motioned to the other officer. "You can go back on patrol, Tim. Keep a lookout for anyone carrying a package about the size of that scrapbook. You never know. We might get lucky if the guy's still on foot."

Tim headed off for his squad car as Jake accompanied Caroline to her Jeep. "I'm going home to change clothes. Do you think the rain's over for the night?"

Jake shook his head. "It's supposed to continue off and on for several more hours. I'm going to stop by

Agatha's place and see if she's home now. I called her when I left the hospital, but there was no answer."

Caroline pondered Mrs. Hagendorf's disappearance as she drove to St. Anne's. It was strange no one had answered the phone at the boarding house. Even if she was still at the wedding, one of Agatha's tenants should have been there to take Jake's call.

"Everything's strange in Rhineburg lately," she murmured aloud. "Anyone who calls this a sleepy little town is just plumb crazy."

Twenty-nine

The phone was ringing when Caroline entered her apartment. She snatched up the receiver, hoping it was Carl on the line.

"Caroline? This is Alexsa Morgan. I hope I'm not disturbing you."

"Of course not." Caroline cradled the phone against her shoulder and peeled off her wet jacket. "How's Bricole doing?"

"I brought her home with me. Jean and Margie are showing her around the house. My granddaughters understand what the child is going through. They had their own problems handling their mother's death."

Caroline could believe it. Elizabeth Morgan's plunge into an icy river had changed her children's lives forever.

"Your daughter-in-law was kind enough to go back to Maria's tent and gather a few things for Bricole. We'll see to the rest tomorrow."

"And how are you doing, Alexsa? You lost a good friend in Mrs. Gregori."

"At my age, one loses friends on a regular basis," Alexsa said wryly. "One comes to expect it after a while. Still, Maria was special. I shall miss her greatly. But I didn't call to talk about Maria. I need to see you, Caroline. Tonight, if possible."

"What about, Alexsa?" Caroline kicked off her damp shoes and padded into the kitchen. She reached into the fridge for a Coke.

"I have some information about Charlie Branch that may assist the police in capturing his killer. I would like to discuss it with you first."

Caroline hesitated. She knew she should advise Alexsa to call Jake Moeller, but curiosity was her strongest suit.

"I just got in and I'm drenched to the skin after being caught in the rain. Let me change my clothes and grab a bite to eat…"

"I'll have a hot supper waiting for you here. Please come as soon as possible."

"All right. Give me twenty minutes."

She disconnected and immediately dialed Carl's number. The professor answered on the second ring.

"Where have you been," he asked. "I've been trying to reach you for over an hour."

Caroline told him about the trip to Charlie's house. "I wish I'd examined that picture more closely the first time I saw it. I have only a vague memory of the other man's face."

"It's not like you knew you'd need to remember it, Cari."

"That's true," she admitted. She went on to relate her conversation with Alexsa. "I wish you could come along, but Alexsa seemed anxious to talk with me privately. I'll call you as soon as I get home."

"Stop by my place instead. I'll have dessert waiting."

Caroline laughed. "I can always count on you, Carl. The sky could be falling, but you'll still make it to the dinner table."

"Hey!" the professor replied in a hurt tone of voice.

"The Duke of Rhineburg had important duties to fulfill today. Unfortunately, satisfying my hunger was not among them."

A little starvation would have helped Carl's waistline, but Caroline refrained from telling him so. Instead she said, "Do me a favor and find out everything you can about Sid Burke, both past and present. I can't stop thinking he's somehow mixed up in these murders."

"Sid's a troublemaker, Cari, but I don't see him as a killer."

"I don't have time to explain. Alexsa is expecting me at her house in twenty minutes."

Atwater agreed to do what she asked and even offered to call the Archangels for help if necessary.

"Thanks, Carl. I'll talk to you later."

Caroline slipped into a pair of black jeans and a maroon turtleneck sweater, donned dry shoes, and grabbed a jacket from the closet. Five minutes later she was on her way to the parking garage. The roads were blessedly empty of traffic, and she made it to the Morgan mansion in good time. Alexsa was waiting at the door when she pulled into the driveway.

"Thank you for coming so quickly. Elvira made a pork roast for supper. I've set a place for you in the dining room."

Caroline followed her hostess down the carpeted hallway that bisected the large house. When they reached the dining room, Alexsa gestured for her to go in.

"There's wine on the sideboard," Mrs. Morgan said. "I'll be back in a moment."

Caroline selected a Merlot from among the array of

bottles lining the shelf. She poured herself a glass of the dark liquid and sipped it slowly while surveying her surroundings.

The dining room was longer than it was wide by at least twelve feet. Three of the walls were creamed-colored and decorated with groupings of small to mid-sized impressionist paintings. A floor-to-ceiling built-in sideboard of carved oak dominated the fourth wall. Its open shelves flanked a recessed mirror engraved with fig and grape leaves set above a set of eight drawers.

A Chippendale table surrounded by twelve chairs occupied the center of the room. Ivory candles in silver holders bracketed a vase of freshly cut tulips in the middle of the table. Above them hung a crystal chandelier composed of cascading teardrop-shaped lights.

French doors at one side of the room led to a flagstone patio encircled by flowerbeds and low cut hedges. Caroline was admiring a walnut and ebony vase stand placed near the doors when Alexsa entered the room carrying a covered tray.

"Let me help you with that." Caroline set her wineglass on the table and took the tray from Alexsa. "I can see you're used to feeding men," she said as she lifted the cover to reveal a plate of mashed potatoes, red cabbage, and applesauce arranged around four thick slices of pork. "This is wonderful, Alexsa, but it's way too much food for me."

Alexsa sank down on an upholstered chair. "It's been a long day. I doubt you had lunch what with all that happened."

"You're right about that." Caroline retrieved her wine,

poured a glass for Alexsa, and joined her at the table. "I was going to open a can of soup for dinner, but this is a hundred times better. Do you mind if I eat while we talk, or would you rather wait until I've finished?"

"This may take some time, so go ahead and enjoy your food."

Caroline saw a look of sadness cross Alexsa's face as she sat there swirling the wine in her glass. It was several minutes before Mrs. Morgan spoke again.

"I asked you to come here tonight because I have information about Charlie Branch that may, or may not, be related to his murder. If what I know becomes public, certain innocent people will suffer because of it. But if I hold back, and it turns out the information is pertinent to his death, Charlie's killer could go free."

"It sounds like you're stuck between a rock and a hard place."

"Yes, I am. That's why I wanted to speak to you first." Alexsa seemed to choose her next words carefully. "You and I made a pact last winter that prevented further tragedy from occurring in this house. At the time, I really didn't trust you to honor our agreement."

"You thought I'd tell Professor Atwater."

The matriarch of the Morgan family nodded her silver head. "It was obvious to me that you two shared a special bond. I feared that bond would prove stronger than your word."

"I won't deny it was difficult withholding the truth from Carl. I knew, though, he wouldn't have approved of the arrangement we made. He would have felt compelled to tell the police."

"I understand. Carl has been a good friend, and lying to him was difficult for me also. Still, I had to preserve what was left of my family." Alexsa drew a deep breath. "These past few months have taken their toll. Over time, though, I've learned one thing. You're not only intelligent; you're also someone I can trust."

Caroline put her fork aside and looked Alexsa directly in the eye. "I'll listen to anything you have to say, Mrs. Morgan, but don't ask me to withhold information from the police again. I have a vested interest in these murders. In fact, I may be partially responsible for at least one of them."

Caroline told Alexsa about her conversation with Charlie the day the rune stone was discovered. "If I'd kept my mouth shut, Charlie might not have gotten drunk that night and gone off to see Emma Reiser."

"If you hadn't told him about the rune stone, someone else would have. I don't believe Charlie killed Emma, and neither do you. I have a story to tell you, one that may be more relevant to Charlie's death than that rune stone of yours. Will you hear me out?"

Caroline stared at Alexsa in silence. Mrs. Morgan was right about Branch. He would have heard about the rune stone sooner or later. His reaction probably would have been the same no matter who told him. She was foolish to blame herself for his death.

"I'm all ears," she said as she picked up her knife and fork.

"Good." Alexsa stood up and went over to the sideboard. She brought back the bottle of Merlot and refilled Caroline's glass. "Last night I mentioned that Julie

Branch had worked for me."

"I remember."

"Elvira has always been my regular housekeeper, but Julie came in twice a week to help with the heavy work. She also assisted Elvira at dinner parties and other large gatherings here. I got to know the girl quite well. I was very concerned when she fell ill. She'd been losing weight and seemed distracted or depressed for weeks before she finally took to her bed.

"One day I drove over to visit her. Charlie was working at Bruck and Julie was alone in the house. When I walked up the path, I could hear her crying through the open window. She wouldn't answer the bell, but I let myself in anyway. I found her curled up on the couching, sobbing."

"Poor thing," Caroline murmured.

"Poor thing indeed," replied Alexsa. "I gathered her in my arms and held her until she stopped crying. When she finally began to speak, the words tumbled from her lips as if she couldn't control them. I don't think she meant to tell me the whole story, but once started, she couldn't stop."

"Julie said Charlie had made a lot of money doing something illegal. She wouldn't go into details, but she kept repeating that he would go to jail if they didn't give back the money. Apparently Charlie believed he was in no danger of being caught. He told Julie he'd hidden the money where no one but he could find it. He was using it to pay for their sons' education, and that really upset her. Julie said she'd never had a head for money, so Charlie paid all the bills and handled the bank account. She assumed they lived as well as they did because both of them were working."

"Julie was a bit naïve, wasn't she?"

"No more so than a lot of wives I know. There are many women who leave financial matters solely in the hands of their husbands. When their men die, these ladies are up a creek without a paddle."

Caroline grinned at Alexsa's use of the old expression. The smile quickly faded from her face, though, when she remembered Charlie's scrapbook.

"I offered to repay the money," Alexsa continued. "Julie refused my help at first. Then, when I agreed it should be looked on as a loan, she gladly accepted. I took her to the bank that very day and withdrew what she needed."

"How did Julie return the money?"

"I don't know. She left town a few days later, supposedly to see her sister in Chicago. When she returned, she was gravely ill."

Alexsa stood up and walked to the French doors. She appeared lost in her memories as she stared at the rain falling in earnest outside.

"I went to see Julie a few days before her death. She was little more than skin and bones by then. That's when she asked me to look out for her husband and sons. I didn't question her about the money. At one point in the visit, though, she took my hand and squeezed it. She told me not to worry. No one would be coming after Charlie."

"I was told Julie died of cancer, but you said it was heart disease."

"Oh, no, Caroline," Alexsa said softly. "I told you she

died of heart trouble, and she did. Julie loved Charlie too much. She couldn't believe he'd deceived her all those years. When she found out he had, she couldn't handle the pain. Julie turned all the hurt inward on herself. Charlie broke her heart, and she destroyed herself because of it."

Caroline folded her napkin and pushed away from the table. "I think I know why Charlie was killed."

Alexsa glanced back at her guest. "Charlie's paths of gold," she said quietly.

Caroline nodded. "Jake Moeller has to know about this."

"Charlie's sons are coming home to bury their father. They should all be in Rhineburg by the morning."

"It can't be helped, Alexsa. They'll have to be told."

"They had nothing to do with it! After all, the money's been paid back."

Caroline hung her head and considered her options. "Jake's a good man," she finally said. "Maybe he can figure out a way to handle all this without involving Charlie's sons."

Alexsa looked out once more at the rain pelting the patio.

"I leave it in your hands," she murmured.

Thirty

So Charlie Branch was a bank robber. Caroline shook her head in wonder as she drove to the police station. Now she understood why he'd kept a scrapbook full of old news reports. They'd all been about him and the clever ways he eluded capture.

Poor Julie. She'd probably discovered the scrapbook while cleaning Charlie's favorite room. Her life had been turned upside down within a matter of minutes when the awful truth came out. She'd made amends with Alexsa's money, but that hadn't saved her marriage, or her life. And now Charlie was gone too. What a terrible price to pay for five college educations.

If Caroline was guessing correctly, Branch hadn't used up all his money on his sons' schooling. She bet there was still some buried in the ground beneath his precious daffodils.

Paths of gold. How had Sid stumbled on the truth? Branch had told him, of course. Caroline recalled her conversation with the gardener the day the rune stone was discovered. 'I tell all the boys who work for me, but none of 'em understand. Not even Mr. Smarty Pants.'

But Sid had understood. He must have sensed there was more to it than just a love of flowers when Charlie erupted in rage over the idea of an archeological dig on Bruck Green. He lured the gardener to the Blue Cat Lounge with only one purpose in mind: to get the man to talk. Plying him with liquor had done the trick.

Caroline reckoned Sid had found the scrapbook while she and Carl were upstairs putting Branch to bed. It didn't take a rocket scientist to figure out Branch was the infamous thief. Backed up by Charlie's drunken disclosures, the news report would have been proof enough for Sid.

The boy was also smart enough to know that digging on the Green could spell disaster for Charlie Branch. No man buried money in a flowerbed unless he wanted to conceal its existence. The police would certainly start asking questions if some rock hound discovered a package of cash stashed beneath a row of posies.

The problem was time. There was no way either Branch or Sid could retrieve the money safely once the Festival of Knights began. The Green would be swarming with people, and while Branch might find a way to work around the crowds, Sid would have no excuse for digging in the beds. Added to that, it would only take one news report to draw the feared treasure hunters to Rhineburg. Once they started digging holes, all bets were off.

Sid had no choice but to attempt the feat at night. Even then, he had little chance of success. There were thousands of daffodils lining the paths on the Green, and it was unlikely that in his drunken state, Branch had revealed the exact location of his cache.

Sid must have decided to steal the rune stone from the post office. That would have delayed, if not put an end to, a dig on the university grounds. Caroline suspected Emma Reiser's murder was unintentional. Most likely the postmaster had heard Sid rummaging around downstairs and had gone to investigate. The boy probably reacted in a panic, lashing out at her with the stone. Then, when he discovered he'd killed her, he placed her body near the steps to make it look like she'd fallen.

Caroline figured Sid had waited until after the banquet before stealing a tool from the gardening shed to dig up the daffodils. Charlie discovered the damaged flowerbed only minutes before the start of the Grand Parade. He must have guessed Sid was the culprit. Because both men were riding in the procession, he couldn't confront Sid until after reaching the jousting field. He probably told the boy to meet him near the fortuneteller's tent. With most of the visitors watching the combat between the knights, there was little chance their conversation would be overheard.

Caroline pulled into a parking spot near the police station, switched off the engine, and sat thinking about Sid and Charlie. Jake had said a friar's costume was stolen from one of the changing tents. She bet Sid had taken it to wear at the meeting with Charlie. He must have known the situation could turn ugly. By disguising himself, he could avoid being recognized by other students.

But Maria had seen him. With her dying breath, she had uttered the word 'mon'. She'd been too weak to pronounce the last consonant, but Caroline was sure she'd been trying to say 'monk'. Few people thought of friars any more, but everyone recognized a monk in his brown habit.

Maria probably heard the two men arguing outside her tent. Maybe she'd drawn her sword to scare them off, or maybe Sid had threatened her and she brandished the weapon in self-defense. Sid must have grabbed the sword, pushing Maria to the ground in the process, and then stabbed Charlie with it.

It all made sense to Caroline now that she knew about the money hidden on the Green. Sid was a troublemaker from way back. Having put two and two together, he'd seen an easy way to make himself a few bucks at Branch's expense. Whether or not he'd bargained on committing murder, she'd never know unless Sid confessed. One thing was for sure. Jake had to be told the entire story so he could go after the young man before anyone else was hurt.

Caroline climbed out of the Jeep and dashed through the rain to the police station. Lights glowed in the pink stone building, and through the big plate glass window she could see Madeline Moeller deep in conversation with Annie Holtzbrinck. The two women looked up in surprised when she rushed in.

"Caroline! We thought you were over at the Morgan place."

"I've just come from there," Caroline told Madeline. "Is Jake in? I need to talk to him."

"Oh, no," said Maddy, shaking her head. "He took off with Professor Atwater about five minutes ago. They're looking for Sid Burke."

"Now what's happened?"

"The professor arrived here with some information on Sid Burke," explained Annie. "Since it was based on rumor, he wanted to check it out with Chief Moeller before he told you about it."

"What information," Caroline asked with a frown.

"Michael Bruck heard that Sid was picked up by the

Chicago police over winter break. Supposedly he'd had a fight with a guy in a bar there, and the other fellow was injured pretty badly."

"Jake made some phone calls to Chicago and confirmed the story," said Maddy. "Sid would be sitting in jail right now if his father hadn't come to his rescue. Apparently Congressman Burke paid off the victim big time, and the man dropped his complaint against Sid."

"So Sid can be vicious."

"It looks like it," replied Annie. "Of course, Edmund Burke has enough money to pay off anyone he wants. When he sold his daddy's trucking company…"

"Carl said you think Sid is mixed up in Charlie's murder," interrupted Maddy. "Jake wants to pull the boy in for questioning, so they went to the university together to find him. So tell us. What did Alexsa have to say?"

"Not much, really. She wanted to talk about Maria and Bricole Gregori." Caroline didn't feel free discussing anything in front of Annie Holtzbrinck. Given Annie's gossip record, the news would be all over town in a matter of hours. "Did Jake get a chance to interview Agatha Hagendorf?"

"Would you believe, she and Emily still aren't home."

"That's pretty strange, Maddy, unless they're staying over in Newberry due to the storm."

"That could be," agreed Annie. "But you'd think at least one of her boarders would answer the phone. All I keep getting is Agatha's answering machine."

"For some reason that makes me very uneasy," said Caroline. "Annie, why don't you call Bertha Meyer. She a good friend of those ladies. If anyone knows where they are and what they're up to, it would be her."

Annie bobbed her head and quickly reached for the phone. A minute later she was connected with Meyer's Bakery.

"Hello, Bertha. It's Annie over at the police station. I'm so glad you're home." Annie exchanged views with her friend on the weather, the success of the festival, and the health of Bertha's family before finally coming to the point of her call. "By any chance, did you hear from Agatha or any of her boarders today? I know Agatha drove over to Newberry this morning for her cousin's granddaughter's wedding, but... What's that, Bertha? The wedding was two weeks ago? Then why would Agatha say... No, I'm sure that was the message on her answering machine. No one else seems to be at home there either. Are you sure you haven't spoken to... No, Bertha, of course I don't doubt what you say. But maybe you forgot... Bertha? Bertha, are you there?"

Annie stared at the phone in shock. "She hung up on me. I can't believe she'd..."

"What did Bertha say?" Caroline asked impatiently.

"What did she say? Oh! Right. Bertha claims she was too busy working their bakery stall at the festival to keep track of Agatha or anyone else. She also claims the wedding took place two weeks ago, not today. She can't understand why Agatha left that message."

"Something's very wrong, Maddy. We have to get over to Mrs. Hagendorf's right now."

Caroline flew out the door into the rain. Madeline told Annie to contact Jake, then she grabbed her coat and ran after her friend.

"Why would Agatha want to protect Sid Burke?" Caroline called over her shoulder as she ran down Wilhelm to Kaiser Street. "She must have seen him enter the post office the night Emma was killed, but why wouldn't she say so?"

"I don't know," panted Maddy. "Maybe she's afraid of him."

Caroline rounded the corner and cut across the wet street. She took the stairs of the Rhineburg Boarding House and Home for Gentle Women two steps at a time. Not a light was on in the house. When she rang the doorbell, it echoed back unanswered.

"Agatha!" Caroline pounded on the door while Maddy peered through the rain streaked front room window. Maddy turned to Caroline and shook her head.

"I can't see a soul in there. Try the door, Cari. Maybe it's unlocked."

Caroline twisted the knob to the right. She heard a click and felt the door give way under her hand. "Got it, Maddy. Come on."

The two women entered cautiously. The foyer lay in darkness, as did the rooms on either side of the hall. What light there was came from a shaded bulb glimmering at the top of the staircase. Caroline walked over to the steps and called out, "Anyone home?"

"Back here," someone answered from down the hall.

Maddy touched Caroline's arm. "The kitchen," she whispered. She pointed to a stream of light illuminating the base of a door at the end of the corridor.

Caroline put a finger to her lips, hushing Maddy. Staying close to the wall, she tiptoed down the hallway.

Maddy scurried in front of her and raised her hand. "Maybe we should wait for Jake," she said hesitantly.

A sudden clatter of dishes caught both of them off guard. The sound of soft laughter came from the kitchen and dance music floated back to them from a radio turned low.

"I guess I was worried for no good reason," Caroline said, shrugging her shoulders. "Come on. Let's go join the others."

She walked to the kitchen, Madeline following at her heels, and opened the door.

"Sorry to burst in on you, but we... Oh!"

"Come in, Mrs. Rhodes. And you too, Mrs. Moeller."

The man in the hooded monk's habit was holding a gun. He pointed it at the two women and motioned them to move farther into the kitchen. With his free hand, he turned off the radio.

"That's better. The music helped draw you to me, but I hate distractions when I'm talking." He pulled the hood away from his face and smiled. "Surprised, ladies?"

"Edmund Burke," exclaimed Madeline. "But I thought you were..."

"My son?" Burke laughed unpleasantly. "Sid may be able to hold his own in a bar fight, but he hasn't got the guts for murder."

"And you do," Caroline murmured.

"It's called self-preservation, Mrs. Rhodes. I've worked too hard to get where I am. I'm not about to lose everything because some stupid gardener would rather bury his money than spend it."

"Charlie was your friend. I saw a picture of you in his

257

house."

"The shot of us standing by the motorcycle?" Burke shook his head. "When Sid said he'd recognized me in the picture, I was afraid you might have also. It's a good thing I persuaded him to break into Charlie's place and steal that photo."

"He took the scrapbook, too. Why was that, Congressman?"

Caroline's heart was working overtime, but she knew their only chance to survive depended on the use of delaying tactics. If she could keep Burke talking until Jake and Carl arrived...

"I think we've talked long enough, Mrs. Rhodes. Why don't you and Mrs. Moeller head downstairs?" Burke opened the door leading to the basement and motioned with the gun. Circling them like a sheep dog, he herded them towards the steps. "Don't keep your friends waiting. I promised we wouldn't start the fireworks without you."

Maddy grasped Caroline by the arm, her eyes wide with fear. "Cari, I can't..." She choked back a sob as Burke poked her in the back with the gun.

Caroline patted her friend's hand. "We'll be all right," she whispered. "Just do what he says."

She started slowly down the stairs, her fingers clutching the banister for support. A wave of nausea swept over her as she realized time was running out. The university was only minutes away, and the Chief should have been here by now if Annie had contacted him. Maybe Sid hadn't been in his dormitory. Maybe Jake and Carl had driven somewhere else looking for the boy.

"Over by the wall." Edmund pointed to the far end of

the basement where a bare light bulb dangled from the ceiling. Sitting beneath the light, their hands tied and their mouths covered with duct tape, were Agatha and her five boarders.

All six women began struggling when they saw Edmund with his captives. Agatha Hagendorf made little mewing noises, but kept her worried eyes glued firmly on Caroline. The other ladies looked to be in varying degrees of despair, fighting against their bonds while uttering incomprehensible words.

"I thought I told you to keep quiet," Burke snarled. He shifted the gun to his left hand and grabbed a folding chair with his right. "Sit down," he commanded Caroline. He pointed to Maddy. "Get down on the floor and lie still."

The two women did as they were told. Burke walked behind Caroline and quickly taped her wrists together. Then he opened another folding chair and repeated the process with Maddy. When he finished with their wrists, he taped their ankles to the chair legs.

"Now isn't this a cozy arrangement?"

Caroline watched in horror as Burke walked over to a shelf and lifted down a container of gasoline.

"What do you intend to do with us?" she asked.

"I intend to kill you," Burke answered sarcastically as he removed the cap from the container. "It'll only take one match to turn this old house into a torch."

"You never answered my question. Why did you have Sid take the scrapbook?"

Burke paused and smiled at her. "You read what was in it, didn't you? Do you really believe Charlie was clever enough to pull those jobs off by himself?"

Caroline remembered Annie saying something about Burke's father and a trucking company.

"You were a truck driver too, weren't you?"

"My father owned the company, Mrs. Rhodes, but he wanted me to start at the bottom. Yes, I drove a truck. I was Charlie's partner."

"Did you ride the motorcycle, or was that Charlie's job?"

Burke set the gasoline container on the floor and walked over to Caroline. "My, my. Aren't you the curious one. You seem to have put two and two together, so I'll fill in the blanks for you. Charlie rode the bike and made all the heists. I simply waited for him at some conveniently quiet spot. When he'd arrive with the money, I'd jump out and drop the ramp. He'd steer the bike up into the truck, and off we drove, two innocent fellows with a load of goods to deliver."

"No wonder you eluded the police for so long. But you won't escape them now, you know. Chief Moeller knows Agatha saw you outside the post office."

That had to be it, Caroline thought as she watched Burke's face contort in anger. Agatha had seen Sid's father the night of Emma's murder. Being who she was – a woman of yesteryear raised to believe all public servants were honorable people – the gentle Mrs. Hagendorf couldn't imagine her Congressman killing anyone. She'd probably assumed Burke was visiting Emma to place a bet. Her old school training had kicked in, and she'd decided to protect Burke's reputation by concealing his name.

"Sid must have mentioned the rune stone when he spoke to you about the picture hanging in Charlie's house. He told you about Branch's 'paths of gold', didn't he? Your son figured out where that money came from, and he knew it would be found if people started digging on Bruck Green. He tried to warn you, didn't he?"

Burke snorted in disdain. He picked up the gas can and poured the fuel on a pile of rags under the stairs.

"You give that boy too much credit, Mrs. Rhodes. Sid is a whining little fool who comes crying to me every time he's in trouble. If it weren't for his mother, I'd have written him off long ago." Walking over to Agatha, he dismissed the terror in her eyes with a wink before pouring gasoline on her skirt. "The only good thing about Sid is, he's not really my kid. Jeannie was pregnant when I married her. That was a no-no for a girl whose daddy was a big shot politician. I saved Jeannie's reputation. She repaid the debt by introducing me to the right people."

"So now I know all your secrets."

"That's right, Mrs. Rhodes." He poured gasoline on Sarah Sonnenschein, then on Eleanor Naumann." But I'm not worried you'll tell anyone. In fifteen minutes this house will be in flames, and you and your friends will be too dead to talk."

"Maybe not, Dad."

Burke spun around. He hadn't seen Sid standing on the basement stairs, listening to every word he said. Caroline, though, had watched the boy creep down the steps and pick up his father's gun.

"Put that down," Burke commanded. "Better yet, give it to me."

Sid backed away from his father.

"I don't think so," he sneered. "Remember, Dad, I'm just a whining little fool. Fools do dumb things, and I may do a dumb thing with this gun if you come one step closer."

Burke recoiled as if he'd been shot. "I was just talking, boy. Just blowing off steam with these women."

"Before you killed them, right, Dad? Like you killed Emma Reiser and Charlie Branch, never even giving them a chance to defend themselves. Well, I can defend myself, Dad. Or should I call you 'step-Dad'?"

"Now listen, Sid…"

"Put down your weapon!"

All heads turned at the sound of Jake Moeller's voice. The chief stood poised at the top of the stairs, a gun clutched in his hand.

"Jake!" Maddy cried out.

Jake's head jerked in the direction of his wife. In that split second, Edmund Burke recovered from his surprise and lunged forward. He caught Sid's hand and dragged the gun away. Then he spun the boy around, caught him by the neck, and pointed the weapon at his head.

"You've got him," said Jake as he lowered his own gun and ran down the stairs.

"No, Jake! It's not Sid!" screamed Caroline.

"Shut up!" yelled Burke. "Stop right where you are, Chief Moeller, or I swear I'll kill him."

Jake halted a few feet away from the Congressman, obviously confused. "What's going on?"

Burke tightened his hold on Sid's throat. "Stay back!" he shouted as he pulled his son towards the door leading to the back yard. He fumbled with the handle, then pushed the door open with one foot. He leaned into Sid and shoved him forward. The boy collided with Jake as Burke turned and bounded up the outside steps.

He ran right into the arms of Michael Bruck.

Thirty-one

"Sir Sidney of Rhineburg."

Sid Burke spurred his horse into a gallop and, to the applause of the spectators, joined a half dozen other knights on the jousting field. He extended his left arm, raised his shield above his head, and bowed to the people in the stands.

The festival herald continued announcing names until the center of the field was filled with brightly dressed horsemen, squires bearing banners, drummers, trumpeters, pages, and a full company of armed soldiers and archers. When the entire group was assembled, they fell into line and circled the makeshift arena. To the continued cheers of the audience, they lined up in rows in front of the main pavilion where the Duke and Duchess of Rhineburg stood waiting.

"Good people of Rhineburg!" Carl called out. "You see before you the bravest of the brave. These knights have acquitted themselves well both on and off the field of battle. We honor them here today."

Another cheer arose from the crowd. Carl paused briefly, then raised his hand for silence.

"Our great poet Chaucer described a knight as valorous, prudent, and meek in his bearing. It is our hope that these virtues were witnessed by all who visited us this week. We invite you to return to our fair land at this same time next year when we will once again bestow knighthood on one of our own. And now, my friends, I declare a close to this great tournament and to the Festival of Knights. I bid you, return to your homes in harmony and peace."

Caroline stood and applauded along with the rest of the throng in the bleachers. People seemed reluctant to let the celebration end. When they finally exited the stands, many of them wandered back to the area where the crafters and artisans were closing down their booths.

"They don't want to leave yet," she commented as she made her way down to the field alongside Martin and Nikki.

"It's always like this on the last day," said Martin. "Reality can seem pretty dull after you've lived in a fairy tale world for a week."

"But it's different this year," Nikki reminded him. "How often has murder intruded on the Festival of Knights? I think folks just want to unwind today. It's like they're shell-shocked. They need to remind themselves that Rhineburg is basically a safe place to live."

Martin wrapped an arm around his wife. "If that's what you want to think, honey, go right ahead. But you're being naïve, you know."

"Now why would you say that?" Nikki asked crossly as she pushed him away. She stalked over to a picnic table and sat down. "Give me two good reasons for your cynical attitude."

Martin looked to his mother for support, but she only raised her eyebrows in response.

"Okay," he sighed. He settled down on a bench across from Nikki. "Reason number one: Emma Reiser's funeral. Reason number two: Charlie Branch's funeral."

Nikki's eyes narrowed. "Explain."

"You attended both of them, Nikki. Did you see any real sorrow expressed at Emma's funeral? And outside of his sons, was anyone really mourning the loss of Charlie?"

"Lots of people came to both services."

"Lots of people came to the Festival of Knights, too."

"Oh, Marty! How can you equate the two?"

Martin gazed up at Caroline again. This time she decided to step in.

"What Marty's trying to say is, neither Emma nor Charlie had any true friends here in Rhineburg. People knew Mrs. Reiser either as their postmaster or as their bookie, but not as the person she really was." Caroline paused, searching for the right words to express her thoughts. "Emma lived a secret life up on the second floor of the post office. There wasn't a person at her funeral who admitted ever being invited upstairs."

"People attended the services out of curiosity, Nikki," said Martin. "The same goes for Charlie's funeral."

"Julie Branch was well liked by the women I talked with, but everyone said Charlie was a loner. He, too, was protecting a secret, and secrets have a way of isolating people from those around them."

"What an awful way to live," said Nikki. "I'd hate to die without leaving even one person to grieve for me."

Caroline thought of Maria Gregori. Her funeral had been sparsely attended compared to Emma's and Charlie's, but those who were there had loved and respected the woman. Sorrow had forged a bond between Alexsa Morgan and little Bricole Gregori. They were inseparable now, and both would live happier lives because of it.

"Here comes Professor Atwater," said Martin. "And Mrs. Moeller and the Chief."

Carl had exchanged his royal robes for street clothes. He looked more at ease in his plaid shirt and corduroy pants. Caroline commented on the fact when he greeted her.

"Can't say I'm sorry to be done with that costume," he replied. "It weighed a ton, and it was much too warm for this weather."

"I thought you looked great in it," said Nikki. "Very regal and authoritative."

Carl stroked his beard to hide his pleasure. "It did fit me quite well," he purred.

Martin rolled his eyes. Fortunately, the professor didn't notice.

"I thought all the costumes were beautiful," remarked Madeline. "I have to study up on all this medieval stuff so I know what the decorations stand for."

"The decorations?"

"You know what I mean, Professor. The symbols on the shields and banners."

"Those are called devices, Mrs. Moeller," explained Martin. "Back in the old days, knights had a custom of emblazoning devices on their shields and surcoats so their followers could find them on the battlefield. The surcoat was the original coat of arms."

"How interesting. So tell me what some of those devices mean."

"It's pretty complicated," laughed Carl. He turned to Martin. "Did you notice Sid Burke altered both his costume and his shield?"

Martin nodded. "On the first day of the tournament, Sid wore a surcoat with two diagonal bands crossing his upper torso. His shield was painted with the same device. He must have removed one stripe, though, because today his costume and shield bore only the band crossing from the upper left to the lower right."

"Sid's new device is called the 'bend sinister'. People used to consider it a sign of illegitimacy."

"It must have come as quite a shock to Sid when Edmund said he wasn't the boy's real father," said Caroline. "Tell me, Jake. How does Sid stand with the law?"

"Edmund confessed to everything," Jake replied. "He asked Sid to steal the picture and scrapbook from Charlie's house, but he didn't give him the real reason why. He told the kid he'd hardly even known Charlie, but he said he'd be embarrassed politically if the man's thievery became public knowledge."

"Do you think Sid believed that?" asked Carl.

Jake shrugged. "I think he did at first. Sid admitted to calling his father the night of the murder. He told him about the rune stone and Charlie's obsession with the flowerbeds. He also told him what he'd seen in the den. Edmund asked Sid to burglarize the house that same night, and apparently Sid did try. He got scared off when Branch walked outside and saw him hiding by the garage."

"Charlie must have been on his way to the post office."

"I think so, Caroline. Branch never saw Emma, though. Professor Littlewort has finally admitted to being at the P.O. He had second thoughts about sending the rune stone to the museum and went there in hopes of getting it back. He saw Charlie, and Charlie saw him. They both lost their courage and ran off. Evidently Edmund arrived only minutes after those two left. He broke in and found the stone, but Emma heard him and came downstairs. He claims he hit her in a moment of panic."

"What happened to the rune stone?" asked Caroline.

"Burke threw it in the river when he drove out of town. Evans has his people looking for it. Maybe they'll get lucky yet."

"What about the time I saw Burke talking with Charlie?"

"Edmund was angry that Charlie had been dumb enough to talk to Sid. He wanted Branch to stay away from his son. He also wanted to know what Charlie had told the police."

"Remember the night of the banquet when I said someone was watching us? That was Sid," said Maddy.

"His father was upset that Garrison Hurst asked you to investigate. He told Sid to follow you and learn anything he could."

"Alexsa showed me her sword cane that night," said Caroline. "She said it was just like the one Maria had."

Jake nodded. "Burke set up a meeting with Branch. He claims it was only to talk, and things got out of hand. I suspect he came prepared, though. Alexsa called me today. She talked with Bricole, and the kid says she saw a monk go into her grandmother's tent. She thought he was a customer, so she stayed away. Later, she returned and couldn't find Maria. By the time she did, her grandmother was in pretty bad shape. As for the monk, he'd disappeared."

"Burke stole the friar's habit from the changing tent."

"Right, Martin. He didn't want to be seen meeting Charlie. I don't buy his story about Charlie's death. I think he planned all along to kill Branch. And I think he went into Maria's tent to find a weapon because he wanted to throw suspicion for the crime on her. He was relying on that old prejudice against gypsies to throw the police off track."

"And it nearly did," said Caroline. "Agent Evans was more than willing to lay the blame at her door. I bet Burke surprised Mrs. Gregori and she drew her sword. He pushed her down, grabbed the sword, and took off to meet Charlie." A sudden thought hit Caroline. "Maria couldn't have gotten outside by herself, not with that broken hip. Burke must have carried her out and placed her behind the tent either before he met Charlie or after he killed him."

"He really is a cold-blooded murderer," Maddy said with a shiver.

"He hung onto the monk's habit because by that time he knew he had to kill Agatha Hagendorf." Jake turned to Caroline. "Sid overheard you and Maddy talking about going to see Agatha. He told his father, and Burke decided to follow you. He saw you in the window with the telescope, and he watched as Professor Atwater walked up and down the street. He figured Agatha had spotted him the night of the murder, but he couldn't understand why she hadn't told me about it.

"He went to the house after you left. Agatha was pleased as punch to see him. She thought he was going to explain what he was doing at the post office with Emma, but instead he forced her into the basement and tied her up. Agatha didn't go quietly, though. Before he knew it, Edmund had a whole bevy of women on his hands. He really did panic then. He left all of them tied up in the basement while he went back to his motel to plan his next move."

"That was before he stole the habit and killed Charlie."

"Yes, Caroline. He knew he had to return to Agatha's house and deal with the six women. The habit had served him well so far, so he wore it when he went into town. With the hood hiding his face, he figured no one would recognize him if he was seen."

"You still haven't told us where Sid stands in all this," said Carl. "Will he be charged as an accessory to murder?"

"Not in Emma Reiser's death. Agent Evans says there's no evidence to prove he knew what his father intended to do. Sid is cooperating, but I'll have to talk with him a few more times before I decide whether or not to charge him in Charlie's murder."

"I don't think he was involved," argued Caroline. "I saw him confront his father that morning, and he was very angry with Edmund." She told Jake about the package Sid had thrown at the congressman's feet.

"Sid's explained all that. He was the one who dug up Branch's daffodils. He unearthed some of Charlie's loot from the bank robberies, and he claims that's when he first suspected his dad was lying to him."

Caroline looked at her son. "Maria told me there was something wicked in the air here in Rhineburg. It seems she was right."

"I wish you'd listened to her, Mom," said Martin. "You almost got yourself killed again."

"Don't worry about her, Marty," said Carl. "Cari's just fine. As for life in Rhineburg, it'll get back to normal in no time flat."

A big smile spread over Jake's face. "Not for me, it won't. Michael Bruck found information on Emma's computer about a safety deposit box Mrs. Reiser kept in a bank in Newberry. Evans got right on to it. This afternoon he called me to say he'd found Emma's will. Seems Mrs. Reiser left all her worldly possessions to the city of Rhineburg."

"That's wonderful, Jake," said Caroline. "But what about the RICO Act? I thought the FBI was going to confiscate everything Emma owned."

"They'd first have to prove she'd bought it all with money made illegally through gambling. While Emma kept a record of her customers' names, it seems she was too smart to list what they or she had earned. The government would have a hard time proving a case under the RICO Act. There's something else," added Jake, blushing slightly. "I promised Evans I wouldn't report how he'd botched this case if he'd forget about what he found in Emma's apartment. I also told him I'd give him full credit for catching Burke."

"Oh, that'll make his day," said Carl. "Think of the great publicity he'll get when Burke goes to trial. He'll probably get a promotion out of it."

"Maybe he'll be transferred to Washington," Maddy said wistfully. "That would make my day!"

"Does Mayor Schoen know about the will," asked

Caroline.

"Oh, yeah," Jake laughed. "When I showed it to him, he was ecstatic. He started right then and there making plans on how to spend the money. He didn't mention giving one red cent to the police department until I pulled out the list of Emma's customers. When he saw his name in bold letters right up at the top, he changed his tune real quick. It looks like I'm getting two more officers and a brand new squad car. Plus a raise for Annie Holtzbrinck."

Caroline gave the Chief a hug. "That's the best news I've heard today, Jake. If I were you, I'd hold out for a few more perks. Ask for something really outrageous, like an all-expense-paid vacation with your wife."

"Sounds good to me," piped up Maddy. "I wouldn't mind a couple of weeks cruising the Caribbean."

"Neither would I," agreed the Chief. "Of course I wouldn't leave Rhineburg unprotected. I'd appoint Caroline interim Chief of Police. Professor Atwater could be her second-in-command."

"I like that idea," said Carl enthusiastically. "We could…."

Caroline put her fingers to his lips and firmly shook her head. "Don't even consider it, Carl. Our days as detectives are over. From now on we stick to what we do best. It's teaching for you, and nursing for me."

Carl looked crestfallen, but he brightened considerably when Caroline suggested the group drive into town for dinner.

"Remember," she said with a twinkle in her eye, "Duke Richard hasn't had a bite to eat since lunch. The poor man's likely to keel over if we don't hurry up and get a menu into his hands."

Carl grinned broadly. "I knew there was a thread of compassion running through that diet-conscious soul of yours, Cari." He linked his arm in Caroline's and strolled towards the parking lot. "How about burgers and beer at the Blue Cat Lounge? While we're eating dinner we can discuss a case I read about in the Newberry newspaper. It seems this fellow walked into the bank and…"

The End

Mary V. Welk has drawn on her experience as an ER nurse to knock off sixteen characters in her Rhodes to Murder mystery series, a Love Is Murder Readers' Choice Award winner for Best Series.

A Merry Little Murder, Mary's debut mystery garnered a finalist position in the Hemingway First Novel Competition under the working title "Four to Go." It also received a Readers' Choice Award for Best First Mystery.

A native of Chicago, Mary is a member of Sisters in Crime. She served on the Board of the Midwest Chapter of Mystery Writers of America and as a reviewer for Library Journal, Mystery Scene Magazine, and Reviewingtheevidence.com. She currently tours with fellow Mystery Mavens Luisa Buehler and S. D. Tooley.

Printed in the United States
217204BV00005B/9/P